W9-CUB-158

UNDERWATER DELUSIONS

I swam past the dead, my air bubbles shimmering in a tunnel of gloom. A few small reef sharks had made their way through the broken cockpit window and were already swimming into the cabin. Three were fighting over the bleeding couple, and another was making its way down the aisle right toward me.

I could see more sharks schooling outside the aircraft. I was going to have to swim right through them. I grabbed the sides of the doorway and was just about to pull myself out and away from the carnage when I heard it. A meowing sound. Hallucination? Possible. At sixty feet under, the ocean can play games with your head. . . .

Praise for the Underwater Investigation Series

Dangerous Depths

"Exciting. . . . Armchair travelers beware! Once you read this book, you'll want to hop on a plane and visit the unspoiled British Virgin Islands." —*Midwest Book Review*

"White-hot writing, a charismatic heroine, and crackling tension flawlessly merge. . . . Lush atmosphere. . . . As satisfying as finding buried treasure." —*Romantic Times*

"As always, the author writes about the gorgeous area of the British Virgin Islands in such an evocative way that you'll feel like you've had a vacation, complete with underwater investigations, without leaving your favorite armchair." —The Romance Reader's Connection

continued . . .

Dark Water Dive

"A compelling whodunit."   —*The Colorado Springs Gazette*

"A lush, atmospheric look at the British Virgin Islands. . . . Assuredly plunges into a solid tale. . . . [An] exciting, well-crafted beach book."   —*South Florida Sun-Sentinel*

"Landlocked Coloradoans with a yen for yachting will find their hobby in full sail."   —*Rocky Mountain News*

"Should satisfy the most jaded appetite for thrills."
     —I Love a Mystery

"Smooth writing, great island characters, a spunky heroine, and a complex plot."   —*Mystery News*

"Readers will feel the sun on their backs and the sand between their toes."   —*Springs* (Colorado)

"A perfect way to spend your surface intervals."
     —The New York City Sea Gypsies

"A book to . . . reread in the dead of winter, when the sun and sand seem a distant memory."   —Reviewing the Evidence

"A satisfyingly suspenseful dive adventure."
     —Cozies, Capers & Crimes

Swimming with the Dead

"A likable, exuberant heroine, the fascinating world of scuba diving, and a fast-paced plot. . . . [T]akes hold of you and doesn't let go until the last paragraph. A terrific debut."
          —*New York Times* bestselling author Margaret Coel

"An impressive debut . . . teems with captivating dive scenes, picture-perfect island settings, and a host of colorful characters."   —Christine Goff, author of *Death Takes a Gander*

"In the tradition of Kinsey Millhone and V. I. Warshawski. . . . It's about time a feisty female investigator leaves the [cold] behind and enjoys the slower-paced—but always exciting—life of the islands."   —*American Eagle Latitudes*

"Debut author Kathy Brandt sets the stage for a thrilling, fast-paced series. . . . Hold on to your hats for this one!"
          —Roundtable Reviews

"This book grabs the reader from the start and never lets go. The pace is quick and sure."
          —The Romance Reader's Connection
          (Mysterious Author of the Month)

"An intriguing debut."   —*Deadly Pleasures*

"Brandt puts a twist on the typical mystery novel. . . . Readers' assumptions are turned backward, somersaulted into suspicion, and coaxed into second-guessing. Brandt leads you to the edge and lets you dangle a bit before giving out the secret."
          —*Springs* (Colorado)

Kathy Brandt

Under
Pressure

AN UNDERWATER INVESTIGATION

Ø
A SIGNET BOOK

SIGNET
Published by New American Library, a division of
Penguin Group (USA) Inc., 375 Hudson Street,
New York, New York 10014, USA
Penguin Group (Canada), 90 Eglinton Avenue East, Suite 700, Toronto,
Ontario M4P 2Y3, Canada (a division of Pearson Penguin Canada Inc.)
Penguin Books Ltd., 80 Strand, London WC2R 0RL, England
Penguin Ireland, 25 St. Stephen's Green, Dublin 2,
Ireland (a division of Penguin Books Ltd.)
Penguin Group (Australia), 250 Camberwell Road, Camberwell, Victoria 3124,
Australia (a division of Pearson Australia Group Pty. Ltd.)
Penguin Books India Pvt. Ltd., 11 Community Centre, Panchsheel Park,
New Delhi - 110 017, India
Penguin Group (NZ), cnr Airborne and Rosedale Roads, Albany,
Auckland 1310, New Zealand (a division of Pearson New Zealand Ltd.)
Penguin Books (South Africa) (Pty.) Ltd., 24 Sturdee Avenue,
Rosebank, Johannesburg 2196, South Africa

Penguin Books Ltd., Registered Offices:
80 Strand, London WC2R 0RL, England

First published by Signet, an imprint of New American Library,
a division of Penguin Group (USA) Inc.

First Printing, June 2006
10 9 8 7 6 5 4 3 2 1

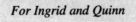

For Ingrid and Quinn

ACKNOWLEDGMENTS

Thanks to Ira J. Rimson, forensic engineer and specialist in aircraft accident investigation, reconstruction, and analysis, for his expertise and patience. He graciously offered his forty-five-plus years of experience to advise this mystery writer who "insisted on crashing an airplane in an out-of-the-way place!" Thanks to Jacky Sach and Martha Bushko for their support and advice. A special thanks to my sister, Sara Palumbo, for her careful reading and perceptive comments on the manuscript and for her undying enthusiasm. (I saved her e-mails and reread them when I was having a bad day.)

I'd be remiss if I failed to recognize the following sources: Arthur J. Bachrach, Ph.D, and Glen H. Egstrom, Ph.D., *Stress and Performance in Diving* (Best Publishing, 1987); Osha Gray Davidson, *The Enchanted Braid: Coming to Terms with Nature on the Coral Reef* (John Wiley and Sons, 1998); Robert G. Teather, *Encyclopedia of Underwater Investigation* (Best Publishing, 1994); and finally, David W. Shaw, *Flying Cloud* (Harper Collins, 2000), for O'Brien's tale of the sea, and Herman Melville's *Moby Dick*, for Capy's whaler's song.

Most important, a huge thanks to my kids for their love and support. And to my husband, Ron, my first reader, my sounding board, and the one who reminds me to eat when I'm so intent on the writing that I've forgotten what day it is, much less what time.

Chapter 1

It wasn't hard to get lost in the crowd, go unnoticed, stay anonymous, especially if you were determined and experienced, shadows who followed, waiting for the right opportunity. The Terrence B. Lettsome International Airport in the British Virgin Islands was exactly the place to do it. Two people, dressed to blend in with the tourists, tailed their quarry to the airport and almost accomplished their task at the curb. In the confusion of luggage being unloaded from taxis and vans, travelers were focused on one thing—keeping track of belongings and getting inside. The stalkers made one attempt, but at the last moment a porter stepped in the way. Without even being aware of it, the luggage handler grabbed a suitcase from their intended target, blocking the quick movement of a determined hand. Too late, and their quarry disappeared through the automatic doors. They followed, stepping into the chaos of the interior.

The terminal was teeming with people. A few were BVIslanders—families or businesspeople going to Puerto Rico or on to the States, Canada, or the UK. Most were tourists just arriving in the islands to spend a week or two sailing the island paradise or on their way home, sunburned and wearing island garb.

Finally, they spotted their target at the ticket counter checking in for Island Air Flight 45 to Puerto Rico. They

tailed their mark to the gate and waited for an opening. It
didn't come. A couple of uniformed cops were standing
around, shooting the shit and watching the endless flow of
handbags and briefcases move through the electronic scan-
ner. Before there was another opportunity, their quarry had
made it through security and into the waiting area, where an
agent would eventually lead the passengers across the already hot tarmac to the plane.

One option remained. They went back to the ticket
counter. A couple, late but too involved in fondling each
other to care, stood at the counter when they got there. They
stepped behind them in line. A baggage handler was grabbing suitcases that were in a pile for the flight and throwing
them onto a cart, unconcerned about what was going into
the heap. Behind the counter, the ticket agent scrambled to
issue last-minute tickets, determined to get the flight out on
time. This was it. There couldn't be more mistakes. Otherwise, they would pay.

Island Air Flight 45 was a fifteen-passenger turboprop
with two pilots. The old Beech 99 was completely refurbished for luxury, with leather seats and soft overhead
lighting. The flights were too short and the aircraft too
small for any inflight service, but each flight was stocked
for creature comforts with everything from the *Wall Street
Journal* and the *London Times* to goody bags filled with
snacks, juices, and even a small bottle of island rum. The
airline was building its reputation based on all the frills.

On that Saturday morning, Flight 45 carried ten passengers, nine adults and one child. It took off as scheduled at
9:32 A.M., lifting off the runway into a cloudless Caribbean
sky and climbing to four hundred feet. It was due to arrive
in Puerto Rico at 10:14. It never made it.

The tower heard the first indications of trouble at 9:36
when the captain yelled, "Pull up, pull up!" At 9:39, Flight
45 plunged into the sea.

Chapter 2

I was on my knees, head buried in the boat locker, ass pointed to the sky, trying to reach one of my diving fins, when the plane went down. I'd been aware of the irritating whine of the engines piercing the morning calm as the aircraft flew low overhead. I'd extracted myself from the tangle of gear in the locker and was considering an obscene and useless gesture when everything turned silent. Then the silver tube took a graceful arc and started falling straight toward our boat.

Christ, it was going to hit us! A vast ocean—and the airplane was going to explode into the one square mile of water where our boat drifted and there wasn't a thing I could do about it. I was still on my knees, fin in hand, when the thing hit not one hundred feet off our bow, sending a tidal wave of water over the rails. I landed in the cockpit in a tangle of equipment, stunned and in denial.

Finally, my mind caught up with what my body already knew. People were out there, dead or dying. When I stood, I could see the plane beginning to sink.

I glanced back to the stern, where Jimmy Snyder, my dive partner, stood dazed and clutching the lifeline. Moments before, he'd switched off his radio and had been standing on the bow, hand shielding his eyes, watching the aircraft take off from the new airport on Beef Island. Nothing bigger than a small jet could make its way on or off that "international" runway, which ended at the water's edge. This plane had been a little twin-engine island hopper.

Jimmy and I had been out at the east end of Tortola on the police boat. I was teaching the kid the intricacies of underwater crime scenes. Chief Dunn, my boss and head of Tortola PD, figured Jimmy was the ideal candidate to become my dive partner in underwater recovery and crime scene investigation.

Jimmy was a quick study but fearless, the latter a liability as far as I was concerned. I wanted someone next to me at a hundred feet down who had as much respect for the ocean as I did. I was of the philosophy that diving was the most unnatural thing a human could do—that every time I went under, I was pushing the limits of what good old Mother Nature would allow. Someday, she'd say *Enough*, and send an air embolism my way or a Portuguese man-of-war. Hell, it could be something as innocuous as a sharp piece of coral that cut my hose.

We'd just been suiting up for the first dive of the day. Jimmy had had the damn radio blaring. If it hadn't been Bob Marley, I'd have complained. Something about suiting up to Marley's "Please don' ya rock my boat, 'cause I don' want my boat to be rockin'" put me in the right frame of mind—that being *Lighten up, Sampson, he's just a kid. He'll figure it out*.

Every hour on the hour the weather forecaster came on to report what everyone already knew. It was a beautiful day in paradise. The only glitch was the tropical storm forming a thousand miles off the west coast of Africa. It was September—off-season in the British Virgin Islands. A sailboater's paradise, it was abandoned now. Only a few sails dotted the horizon and everyone monitored the weather. It was hurricane season in paradise.

But today was a sunny, blue-sky day, and plenty hot. The water was as clear as crystal. It had been a glorious morning until the plane went down. It floated for just a second, then tipped. The nose pointed down and it headed to the bottom, tail jutting skyward.

Suddenly the aft cabin door burst open and a woman appeared. We were so close I could see the desperation and horror in her eyes. Her fingers gripped the side of the door as she tried to push her way out against the water that was rushing into the aircraft. In sheer panic, she kept fighting, straining against the surge. Then a man came into view right behind her. He wrapped one arm around the woman and plunged into the maelstrom. But the plane was sliding fast now. Water gushed into the open door and they vanished in a raging turmoil of foam. Then water swirled around the tail and the whole plane disappeared in a confusion of angry water.

I scanned the froth, watching for any signs of them. Nothing but a cauldron of bubbling water. Then in the next instant heads popped up, the man with one arm still locked around the woman.

Jimmy threw him the yellow horseshoe and the guy managed to swim to it, still holding fast to the woman. They were okay. The guy gave a wave. No way I was taking the time to fish them out and pull them aboard the *Wahoo*. I knew that other boats would be converging on the area quickly. The two victims in the water would be fine until then.

I shouted instructions to Jimmy as we pulled on our dive gear.

"We need to get to that wreck fast. I'll go in and start hauling people out. You stay by the plane door and get them to the surface." Pretty simple plan. It would get a whole lot more complicated once we got down there.

I was in the water within minutes, Jimmy right behind me. I hoped he was up to what lay ahead. I couldn't afford to have a diver in trouble right now.

We headed down. I knew the bottom was only sixty feet

below and sandy. God only knew whether we could get to anyone in time. We dove into a rush of bubbling water. It gushed around us, trying to force us back to the surface. I could barely make out the dark shape of the plane through the swirling brown clouds of sediment. The aircraft was just settling on the bottom, tail raised, air still captured in the back section. I kicked hard, forcing my body through the mayhem of turbulent water.

Finally I found the dark square that was the door. It was still open. I was about to head into the cabin when a passenger swam right into me, arms and legs working hard. It was a woman, her eyes determined black marbles set in a pale face. A red mane of hair floated around her head. She was clearly going to claw over me or anyone else who got in her way. I shoved her toward Jimmy. He grabbed her, jammed his extra regulator into her mouth, and headed to the surface.

I prayed that by now there were people up top ready to assist. I needed Jimmy back down here fast. I shone my light into the darkness and started into the cabin. It was a relatively small plane, one cabin with five rows, one seat on each side, stretching into what seemed like eternity to the cockpit door. In the aft section another two rows of seats were affixed two abreast and then a door marked "Restroom" was tucked way back in the tail section.

I could see six people still in their seats. Way up in the front row, two passengers slumped in their chairs. A black swirl of water drifting around them turned red in the beam of my light. They would probably have bled to death by the time I got to them. But hell, they might already be dead. I knew the only logical approach to the rescue was to make my way down the aisle, get to the closest victims first, and start pulling people out before they drowned. I swallowed the fear working its way up my throat and headed to the first occupied seat.

Damned if the guy didn't look right at me, more confused than panicked. He was bald with a fringe of hair all the way around the edges of his head and a shirt with green fronds and parrots that had "tourist" written all over it. He held his mouth clamped tight, trying to trap precious air in his lungs and keep the seawater out. He was fumbling with his seat belt, trying unsuccessfully to get it off.

I pointed to my spare regulator, indicating that he should put it in his mouth. He ignored me and went on with his single-minded struggle with the seat belt. Realization, and with it panic, had set in. All he knew was that he wanted out. I jammed the regulator into his mouth and nodded, trying to keep him calm. He looked at me muddled, then took a deep rasping breath of air. I could see him relaxing a bit, some coherence returning. I didn't have the time to coddle the guy though.

I released the belt, grabbed him around the arm, and swam to the doorway. He had a death grip on my dive vest when Jimmy got there. Still way over the edge of reason, he wanted nothing to do with giving up my regulator or letting go of my vest. I couldn't blame him. He had an ocean of water above his head and I was asking him to relinquish his only connection to an air source. I yanked the regulator out of his mouth, probably jarring a couple of teeth loose. Jimmy quickly shoved his extra regulator in and headed to the surface with a firm grip on the guy's parrot shirt.

I went back into the gloom and swam to the only guy in the next row. He appeared to be gazing out the window, his head twisted at an impossible angle. I glanced out too and caught sight of a shark swimming by. The guy wasn't worried though. He was dead.

I moved on to the next seats forward, where a young couple sat, deeply tanned, hands interlocked across the aisle. A shiny gold band graced the man's left finger. She wore a sundress and her hair was woven into island braids and adorned with colorful beads. He had a baseball cap clutched in his other hand. Their heads were propped back in the seats. Both were unconscious. No doubt their lungs were already filled with water.

It seemed to take forever to release their seat belts, his first. I pulled him out of his seat, let him drift there, and released her seat belt. Somehow I managed to get hold of both of them and pushed him in front of me while pulling her behind by her braids. When I got to the door, I could see Jimmy coming through the blue, ignoring the growing swirl of sharks. He nodded, grabbed the guy's collar and her dress, and disappeared again.

Time was really running out. I had serious doubts I'd get anyone else out alive. How long had it been? Fifteen minutes? More? I checked my pressure gauge. I'd been using my air fast, breathing hard and sharing it with the panicked guy in the parrot shirt. I had enough for maybe twenty more minutes.

Just the one couple was left now, way up at the bulkhead. Beyond, the cockpit door was closed. With luck maybe the pilots had made it out a cockpit window. About the time I reached the front of the cabin, the plane shifted. The air that had been caught in the tail was leaking out.

The passengers in the first row were a distinguished-looking pair—even waterlogged. Her fingers, nails polished a bright red, clutched a handbag. She wore a white linen suit and a red necklace, complemented by matching lipstick. Her mascara hadn't even smudged her cheeks. A copy of *Cruising World* was lying in the man's lap, held in place under his arm. It was open to the newest and most expensive advances in sailboats.

A cloud of pink water still circulated around them. At first glance, they looked unscathed, sitting there. Then I realized that their legs had been severed just below the knees and a sharp piece of metal was embedded in the flesh. Evidently it had once framed the plane's outer shell. How the hell it had managed to end up slicing through their legs was a question for a physicist or, more aptly, for someone who could explain the unexplainable. It would be a "guess their time was up" kind of explanation.

I left them where they sat and tried the cockpit door, twisting the handle. It turned but didn't open—jammed. I pushed, pushed again, and the thing gave way. Damned if I didn't see Jimmy through the cockpit window. He had smashed a rock through the glass and was pulling the copilot out of the right seat. I gave him the thumbs-up and indicated I'd get the other—the captain, I presumed. Jimmy just shook his head. I knew why when I swam inside and got a good look at the guy from the front. His face had been shoved into his skull on impact.

I left him where he was and headed back through the cabin. I swam past the dead, my air bubbles shimmering in a tunnel of gloom. I would return for the bodies later. I never risked my life for the dead. God knows how many at the surface would pull through. I made it to the doorway and hovered there, taking one last look down the length of the cabin.

A few small reef sharks had made their way through the broken cockpit window and were already swimming into the cabin. Three were fighting over the bleeding couple, and another was making its way down the aisle right toward me.

I'd never heard of a shark attacking a diver anywhere in the Caribbean except when some asshole decided to grab the tail of a resting nurse shark or hand-feed a lemon shark. I'd say the diver deserved it. In most instances, a shark will take off at the first sight of a diver. But that didn't mean I was going to push it, especially in an airplane that was turning into a feeding ground. I wanted to get out of the damn plane before I was considered lunch.

I could see more sharks schooling outside the aircraft. I was going to have to swim right through them. I grabbed the sides of the doorway and was just about to pull myself out and away from the carnage when I heard it. A meowing sound. A cat? No way. Hallucination? Possible.

I'd been down now for close to thirty minutes, not that long to be breathing compressed air except for the fact that conditions had been extreme. High doses of adrenaline had coursed through my veins from the moment I'd jumped in the water. Perhaps my mind was playing tricks.

Then I heard it again. There was no ignoring it. The sound was coming from somewhere in the tail section. I twisted away from the door and peered into the dark recesses of the plane. Debris floated all around me—Styrofoam cups, pieces of paper, a CD. I found no explanation for the sound. I knew I'd heard something, but at sixty feet the ocean can play games. Maybe it was simply a final air pocket filling or the scraping of metal against a rock.

I held my breath, working to silence the bubbles and the rasping noise of air intake. I listened. I'd made a mistake before—taken my situation and the underwater environment for granted. Only once. I'd never let it happen again. So I waited. A shark brushed past and swam out the door. I closed my eyes, hovered, focused, and waited some more. Just a couple of seconds longer and I'd get out.

The plane shifted slightly and I heard it again—a whimper, coming from the tail. I hadn't worried about anyone being in the bathroom. The plane had been just taking off. No one should have been moving around the cabin or in the john. I swam to the door and pulled it open.

I caught a sudden flash of red and then a glancing blow hit the edge of my mask, followed quickly by another. This one hit me square in the nose. When my vision cleared, I saw it—a red high-top tennis shoe. It was a kid. He had managed to wedge himself up into the ceiling. He was kicking his feet like crazy and sucking on the last pocket of air in the space. He wasn't ready to give up his position either. When I grabbed his leg, he kicked again. This time I was ready. I grabbed his ankle and tried to pull him down toward me. He didn't budge. He was stuck on something. I swam up into the air space and wedged myself in next to him. He had his head tipped back and was gasping for every breath. His eyes were wild with fear. No kid should have to experience this kind of fear.

He had a camera wrapped around his shoulder. The strap was caught on a hook and the kid was hanging on to it for dear life. The thing had probably saved him. It was keeping him in the air pocket. He wasn't about to let me release him.

I looked him in the eye and forced him to focus on me. He was fighting me all the way. I grabbed his face in my hands and shook him. Then I took my regulator out of my mouth and took a breath of stale air. Seawater bubbled up round us. In seconds the kid's only source of oxygen would be gone.

"Kid—kid, we've got to get out of here," I said, shaking him again. "I'm taking you out. I've going to untangle the strap. When I release it, you'll sink under the water, but I'm going to give you this thing to breathe through." I showed him my spare regulator.

He took a quick look at it and nodded.

"The water will sting your eyes, but it will be okay. All you have to do is breathe. I want you to grab my tank and hold on. Are you ready?"

I put my arm around him and waited. He nodded, took the regulator, and put it into his mouth. I watched him take a breath, then another. He learned fast—nothing like a kid. I untangled the strap and he grabbed me around the neck. I found my regulator, breathed through it once, then we sank together into the water, swam through the bathroom door, and out into a gathering of gray sharks.

I could feel his fingers digging into my neck. This had to be a kid's worst nightmare—swimming into a pack of jaws. These were no great whites, but to this kid they probably looked it.

A small lemon shark came right at us. I punched it with

a fist and it veered, its dorsal fin skittering along my belly
as it swam away. I could see it coming around for a second
look, another shark right behind it. If I could have spoken,
I would have told the kid not to worry, that the damn things
looked ferocious but would not bother us. It was raw bleeding flesh that they were after. Instead, I kept moving up.

Chapter 3

When we broke into daylight, a pair of sinewy black arms grabbed us and lifted us together in one swift motion into the *Wahoo*. It was Stark. He helped me out of my gear with the kid still clinging to me.

"It's okay, kid. You're okay. You're out. You're okay," I kept saying, probably as much for me as for him. Only minutes before, we had been gasping for breath in the last air pocket of a plane under sixty feet of water. Now we were standing in tropical sunshine, a warm, fragrant breeze brushing our faces.

I'd been here before. It was mind-jarring to realize that we had just escaped death.

The kid didn't let go. I wrapped my arm around him, pulled him in, and held him, waiting for the shaking to stop while Stark stowed my gear. Jimmy appeared with a blanket and managed to get the kid bundled up with me in it.

Stark came back over, handed us each some water, and sat down next to me.

When I wasn't on a dive-related investigation, Stark was my partner in the PD. Though we were officially assigned to homicide, Stark and I got called out on anything that needed special investigative skills, from burglary to drug running.

Stark was a native islander, had done a three-year stint in

Miami as an undercover narcotics officer, and had spent his entire life with the ocean outside his window. Yet he'd rather have a killer holding a .357 Magnum to his temple than put his big toe in the water. The guy avoided anything deeper than a glassful of island rum.

Right now he looked like his stomach was somewhere in the back of his throat and his mahogany skin had turned an ashy charcoal. He never set foot on a boat without a life jacket and today was no exception. Stark was a big guy, six-five, all muscle, his head shaved. The life jacket barely made it across his chest.

The kid and I sat huddled on a bench as chaos reigned around us. By now there were a dozen boats circling, with everyone trying to help out.

Dunn was standing in the cockpit of the *Wahoo,* hands on hips, surveying the situation and directing the scene in his calm, chief-of-police voice. I had never heard Dunn raise his voice. He never had to. People did what Dunn said. He'd been running the police department with his regal authority for more than fifteen years now, and at times like this I was glad he was around. Though Dunn and I had butted heads on more than one occasion, I respected him and called him a friend.

Several other official boats were tied up alongside the *Wahoo.* James Carmichael and Tom Mason, one of his dive masters, were standing on the deck of the BVI Search and Rescue vessel. Both were experienced divers and volunteers for search and rescue. They were pulling on dive gear and getting ready to go in to assist.

"No need for any divers to rush back down there," I said under my breath to Stark. "We're in recovery mode now."

I snugged the blanket around the kid, stood, and motioned Stark to the cockpit to talk with Dunn, who at the moment was threatening to arrest a tourist who had motored over with dive gear and thought he had every right to dive to the wreck.

"Hannah," he said. "Unbelievably lucky that you were out here when the plane went into the water and got to the passengers so quickly."

"Almost too lucky," I said. "Damn plane almost hit the *Wahoo*."

"What's the situation down there?" Dunn asked.

"Jimmy and I got everyone out except for the four still inside who died on impact."

"You sure there's no chance?"

"Yeah, I'm sure," I said as I flashed on the image of that couple sitting in their seats while sharks moved in.

The victims that Jimmy had brought up were lying all over the deck. Christ, I'd lost count. How many had been rescued? Only eight—the copilot and seven others, including the kid. It wasn't clear how many would survive. The copilot had already been pronounced dead. His body lay under a tarp ready to be transported to shore.

A couple of emergency techs were working over the blond woman in the sundress and her husband. Other passengers were being loaded into a powerboat to be taken to the hospital.

The man, along with the woman he'd pushed out of the plane before it sank, was already aboard. The man smiled and gave a little salute. He held his right arm close to his body and it was obvious he was in a lot of pain. He was drop-dead gorgeous, maybe thirty-five, tanned, square-jawed, heavy eyebrows, and bedroom eyes. I knew him from somewhere. The woman was older, fifty-five, maybe sixty, and looked like she was in shock. The guy with the parrot shirt huddled next to them.

Finally, the techs loaded the blond woman onto the boat. She was still unconscious. Her husband had come around, coughing half the ocean out of his lungs.

The woman with the red mane who had been fighting her way out of the plane was standing on the deck, arms locked across her chest, breasts spilling over the top of a form-fitting black shirt. She couldn't have weighed more than a hundred pounds. She was tiny, lean, top-heavy and flaunting it. She was well aware of the fact that every guy on the boat who was conscious had his eyes glued to the cleavage. She was determined not to go to the hospital and was stating that fact in no uncertain terms until Dunn made it clear he wasn't giving her a choice. Reluctantly she climbed aboard.

The kid needed to go with them. He was in shock. Color like fresh snow. He was still huddled under the blanket near the back of the boat, looking small, alone, and haunted. I went back, sat next to him, and wrapped an arm around his shoulders.

He looked like he was about ten. In other situations, I was betting, the last thing he'd want was some strange woman acting like his mother. Not now though.

"Hey, I'm Hannah. What's your name?"

"Simon Redding," he said, voice quaking.

"Were you traveling with someone?"

"My dad. Where's my dad?" he asked, sitting up, reality taking hold, and with it renewed panic.

"Was your dad with you on the plane?"

"Yeah. He was sitting right across from me. He didn't want me to go to the bathroom, but I told him I couldn't wait."

"What does your dad look like?"

"He's old, got some gray hair, wears those wire-rim glasses."

"How old is he?"

"I guess he's maybe forty or something." I guess I thought forty was old once too. Now old is ninety.

"What about your mom?"

"She died a long time ago," he said.

"Look, I want you to go with these people in the boat and let the doctor check you over."

"Can't I stay here with you till you find my dad?"

"No, Simon. I've got to go back in the water."

"And you'll find my dad?"

"I don't know. I'm not sure where your dad is." I wasn't about to lie to the kid, tell him his dad would show up. I was pretty sure he wouldn't. I thought about the dead guy down there staring out the window at the sharks.

"I'll come to the hospital as soon as I can. Meantime, you go with these folks."

I walked him to the waiting boat and one of the techs lifted him aboard. The good-looking guy made room and Simon settled in next to him.

"Hey," Simon looked at the man, his eyes lighting up for an instant. "I know you. You're the Avenger!"

The Avenger. Jeez, the guy was a film star. There had been a movie, a couple of sequels. The Avenger was a one-man force against evil.

"Yeah, kid. Stick with me. You and me, we'll take care of things."

As Dunn released the boat line, the kid gave me a lost look and pulled the blanket tightly across his body as if to protect himself from the inevitable. I figured he already understood that he wouldn't see his father again. In spite of the fear and the shock, the kid knew the score.

"I'll see you at the hospital," I called before the engines roared and the boat sped toward shore. At the time, I never would have imagined that saving the damn kid would change everything. But like my old partner in Denver Homicide said every time the unexpected occurred: "Life is what happens when you have other plans." He always followed it with, "Shit happens."

Chapter 4

I found Jimmy in the stern of the *Wahoo,* untangling dive gear. I recognized the syndrome. Keep busy enough and maybe you could wipe out the horror of the dive, muffle the fear, and forget how terrified you'd been so that you could get back in the water.

He and I both knew we were going back down. We had no choice. We needed to bring the bodies up and we couldn't leave it to the volunteers on the BVI Search and Rescue team, who were not qualified in underwater investigation. Things needed to be done by the book. That's what I'd been training Jimmy to do—analyze the scene, handle the evidence, bag the bodies, and document everything.

I'd been worried about how Jimmy would perform under pressure. He was so young, with all the recklessness that came with it. But he had really come through today under the worst possible conditions.

"Sit down, Jimmy. Leave that stuff for a minute. We've got time before we go back down."

He sat, put his arms on his knees and his head in his hands, and gazed at the wet floor.

"You were unbelievable down there, Jimmy," I said, hoping to divert the doubt. Too late.

"I don't know 'bout dat, Hannah," he said in his island accent and then grew quiet. I knew he was reliving the entire last hour, play by play, kicking himself for what he thought he could have done better. I'd done it plenty of times myself.

I leaned back and lifted my face to the sun, trying to regain my own equilibrium. The scene had been like a Dali painting, surreal and frightening. Now, sitting in the back of the *Wahoo,* I could almost convince myself that I'd fallen asleep and dreamed it all, that it was just another day in paradise.

I could see a big cruise ship docked over in Road Harbor and sailboat masts jutting into a sky dotted with cotton puffs. Nearby, a flock of terns chattered and splashed in the water, feeding on a school of small silversides. The water sparkled like a sapphire crystal, except around the police and rescue boats, where everything looked mean and ugly brown. A dark foam of flotsam—life jackets, seat cushions, even a few pieces of luggage—was finding its way to the surface.

"I be thinkin' a couple a dem folks not be pullin' through," Jimmy finally said, lifting his head. "Maybe I coulda been gettin' dem up top quicker. Maybe I shoulda been spendin' more time givin' dem CPR on the surface before I be goin' back down. When I be comin' up da first time with dat redheaded lady, no one be out here yet. I be leavin' her with dat guy and da older woman. Dey be hanging on to the *Wahoo.* The next time when I gets up with dat fella with da parrot shirt, the place be swarmin' with boats. I just be handin' da guy over to da closest boat and going back down.

"Mon, I be one happy fella da next time I come up with dat couple and be seein' da chief, Stark, and Carmichael on the Search and Rescue boat. Still, dat young blond woman be lookin' real bad. Maybe if I be gettin' her up to da top faster, she be conscious now."

"You did everything exactly the way I would have, Jimmy. No one could have gotten them up more quickly.

And you had to leave the victims with whoever was on the surface. It was just the two of us to get those people out. You know what would have happened if you hadn't been back at the airplane door every time I needed you there? I'd have had to head up with the victims or release them into the water and hope they'd make it to the surface. Christ, you saved people down there, Jimmy. I don't know what I would have done if you hadn't been there. You kept your head and did your job. You're one hell of a diver."

"I be havin' a good teacher," he said with a quick smile.

About then Carmichael and Mason came back to the stern and we developed the recovery plan. I'd never dived with Mason but had gone down with Carmichael many times. He was an exceptional diver—professional and levelheaded. The first time I ever dived with him, almost two years ago now, a killer had trapped me in a wreck. I was breathing the last of my air when Carmichael showed up and shared his air until we made it to the surface. We'd been friends ever since.

Carmichael owned his own dive shop, Underwater Adventures, one of the most reputable operations in the islands. He never took anyone out on a dive that they weren't qualified to make. And he wouldn't put up with the bullshitters—the ones who bragged about all the macho diving they'd done, going down one hundred fifty feet and into the middle of a pack of hammerheads, a knife strapped to each leg. That kind of bullshitters. Carmichael told them to find another shop.

Both Carmichael and Mason had been on call for BVI Search and Rescue this morning when the plane went down. Their boat had been one of the first on the scene.

I filled them in on what we were likely to encounter down there. All four of us would descend to the aircraft, Carmichael and Mason ready to assist as needed.

Dunn and I had talked over the procedures. Since we had no idea why the plane had crashed, we agreed that this would be treated like every other underwater crime scene. That meant recording what we saw, assuming the victims were possible targets and that there might be evidence that needed to be preserved.

I would photograph as we circled the exterior of the aircraft. Then Jimmy and I would go inside. I'd take close-ups of the bodies. Then we'd bag them and pass them out to Carmichael and Mason, who would swim them to the surface. I warned them that by now the area would be thick with sharks.

"Not a problem," Carmichael said. "Got just what we be needin'. I be dyin' to try des things out." He jumped into the BVI Search and Rescue boat, pulled a nest of equipment out of the hold, and shot a smug smile our way.

"One of da local banks be donatin' des to da team. They be called Shark Shields, made by an Australian company. Things are supposed ta send out a protective electrical field dat sharks be detectin' through da sensory receptacles on der snouts. Shark hits dat electronic barrier and takes off. Doesn't hurt da shark, doesn't bother any other kinds of fish. Puts a circle of protection around da diver."

"Jeez, Carmichael. You say you haven't tried one out yet?" I said. I admit it. I'm a born skeptic, especially when it comes to guarantees about jumping into a sea full of sharks.

"Come on, Sampson. They be better den nothin', which is what we'd be havin' otherwise," he said, handing each of us one of the devices.

"Okay, but let's not just assume that these things will make everything okay down there. We need to stay alert," I cautioned.

Carmichael showed us how to put the things on, strapping the main housing unit onto his thigh, then attaching one of the antennae units to his tank and the other around his ankle. A snakelike appendage dangled from the unit. I didn't like it. Until I got in the water.

A couple of sharks in the eight-foot category were swimming right around the boat and more were gathering around the wreck. Carmichael headed right toward a big reef shark and it immediately turned tail and swam away.

Okay, so maybe the Shark Shields did work, but perhaps it was Carmichael's human countenance that sent the thing running. I wasn't about to take any chances and I didn't want the others to either.

I signaled that we needed to head to the wreck, which was only a dark shadow in the water. We could barely make out the logo on the tail, a palm tree with a setting sun. The plane had completely settled on the bottom now. I snapped off several dozen shots as we swam around the aircraft, close-ups of the engines, tail, wings. Everything seemed intact, but then I know nothing about mechanics. I don't even consider lifting the hood on my old Rambler.

The entire nose section was crushed in. No wonder neither of the pilots had survived. Hitting the water at the speed the plane had been falling out of the sky would have been like slamming into a brick wall at a hundred miles per hour. It seemed amazing that it hadn't broken apart. The fuselage had accordioned all the way back to the first row, sending metal into the couple seated there.

Exterior photos taken, we swam back to the cabin door. Jimmy was in the lead. About the time he got to within fifteen feet of the opening, a flurry of sharks, clearly desperate to escape what had to be the electrical current emitted from his Shark Shield, found their way out of the aircraft and disappeared. Then one last shark darted through the door, a foot gripped in its teeth—a woman's foot with a sandal strapped around the ankle, toenails glistening with red polish.

I could see the horror cross Carmichael's face. Then Mason started upchucking in his regulator. Jimmy hung in there, maintaining his composure. We hovered for a few minutes, waiting for Mason to purge his regulator. I had to hand it to him. He took care of it without a problem and signaled he was okay.

Finally, Jimmy and I swam into the gloom. He stayed out of the frame while I took wide-angle photos to capture the context—the entire layout of the plane and the location of the victims. Then I took close-ups of each row of seats, the interior walls and ceiling, and the cockpit.

When I'd finished photographing, Jimmy swam into the cabin with the body bags. They were designed with open mesh panels so that water would flow out as the bodies were brought to the surface. This would be the first time that Jimmy had encountered a body underwater. I'd tried to tell him what to expect, but words rarely painted a complete picture.

Jimmy had sloughed it off at the time, but the kid was way at the other end of the spectrum from emotional zombie. I worried about how he'd handle it.

The first guy was in pretty good shape. No open wounds to draw a flurry of predators. I was sure this was Simon's father. In the seat pocket across the aisle, I could see a Walkman I figured was Simon's. I wondered what his father had been thinking, with his son back in the bathroom and the plane going down.

He was about forty-five, wearing khakis and a plain blue short-sleeved shirt with a pocket protector that still held pens in place. Wire-rimmed glasses were propped on his nose, shattered now, the bows holding them tightly against his face. The guy exuded nerd. Nothing flashy about him and nothing about his appearance that said vacation. I wondered what had brought him and the kid down here.

I was guessing that he had followed directions and grabbed his ankles when the plane started down. I could never figure out why anyone thought that was a good idea. He'd clearly jammed the top of his head into the seat in front of him when the plane hit. His neck had snapped.

There was a deep indentation in the seat in front of him where he'd hit.

Jimmy unbuckled the seat belt. We slipped the guy's feet into the body bag and the rest of the body followed. We zipped it up, then we each took an end, swam to the door, and handed the body off to Carmichael and Mason.

That was the easy part. Next was the couple up at the bulkhead. It was not going to be pretty. I signaled Jimmy and we started forward. The sharks had done their work. The lower limbs were gone. The torsos were still complete, but other smaller, though no less ferocious, scavengers were at work—already a few fish were nibbling around the wounds. They scattered when we unbuckled what was left of the bodies.

Jimmy never flinched. We bagged them and hauled them out of the plane. Carmichael and Mason had already made it back down and took them to the surface. Finally, we pulled the captain out of his seat in the cockpit, got him zipped into a bag, and headed slowly through the turquoise water to the surface. Not far off I could see a coral head, home to a flourishing colony of life. Sea fans swayed in the gentle current, a couple of French angelfish darted around the rocks, and a sergeant major diligently guarded the purple circle of eggs that decorated a rock face.

Just yards from the wreckage was a separate world, one unconcerned with the human drama that had unfolded nearby. It made me feel stupid somehow. Such ridiculous activity. Such fools to be making a world where airplanes fell from the sky and where bodies were hauled from the sea.

Once up top, we inflated our buoyancy control devices, or BCs in diver's shorthand. The hissing noise brought me back to reality. Carmichael and Mason were on board waiting to assist and pulled the last body into the boat. We swam to the ladder, removed our fins, threw them onto the transom, and climbed aboard.

The coroner had already arrived and was unzipping the

first body bag that Carmichael and Mason had brought up. He'd do a quick examination before the effects of exposure to air took hold, though it was pretty apparent the guy had died from the impact when the plane had slammed into the water.

"The guy's neck is broken," he said without emotion.

"Any ID?" I asked.

"Just a second, let me check." He reached around to the guy's back pocket, pulled out a wallet, and handed it to me.

Inside I found a water-soaked driver's license issued to Lawrence Redding. I pulled a plastic picture holder out of a side compartment and opened it to a smiling family photo of Redding and a petite, slightly overweight blond woman. Simon stood between them.

Chapter 5

Dunn and Stark were at the hospital by the time I got there. I told them that Simon's father had been on the plane and that we'd pulled his body out. God knows why I thought I should be the one to tell the kid.

He was sitting up in bed fooling around with the TV remote when I went in. His face actually lit up when he saw me. This was not going to be easy. I figured I was about to crush his world.

"Hannah," he said. "You came."

"I told you I'd be here."

"Yeah, but grown-ups tell you stuff like that all the time."

What was that about? It sounded like the kid had been disappointed a lot in his short life.

"Hey, I always do what I say I'm going to do," I said, sitting next to him on the bed. "Don't forget it."

"Did you find my dad?"

I hesitated, wishing I could tell him his dad was fine. Was there any right way to tell the kid his father was dead? If there was, I didn't know it.

"Jeez, Simon. I'm so sorry," I stammered. "Your dad didn't make it."

He sat there for a minute flipping madly through the channels, trying to hold it in. Then a tear slipped down his cheek and his face crumpled. I pulled him to me. He buried his head in my chest and sobbed, deep, racking sobs.

A couple of minutes later a nurse came in, checked Simon's vitals, and handed him a sedative and a glass of water. He took it without question. She told me she'd be at the nurses' station if I needed anything.

Soon Simon's sobs turned to whimpers and he lay back on the pillow.

"How old are you, Simon?"

"Nine, but I'll be ten next month."

"Any brothers or sisters?"

"Naw, just me. My mom died in a car accident when I was six. It was just my dad and me," he said, more tears sliding down his face.

"Were you on vacation down here?"

"It was kind of a vacation, but my dad, he's always real busy with his job. He gives people money, has to check on them all the time."

"What kind of people?" I asked. Now the kid had my interest. Checking up on people he gave money to could lead to all kinds of trouble. Though there was no reason to believe that the plane crash was anything but accidental, I could never let a weirdness pass without note. This was definitely a weirdness.

"Scientists, mostly, I guess. For their projects," Simon replied.

"Who did he work for?"

"The Woods Foundation. He asked me to come down here with him. He said it would be like a father/son vacation, but we never did anything fun together except for on our last day. We rented a motorboat. The rest of the time all I did was follow him around while he worked."

"Do you know who he had business with?"

"Some man who's studying some trees."

"Trees?" That didn't sound too sinister.

"Yeah. You know, those mangroves that grow near the

water," he said. He was starting to drift, the drugs taking effect.

"Who should we contact for you, Simon?" I asked.

"I guess you should call my aunt. We never see her much. She and my dad don't get along."

"What about grandparents?"

"My grandma and grandpa were in the car with my mom and dad and me. There's just my other grandma, but she's in a nursing home. My dad and aunt are always arguing about her."

He couldn't keep his eyes open now.

"Okay, Simon. You get some sleep."

"You know I'm not a baby," he said.

"Of course you're not. Why would I think that?"

"Well . . ." he hesitated.

"What is it?"

"Will you stay here just till I go to sleep?" he asked.

"Sure thing. And I'll be back in the morning."

"Promise?"

"I promise," I said. He was asleep in five minutes.

God, I felt horrible. This kid, so slight under the covers, so alone. I sat stroking his head for another few minutes until I heard yelling out in the hall.

"Hey, keep it down out here, for crissakes," I said, stepping into the hall.

A heavyset guy with horn-rimmed glasses and a belly hanging over his belt was on Dunn's case and was actually poking a finger in his chest.

"I would appreciate your keeping your hands to yourself," Dunn said in his typically understated manner, one that the guy couldn't ignore. He backed away but continued his tirade.

"I just saw my wife and I want an explanation for what happened out there today. She said that your people left her floating in the water out at that plane crash."

"You want to tell me who you are, sir?" Dunn said.

"I'm Jack Westbrook. U.S. Senator John Quincy Westbrook," he said, emphasizing the *U.S. Senator* part.

I stepped in. I hated it when someone from my country was an ass. "Look, Senator, Chief Dunn was not on the scene. I was."

"So, why did you leave my wife in the water? She said it was teeming with sharks!"

"I made a snap evaluation of the situation. Your wife was safe. She was lucky to be one of the two people who got out of the plane before it went under the water. You have that movie star to thank. I wasn't about to waste precious time pulling your wife into the police boat. There was a chance I could get the others out of the plane before they drowned. Do you really think I should have done otherwise?"

He blustered and flustered, muttering something about wanting a full investigation, until Dunn interceded.

"Why weren't you on the plane with your wife?" he asked.

"I had plans to fly out later. I had to take care of some business and make sure my boat was secure," he said. "I was down at the marina arguing with that SeaSail owner, O'Brien. I told him I wanted my boat hauled over to the hurricane hole for the rest of the hurricane season or I'd pull it out of his fleet. I rushed out to the airport when I heard the plane went down. They said that victims had been transported here."

I bet he'd threatened every airline official at the airport in the process. The guy was obviously a blowhard who thought he deserved some sort of consideration the rest of the population didn't.

"Was your wife traveling alone?" I asked.

"No," he said. "Our sailing companions, the Rileys, were with her." It was written all over his face. He hadn't even inquired about them and he was embarrassed at the diplomatic snafu. He'd been too busy complaining to think about his friends.

I realized they were the couple in the front of the aircraft. The coroner had pulled a license out of the mangled pocket of the man. It had been issued to William Riley III.

"Are they around sixty? Woman blond, guy almost completely gray?" I asked.

"Yes. Are they here in the hospital?"

"I'm afraid they didn't make it," I said.

"What?" he said, shocked. "You just told me you left my wife floating in shark-infested water to save the people on that plane. Now you tell me you didn't."

"That's exactly what I'm telling you," I said. I was ready to take my turn poking him in the chest. Anticipating my reaction, Dunn took my arm and held me back.

"Look, Senator," I said, taking a deep breath, "we saved some, we lost some. Unfortunately, the Rileys died on impact."

"Jeezus, you know who they were? His family is one of the oldest and wealthiest on the East Coast—right up there with the Rockefellers. He heads a Fortune Five Hundred company. What do you mean, dead?"

"Sorry," I said. "I wasn't considering net worth when I was down there rescuing people." What an ass. I'd pissed him off, though.

"Don't speak to me in that manner, miss."

"It's 'Detective,'" I said. "Detective Hannah Sampson."

Dunn stepped in before things escalated further. "We'd like you to identify the bodies," he said. "We'll need to start notifying next of kin."

"Hell, I can do that. Where are they?"

"They should already be in the morgue downstairs. Let me warn you though. There was substantial injury to their lower torsos," Dunn said.

"Christ, I've seen dead people before. Let's go," he said, not a speck of regret or sorrow at the loss of his friends visible in his expression. In fact, he looked smug and somehow satisfied. I wondered how much this guy really cared about the Rileys. Maybe he was glad that they were dead. Maybe he had something to gain. It was another item for my weirdness list.

"Detective Sampson will take you down there," Dunn said.

I was about to object, but then I decided I might learn something more about the guy's relationship to the Rileys and the crash by watching him.

"Let's go."

We waited for the elevator in dead silence, me still angry, he just oblivious. The antagonistic exchange we'd had in the hallway was probably run of the mill for him, the kind of confrontation he engaged in every day in Washington before they all went to one of those three-martini lunches. I know I'm a bit hostile. I just don't like politicians.

Finally the elevator arrived and we stepped in. I pushed the button for the basement and we stood side by side, staring at our reflections in the elevator door. I looked less than official. I'd showered quickly at the marina after the dive and pulled on a pair of shorts, an orange tank top, and an old pair of Birkenstocks that were in my duffel bag. Sunglasses dangled from a rope around my neck.

My dark hair was sun-streaked and wild. I was deeply tanned in spite of the fact that I was keeping several sunscreen companies in business. There wasn't much to be done about it. By the time I turned fifty, I'd look like a raisin. Even in the reflection in the elevator door I could tell that my dark eyes were haunted by today's dead.

Westbrook was giving me the once-over though he was trying not to be obvious. I was doing the same—sizing him up. He was close to six-two and overweight by about forty pounds. He exuded confidence and money. He too was wearing shorts but with a white golf shirt. Unlike mine, his shorts were ironed and perfectly creased. His white hair was coifed, his nails manicured, and he was deeply tanned. His cologne was overpowering in the confined space.

"So, how long have you been with the police department down here?" he asked, breaking the silence.

"Almost two years now." I'd quit my job in Denver Homicide to take the position as a detective and the only underwater investigator for what I'd thought would be the quiet Tortola PD. Even in paradise though, there was trouble.

"You're American. This is an odd place to end up. Seems like an end-of-the-road kind of place."

"You could look at it that way. I don't."

"You'd be able to make a name for yourself in the States. There can't be too many experts in underwater investigation around, especially as good-looking as you are."

I could not believe the man who had accused me of leaving his wife as shark bait was now flirting. "I'm happy just where I am," I said.

"Sorry if I was rude upstairs. Can I make it up to you. Buy you dinner?"

"Maybe when your wife is up to it," I said. There was no way I'd be caught alone in a restaurant with this guy. He knew what I was saying and changed the subject.

"What was it like down there in that airplane? It must have been some intense diving."

"Yeah." I knew he wanted the gory details, but I wasn't about to elaborate.

"Did you see anything that makes you think this wasn't an accident?" he asked.

"Nope, but we'll be diving out there again in the morning."

"More than likely it was an equipment failure. One thing's for sure," he said, a note of derision in his manner. "No terrorist would bother to sabotage one of these island puddle jumpers. Not much of a political statement."

"There are motives other than terrorism," I said.

Chapter 6

Even Westbrook's cologne couldn't mask the smell of the morgue that assaulted my senses the minute we got off the elevator. Nothing like it. It's trite to say it smelled like death but that was exactly how it smelled—like blood and body fluids muted by disinfectant.

I led the way down a dimly lit hallway to the double doors and pushed through. An attendant in a bloodstained lab coat was sitting at a desk. I showed him my badge and told him we were there to identify the Riley couple. He led us to the back, where the bodies were still bagged and lying on gurneys. It was pretty obvious which were the Rileys—no bulk in the lower half of the bag. The attendant unzipped one of the bags, exposing the face.

"Yeah, that's Bill Riley," Westbrook said. He didn't show a sign of emotion. This didn't bother him in the least. He moved in closer, and before I realized what he was doing, he'd pulled the zipper all the way down, exposing the whole body. One leg was missing at the hip. All that was left of the other was the bloody end of a femur.

"Ol' Riley. At least you kept your pecker," he said, carelessly flipping one side of the bag back over the body. Then he checked out the wife and said her name was Louise. "I'll call the family," he said and walked out the door. The guy never even flinched.

It was past three o'clock when I got back upstairs and tracked Dunn and Stark down in Dr. Hall's office.

Hall is head of the hospital and chief of surgery, "surgery" including everything from a well-placed stitch and a Band-Aid to repairing gunshot wounds. He's patched me up more than once.

Hall was sitting behind his desk tapping his pen against his forehead and flipping through papers. A woman I didn't know sat on the other side. She looked official though, wore a gray suit, a perfectly tailored size eight if I had to guess, with a blouse in subtle gray and navy stripes. She wore navy heels and carried a navy handbag and leather briefcase. She was black, probably forty, and a classy-looking woman.

"Hannah, this is Edith Leonard. She owns Island Air," Hall said. I knew the name. It appeared in the paper at least once a week for some charity event or other. Her husband was a high-powered attorney with clients in offshore banking. The Leonard name was on a dozen businesses around the islands, from mom-and-pop groceries to auto dealerships to the huge office complex in the middle of town. I had little doubt that she was related to most of them. Her family had a lot of clout in the islands.

She stood and took my hand. "Detective Sampson. I can't thank you enough for your heroics today. If you hadn't been out there and acted quickly, no one in that plane would have survived."

"I was in the right place at the right time," I said. "Jimmy Snyder was unbelievably skilled down there and we were lucky. I'm sorry we couldn't save them all."

"From what I've been told, there was nothing you could do. Those that didn't make it died on impact."

She placed the briefcase on her lap, unsnapped the buckles, and pulled out a couple of printed documents. She'd brought the passenger list and the emergency contact information that the airline routinely collected from passengers.

"The airline will notify relatives. We'll need to give them a contact number here at the hospital," she said, getting down to business.

"They can call me directly," Hall said, handing her his card. "That number rings right into my office. They won't have to go through the hospital switchboard."

"Now, what about an investigation?" she asked, turning to Dunn. "I want the airline to be involved and I'd like to be kept informed. I'm convinced that my company is not at fault and I want it proven. You probably know we are a new outfit—not yet three years in business. We just bought our fifth plane. Our target market has been the wealthy traveler who wants red-carpet treatment and it's really paid off. We've managed to capture a select market. I can't afford the negative publicity and I certainly can't withstand a lot of frivolous lawsuits about negligence."

"Red-carpet treatment is one thing, but what about maintenance?" Stark asked. Money and power didn't impress Stark.

"We keep our planes in top condition. The plane that went down was a Beech 99, completely refurbished inside and out."

"You must know that ninety-nine point nine percent of the time these crashes are due to mechanical failure or pilot error," Dunn said. I wondered where he'd gotten that figure.

"More than likely that's the case here," he continued. "For what other reason would that plane have gone down?"

"I can assure you that neither pilot error nor equipment failure is involved in this case. I maintain a strict schedule of maintenance on my aircraft and that plane was gone over from nose to tail just one month ago. Every system was checked."

"What about the pilots?" Dunn asked.

"I hire only the best. Both were highly experienced. The captain has been with the airline from the beginning and his record is impeccable. He flew Beech 99s for Caribbean Airways before coming to us. Additionally, in January both he and the copilot went to do refresher training on the Beech 99 as well as our other aircraft. We require that all our pilots take this training every year."

"What else could be a factor?" Dunn prompted.

"I did heard reports that there was an explosion before the plane went down," she said. "You know what's happening in the world these days. It was just a matter of time before terrorism reached our quiet islands."

This was the second time today that someone had suggested terrorism. Westbrook being the first.

"I didn't hear an explosion," I said. "Where did you get that information?"

"I was told that one of the local fishermen was talking about it on the docks. Word gets around."

"I'd call it rumor," I said.

"Besides," Stark said, incredulous, "why would a terrorist want to bring down a little island hopper in the Caribbean? Not much of a statement there. I mean, come on." He bent his arms out at his side, his hands open, palms up, making a weighing motion. "A 757 into the Pentagon—a turboprop Beechcraft into Drake Channel and a big spread in the *Island News*. I don't think we should waste our time going there."

"I'm sure that my airline is not at fault," she said. "Perhaps there was someone targeted on the plane."

"Let's not jump the gun here," Dunn said. "We need to check out the plane and its contents. Hannah, I want you out there first thing in the morning. Snyder will back you up. I've spoken with the director of civil aviation. He will get in touch with the UK Department of Transport, which handles aircraft accidents in the islands. He'll get back to us as soon as he can make arrangements to get a crash investigator down here. I've already arranged a site in one of the empty warehouses in the harbor. Everything that is brought up will be taken there.

"The sooner we get this resolved, the better for everyone—victims, families, airline, the tranquillity of the islands," Dunn insisted. "Besides, a tropical wave is developing in the Atlantic with the potential to move in by the end of the week. Conditions could get impossible out on the water."

I did not want to dive into that airplane again, but I knew there wasn't a choice. It was times like this that I really missed having an expert team of divers like the team I headed in Denver. Here, we had one experienced underwater crime scene investigator—me—and Jimmy. Most of the time that was sufficient.

We started through the passenger list that Edith Leonard had brought. Dr. Hall referred to the patient files on his desk, updating us on the condition of the victims. Both pilots had been dead on arrival—multiple injuries. The other dead were the Rileys and Lawrence Redding.

The young couple were newlyweds on their honeymoon. Hall reported that though the groom had moderate injuries, a sprained wrist and contusions, his wife was touch and go. She had been without oxygen for probably fifteen minutes before the emergency crew got her breathing out there on the boat, and she had also sustained head injuries. Her husband had already called relatives and her parents were getting the first available flight down.

The woman who had been making her way out of the plane when we got down to the wreck was fine. Her name was Zora Gordon and she was insisting on being released. Hall saw no reason to keep her in the hospital.

Daniel Stewart, the actor, had also been injured. He had a broken collarbone and wrist. He'd been traveling with his agent, Sammy Lorenzo, the guy in the parrot shirt who'd been unwilling to give up my regulator. They'd be released in the morning, as would Debra Westbrook, the senator's wife.

That left Simon. He was physically okay but emotionally devastated. His aunt was listed as an emergency contact. I remembered what he'd said about his aunt. I didn't like it.

Chapter 7

The door to 107 was ajar when I walked past. I couldn't help overhearing the excited conversation on the other side. Okay, I admit it. I eavesdrop. It's my job.

"We can really take advantage of this whole situation," the man was saying. "The tabloids are still picking up on the lies that 'dancer' was spreading around about you. Once we get this story out, those rumors will be old news. You'll be a real-life hero. I can see the headlines. *Movie Star Saves Senator's Wife!*

"Look at the copy that reporter dropped off. It will be on the front page of the local island rag tomorrow morning. By tomorrow afternoon, I'll have that photo in every big paper in the U.S."

I tapped lightly on the door the moment the guy stopped to take a breath. There was silence for a few more seconds. Then another voice invited me in.

A man who looked a lot like Danny DeVito was sitting in a chair, sweeping his arms through a cloud of smoke that circled just above his head, obscuring the "No Smoking" sign. This had to be Sammy Lorenzo. I recognized him as the passenger in the parrot shirt. He quickly tried to put the cigar out, but it still smoldered as he cupped it in the palm of his hand. I couldn't believe he could handle smoke in his lungs after nearly drowning just a few hours ago. I chalked it up to the healing powers of tobacco and let it go.

"Hannah Sampson, Tortola PD," I said, shaking Lorenzo's hand.

"Detective Sampson," he said, standing and gushing. "It's so good to meet you. Man, you really saved my ass down there in that airplane! We were hoping for the chance to meet you. This is Daniel Stewart."

"How are you doing?" I asked, turning to Stewart. He was lying in the hospital bed, his wrist in a cast, his arm in a sling.

"Fantastic. They've got me on some dynamite painkillers." He looked it.

"I wanted to stop in and thank you for taking care of Debra Westbrook out there. It allowed us to get down to that plane fast and pull the other passengers out."

"Hey, we're at your service," Lorenzo said. He was chewing on the unlit cigar, working it into a slimy mess.

"So Betty Welsh has already been here to get the story," I said, picking up a couple of photos that lay on the bedside table with her card clipped to them.

I wasn't surprised. The woman was a dynamo. I hadn't seen her out at the scene, but she'd clearly been there with a photographer. I studied the pictures, one of Stewart in the water holding on to Debra Westbrook, then another of him helping her onto the rescue boat.

Betty had to have been one of the first on the scene. I couldn't help admiring the woman. She always wrote an accurate and responsible account. If someone was scooping the story, I was glad it was Betty.

"Yeah. As a matter of fact, she just left," Lorenzo said. "She spent an hour interviewing Daniel. I told her I wanted to get the story out on the wire and hit the major papers in the States. It will be great publicity! Absolutely fantastic. This couldn't get any better." Lorenzo was nearly choking on his cigar now.

Stewart had hardly said a word. He was looking uncomfortable with the whole concept. *Surprising*, I thought. After all, this is what being a star was all about. He noticed me noticing.

"Sammy is the mover and shaker. That's why I hired him. He does what I can't and he's a good friend," Stewart said. "If it weren't for him, I wouldn't have a career. He does the promotion and keeps me working. All I want to do is act. Funny, huh? Right now it's this *Avenger* gig, but we're about to sign for a major role for a film with a multi-million-dollar budget. That's all because of Sammy."

I'd never met an actor before, but if I'd given it any thought, Stewart would not have been what I'd expect. He seemed pretty humble and low-key for a guy who probably had women hanging all over him. I didn't begrudge him the publicity. It had to have been painful pushing Debra Westbrook out of that plane and holding her up in the water with the injuries he'd sustained.

"Are you up to telling me what you remember about the crash?" I asked.

Stewart replied, "I was sitting in the last row on the right side near the window. There were two seats together back there. The senator's wife moved back right before takeoff and asked if she could take the seat next to me. I told her sure. There was the kid. Christ, I can't believe you got him out. What about his dad?"

"He didn't make it."

"Man, tough break. Is the kid okay?"

"About as you'd expect. He's hurting. Doc gave him something to help him sleep."

"I'll get down to his room to see him," he said.

"He'll like that," I said and pressed on. "So what happened next?"

"Well, we'd barely lifted off the ground when the kid got up and went to the john. He was taking pictures out the window on his way.

"I could tell his father didn't like it. The seat belt light was still on. He kept looking back to see if the kid was okay.

"About then I heard one of the engines sputter and quit. Just minutes later, the captain came on the intercom. Said there was a problem, he'd be heading back to the airport. I wasn't too worried. I knew the plane could make it back easily on one engine. But he'd just begun to turn the plane when the other engine quit. God, what a feeling. It was horrible."

I could only imagine. Everyone on board must have known what was going to happen.

"We kind of floated there for a second, then the thing just started to fall. The pilot came back on. Jeez, I could hear the barely controlled panic as he told us to prepare for a crash landing." Stewart was reliving it and trying to contain the horror.

"We didn't have time to react. I heard the father yelling to his son. He was struggling to get out of his seat to get to the bathroom, but he couldn't get up. The plane was going down too fast. All he could do was stay buckled in and brace for the crash.

"The plane hit the water like a rock. People were screaming and the water was rushing in like crazy. Everything's kind of a blur after that. I don't even remember unbuckling my seat belt. Everyone else seemed kind of stunned. I helped the senator's wife. I got her unbuckled and we stumbled to the door. I don't even remember opening it, but I guess I did."

Stewart couldn't tell the story fast enough now, his words tumbling over one another as though getting them out would end the horror.

"I was trying to push her out when the plane started sinking, sliding right through the water nose first. She was having a hard time fighting her way out the door. I just pushed as hard as I could and suddenly we were in the water. I could feel myself being sucked down with the plane. I held on to her and prayed. Suddenly we were on the surface. That's when I saw you."

"Did you notice anything unusual when you were checking in or waiting to board?"

"No, nothing like that. Are you thinking this wasn't an accident?"

"Not likely, but we've got to check it out. Were you guys vacationing in the islands?"

"Yeah," Lorenzo said. He had been growing paler and more subdued as Stewart described the crash. "Daniel wanted to get away for a few days. Jeez, he's right in the middle of filming *Avenger* number three. I couldn't talk him out of it though. He wanted some sun and tropical breezes.

"A couple of days ago, I decided to join Danny. I couldn't believe it when I got here. Everybody's out on damn boats—boring. Give me a casino and showgirls anytime. When Daniel here up and decided all of a sudden to head back home, I was racing him to the airport."

"I wanted to get off the island before that bad weather hit and we ended up stranded. I've got to get back to the film," Stewart explained.

"How did you choose here?" I asked. "Why not someplace like Saint Barts?" That little island just off of St. Martin was known as the hangout of the rich and famous. It was French, had unbelievably good restaurants and a picturesque port with a few million-dollar boats tied to the docks and moored in the bay.

"That's what I wanted to know," Lorenzo said. "Danny here had no interest in going there."

"Why would I want to go someplace where there are a bunch of other movie stars?" he asked. "Remember, the point was to get away."

"I'll let you two get some rest," I said. They both looked

beat, especially Stewart. I could see that the pain meds were
wearing off. His face was strained, his jaw tight.

"Detective," Stewart said as I stood to leave, "what happens with the plane?"

"I'll be going back down there in the morning. A couple
of salvage divers will help bring the aircraft up. There's an
investigation whenever a plane goes down."

"What about the contents?" he asked.

"Everything will be collected and secured until the investigation is complete," I explained. "It will be a while before anything will be released though. I'd guess the airline
will be responsible for shipping your belongings to you."

"Hey, Detective," Sammy said as I started out the door.
"How about we get a picture tomorrow of you and Daniel,
maybe in the police boat, you in your dive gear. It would be
great press," he said, getting into the idea, working on the
spin. "I can see it now. A follow-up story. Daniel Stewart
assists drop-dead-gorgeous scuba-diving cop. Will it turn to
romance?"

"It's his job," Stewart said, shaking his head.

"I don't think so, Sammy," I said, smiling to myself as I
closed the door. Lorenzo was a real schemer but somehow
likable.

I was on my way past the nurses' station when I recognized the small woman standing there arguing with one of
the nurses. She was unfazed by the fact that the nurse towered over her. It was Zora Gordon, one of the passengers
from the plane. She was a unique but exquisite-looking
woman, olive-skinned, her features finely chiseled, her hair
a deep red mass of curls that cascaded down her back. She
was maybe five-two and didn't look like she'd hit thirty yet.
She wore nylon shorts that showed off muscular legs. The
woman obviously worked out. She was pressuring the nurse
to get the paperwork done so she could get out of there. I
stopped and introduced myself.

"Oh yes, you are the diver. I suppose I should thank you for getting me out of that plane this morning."

"Seems like you were on your way out without any help from me," I said.

"Yeah, well, I'm not the type to simply sit there and drown. Do you know what caused the crash?" she asked.

"Not yet. We'll be out there again in the morning. We'll need to interview all the passengers as well."

"I can't tell you anything. The plane was in the water before I knew what was happening," Zora said. "I really don't want to talk about the whole ugly affair."

"I'm afraid we won't be giving people any choice," I said.

"All right, if it's absolutely necessary," she said as she scrawled her name at the bottom of the release form that the nurse had placed in front of her.

"It is. Where can I find you?" I asked.

"I am vacationing on a yacht in Brandywine Bay. It is called the *Mystic*. You will need to ask the marina security man to let you in. He will unlock the gate to the dock. Please call ahead to let me know when you are coming. Here's my cell number." She grabbed a piece of paper from the counter, jotted down the number, handed it to me, and headed down the hall.

"Thanks. I'll be in touch," I said as she pushed through the front door of the hospital and disappeared.

Stark and I met up back at the Tortola PD. Stark was in his office, a carbon copy of mine. It was a perfect cube, nine by nine with a door, no window, and just big enough to hold a desk and a chair. Stark had the chair, and his bulk alone made the room overcrowded.

Stark, Alvin Mahler, and I were the only detectives who worked out of this office. Mahler was out for the week on vacation down island. Then there was Jimmy Snyder. In addition there were seven uniformed officers, Dunn, and his

secretary, Jean. Our office did all the investigative work
and handled the occasional homicide. Other ancillary offices scattered throughout the islands handled the "routine"
stuff—mostly domestic problems, vandalism, and traffic
violations, which were loosely enforced, to say the least.

The tourist guides say there are forty islands, islets,
rocks, and cays in the BVI. As far as I can tell, a good fifty
percent of them fall into the rock category, a pile of vol-
canic debris jutting out of the water.

The total population of the BVI is around 19,000 people.
Some 14,000 live on the main island of Tortola. Road
Town, where our office is located, is the capital and center
of commerce. Offshore banking is big business in the islands, with tourism in the form of the sailing industry a
close second. The BVI boast of having the largest sailboat
fleet in the world.

Ten miles long and a mile wide, Virgin Gorda is the second most developed island, with a population of some
2,500. To the northwest of Tortola is Jost Van Dyke, named
after a Dutch pirate. Fewer than 300 people live on that island, many of them descendants of Quaker slaves, and
they've had electricity only since 1991. On New Year's Eve
one of the biggest parties in the world takes place on Jost
Van Dyke, at the renowned Foxy's.

A couple of the other little islands have a restaurant or
small hotel and that's about it. Unfortunately, there is
change in the tropical wind—like the big resort that's
slated for Norman Island, once completely undeveloped except for the *Willie T*, an old schooner and floating bar that
hosts the more hardy crews.

Stark and I found Chief Dunn behind his desk waiting
for us. He had the corner office with a big picture window
that looked out on Road Harbor and Sir Francis Drake
Channel. I could see a couple of sailboats out there, sails
full, tipped in a gentle wind. The harbor itself was filled
with boats, at least a hundred masts jutting into the sky.

They were beautiful, a man-made version of a winter aspen grove in Colorado.

The spot where the plane went down was visible from the window. One of our police boats made lazy circles over the site. Someone would be patrolling out there all night and into Sunday morning to ensure that other boats did not approach and that the curious snorkeler or thrill-seeking diver did not disturb the area. Dunn had also instructed the officers on board to keep an eye out for any debris that might surface and to retrieve it before another vessel interfered. He didn't want any valuables, either the airline's or the passengers', being taken and he wanted everything handled as though it was evidence until we determined the cause of the crash.

I told them what Stewart and Lorenzo had said about the crash and about my brief and somewhat brusque encounter with Zora Gordon. Then Dunn went over plans for the morning. A representative from the Air Accident Investigation Board had called him.

"A guy named Joe Harrigan from AAIB will be on a flight into Saint Thomas from London sometime tomorrow afternoon," Dunn said. "In the meantime, he's arranged for a couple of salvage divers to go out to the site to assess the situation and determine what we will need to bring the plane up. They will meet you out there in the morning. I'll be down at the docks right after the early service.

I knew that Dunn's wife never let him miss church on Sundays. Plane crash or not, tomorrow would be no exception.

"Carmichael and Mason are willing to help out," he continued. "Stark, I want you to begin talking to the witnesses and find out what they may have seen or heard before that plane went down. I want this investigation to go smoothly. The local director of civil aviation, the airport manager, and the people at the AAIB—they all want answers. And I don't want any criticism from Edith Leonard about our procedures."

I could see the look of relief flood Stark's face when he realized that he would not have to go out with us in the morning. Someday he'd need to get past his phobia about the water.

"Has someone gotten in touch with Simon's aunt?" I asked.

"Not yet," Dunn said. "It is a bit complicated. The message on her home machine said she was out of the country and would be away for two weeks. She referred callers to her business number. Evidently she heads up a big advertising agency. Her name is Elaine Redding. Her secretary said she left one contact number. She's going to try to reach her."

"Surely there's someone else," I said.

"The secretary didn't know of anyone. She said she's never heard her boss talk about any family but her brother," Dunn replied.

"Let's hope the secretary can reach her," I said.

"We should hear back by the morning."

"Anything else?" I asked. I was exhausted. The diving today had been intense. All I wanted now was a hot shower, a decent meal, and to climb into bed with O'Brien.

Chapter 8

Enok Kiersted sat over at Calico Jack's beach bar, sipping a beer and watching the tourists at Dolphin World. There were five of them in the pen—three kids with their parents. The wife was holding back and watching while her husband coaxed the youngest to touch the dolphin that was swimming nearby. One of the older kids, a boy of about twelve, was trying to jump onto another.

Kiersted was pissed. He wondered what made people think they should be riding on dolphins. It was an insult to the animals. Humans thought they owned this earth and that every other creature on it was here to serve them.

In spite of the objections of the animal welfare community, six dolphins had been relocated to the new dolphin attraction in the lagoon. Dive operators and environmental groups had argued that the noise and vibration from the water desalination plant near the lagoon, the street traffic noise, the silt, the trash, and the dirty water that washed in during rains made the location completely unsuitable for dolphins. Besides, the lagoon was more like a pond, dredged out of a shallow mangrove lagoon. The bottom was silty, the water far too warm.

The warnings fell on deaf ears. No one took action. Now one of the dolphins was dead and another had been isolated and was being force-fed. Kiersted knew she probably wouldn't make it.

It made him sick. Wild dolphins everywhere were being trapped and placed in confined spaces. They often died just so some humans could be entertained and others could get rich in the process.

Few of the attraction's operators ever admitted that people got hurt, but they did. Kiersted had heard reports of dolphins biting and ramming people in the water. And who could blame the dolphins, trapped in captivity? Existence as they'd known it was gone. They became confused, aggressive, and sick. They died from shock, pneumonia, intestinal disease, ulcers, poisoning, and sheer hopelessness.

Kiersted had seen the creatures in the wild, leaping and darting through the water. The very nature of these animals made them uniquely unsuited to confinement. In the wild, they lived in large groups, often in tight family units. Social bonds could last for many years, sometimes a lifetime. He knew they could swim forty to a hundred miles per day. In the lagoon he watched them swim in endless circles. Dolphins are always swimming, always moving. Captivity for these ocean creatures was an absolute tragedy.

Kiersted was furious that the enclosure had been approved. In fact, he was angry about a lot of things that were going on in the islands—about the indifference to environmental issues and about the almighty dollar being placed above the need to protect marine life. He couldn't believe that the grants officer, Redding, didn't agree with him.

He'd seen it again and again. People just didn't get it. Didn't they realize they were destroying the very thing that brought the money here in the first place? The dolphin park was a good example. So was the extension of beachfront property over on the east end of Tortola. That area had been filled in with fine sand that would wash away with the first bad storm and high seas.

Yesterday he'd been back in the mangroves collecting

sediment samples when he saw someone dumping garbage over the side of a boat. He'd tried to get to the water's edge and give them a piece of his mind but there was no such thing as moving quickly through mangroves. With every step, his boots had been sucked down into the muck. Then he'd caught a foot under a root and fallen, his arms buried to the elbows in mud. By the time he got to the place where he'd seen the boat, it had disappeared around the bend. He'd recognized it though and would be watching for it.

Now he had other things on his mind. It was almost dusk. The dolphin park had just closed. He waited another half hour to be sure that everyone had gone. The place was deserted and silent, the water in the lagoon like glass except for the occasional splash of a fin as the dolphins circled, dark shapes in the shallow water.

Kiersted went down to the pen and found the sick female. She was listless, floating on her side. He got in the water and touched her. She was still breathing, barely. He pulled the netting back from her enclosure and guided her out into the main lagoon. She came around a bit when she saw the others and swam to them. One nuzzled her—a young calf, evidently her offspring.

Kiersted swam out to the far side of the pen. He held wire cutters in one hand. By the time he finished, he'd cut the entire ocean side of the pen apart. Moments later, the five dolphins swam out of the enclosure and into open, deep water. The last to go were the mother and her calf. He saw a fin glisten in the moonlight, then disappear.

Chapter 9

Sadie was waiting for me. When she saw me walking down the path to O'Brien's, she raced up, slid to a halt, and sat panting, tail sweeping through the grass.

"Hey, girl!" I crouched and she put a cold nose against my face as I scratched behind her ears. Sadie is a red Labretriever mix that my father was sure I needed for protection. I'd been living alone in a little cottage in Denver then. She's six now and has never protected me from anything but squirrels and the occasional mongoose. I mean, she's a Lab. What was my father thinking? But I love her anyway.

O'Brien was in the kitchen, standing at the stove. He'd just put a wooden spoon to his lips and slurped.

"Perfect," he whispered to himself. He hadn't heard me come in.

I stood and watched him as he went over to the counter and began dicing vegetables, intent on his work. Tonight was Marta's night off.

O'Brien was forty-one and the owner of SeaSail, a charter company with the largest fleet of sailboats in the islands. His parents had started the company with one boat more than thirty years ago. O'Brien had grown up on boats and had built the company into a multimillion-dollar enterprise.

I could watch O'Brien for hours. His face was weathered, the veins in his arms pronounced from all the time he spent winching in sails and climbing masts. He was one of those people who would never slow down and would never be far from the sea.

I'd met O'Brien when I'd first come to the islands and things had gone from casual to intense way too quickly for me. A few months back, he'd talked me into moving in with him. It was a big decision on my part. I'd been living on the *Sea Bird*, a thirty-seven-foot Island Packet, with Sadie and my cat, Nomad.

I loved the boat, my privacy, and the fact that I answered to no one. But I'd fallen hard for O'Brien. I'd put him off for as long as I could because I'd been happy with the way things were, him living in his villa, me on the boat. But O'Brien wanted more. I told him I'd give it a try, but I'd insisted on keeping the *Sea Bird*. The transition had been hard, mostly for me.

"Hi, O'Brien." I'd crept up behind him and wrapped my arms around his waist.

"Hannah," he said, turning and leaning in with a kiss that tasted like curry.

He lowered the flame on the burner and opened a bottle of Chardonnay. We took it out to the patio to watch the sunset. O'Brien's villa was perched on the hillside, just above the SeaSail marina on the eastern end of Road Town, and looked out across the channel to Peter and Salt Islands. We could see a couple of boats anchored over in Deadman's Bay. Their anchor lights looked like low-hanging stars. The water was turning orange and purple as the sun headed to the horizon.

O'Brien and I had been living together for less than a year, but we were a fit—comfortable with one another, and God knows in a lot of ways we were alike. People say opposites attract. Maybe it's true that sexual and emotional tension keeps people stuck together. It doesn't work for me. I've got enough tension in my life. I'd never thought

O'Brien would happen—that I would develop a relationship that was this close, this giving, this comfortable.

We settled into one chaise lounge together. I leaned back against him, finding comfort in the feel of his body next to mine. As I said, we were a good fit. He wrapped his arms around me and we were quiet, sipping our wine and lost in our own thoughts.

"You seem worried," I said finally, breaking the silence.

"I spent most of the day monitoring that storm. It's been upgraded to a tropical depression. It's still out in the Atlantic but moving in our direction. Right now, if it continues on its present course it will hit the BVI."

"When?"

"Midweek. Probably Wednesday, Thursday at the latest."

Already several named storms had moved through the Caribbean. A category three hurricane had grazed Jamaica before crossing Cuba and swirling out to the Atlantic. This year we had made our way through the alphabet to F. Everyone prayed that the season would not mimic the last, when four major hurricanes came through. That year Florida and the Gulf Coast had been hit hard.

Hurricane Ivan had made history, hitting farther south in the island chain than any storm in the past fifty years. It was the deadliest hurricane to hit the Caribbean in a decade, and it pummeled Grenada, where chunks of twisted metal and splintered lumber had been pitched across the hillsides and roads. Power had been out, water contaminated, and trees all over the island had been demolished.

In the harbor at St. George's, Grenada's capital and main port, the hurricane had hit with a vengeance. Ironically, the harbor had been filled with sailors who headed to Grenada every year to escape the hurricanes, which rarely hit the southern Caribbean. In the aftermath boats were piled up four deep on shore and most of the rest were on the bottom of the harbor. We'd seen photos of the devastation. I knew that O'Brien feared the same might happen to his SeaSail fleet.

"It could still veer off or die out, but at this point I've got to assume the worst," he said. "If it continues on its current course, on Monday we'll be notifying the boats out in charter and telling them to come in. It will take the better part of two days to get them into the harbor. There are a few whose itinerary puts them pretty far out. We have a couple boaters making the crossing from Saint Martin."

O'Brien refilled our glasses and gazed out at the water.

"It will be a madhouse," he continued, "finding places to tie them all up. We've got room for about a hundred fifty boats in the hurricane hole at Paraquita Bay. Every dockhand will be at work, removing sails, biminis, and taking booms down as each boat comes in. The office staff will be trying to find hotels and guesthouses for people to stay. Those last in will end up sleeping on cots in the marina, my office, any place safe from the winds."

I took his hand and lifted it to my lips, then pulled his arms tightly around my body. "It will be okay, O'Brien. By the end of the week, we'll be sitting out here wondering what all the worry was for."

"I hope you're right. I have a bad feeling about this one. People are getting nervous. Damned if I didn't have to spend an hour arguing with Jack Westbrook about his boat. He'd just come in from a week of sailing and he wanted the boat moved over to Paraquita Bay immediately. He's owned several boats in my fleet, upgrading every couple of years to bigger and better. But he is a pain in the ass."

"You know his wife was on that plane?" I said. "She got out, but the couple they were sailing with are dead."

O'Brien had already heard all the gory details about the crash. News travels fast in the islands and he'd been able to see things unfolding out at the site from his office window. He knew I'd be out there—I'd called him from the hospital to let him know I was okay. O'Brien hated the way I made my living.

"You know, Hannah," he began.

"Let's not have that conversation now, Peter." I knew what was coming. Tonight was not the night. We were both tired and on edge, and after pulling bodies out of that wreck today, all I wanted was to escape. I wasn't up to an argument.

But O'Brien couldn't let it go. "The diving you did today," he said, "you know how dangerous that is. Sooner or later your luck is going to run out. It happens to almost every diver who does the kind of diving that you do. And Christ, pulling mutilated bodies out of the ocean. It gets to you, Hannah. You know it does."

What O'Brien said was true. Most extreme divers did eventually die under the water. They got too casual, maybe grabbed the wrong tank, or pushed the limit, going too deep or swimming too far into a complex underwater cave system, getting lost, running out of air, and getting the bends. It was all about air and the effects of breathing it at depth or not having it at all.

But I wasn't careless. And I didn't consider myself lucky. I was skilled and I was careful. I also had a healthy amount of fear and respect. At a hundred feet in an ocean that is always unpredictable and with equipment that can fail, I counted on something going wrong. When it didn't, well, that was lucky. When it did, I was ready for it. The other part, the part about retrieving the dead? I'd learned to live with it.

"Quit the job, Hannah. Let's have a kid before it's too late."

"Christ, O'Brien. I'm thirty-eight years old. I love my job. I don't want to be pregnant, have a kid. You know that. How many times are we going to go over it?"

I was angry now, angrier than I should have been, I guess. But O'Brien kept pressing. I knew he could see the impact the rescue and recovery had had on me today and he was concerned. I'd tried to hide it, but O'Brien knew me too well.

"Don't you think our relationship needs to evolve?" he asked, pulling his hands away and deliberately setting mine in my lap.

That pissed me off. Call me sensitive, but the rejection hurt. "Why are you so dissatisfied?" I asked, defensive now.

"Because I want more," he said. "Maybe more than you can give, Hannah." He swung his legs off the lounge chair and moved into another chair.

"That's right, O'Brien," I said, standing and glaring down at him, seething now. "It's more than I can give." I emptied my wineglass, tipped the rest of the bottle into my glass, and consumed it in one long swallow. Then I grabbed the empty bottle and stormed inside for another. I intended to wash this conversation away in alcohol. A mistake, but dammit, I didn't need this now.

I was in the process of shredding the cork in a bottle of Cabernet when O'Brien came in.

"Let me do that," he said, reaching for the bottle.

"I can get it, O'Brien," I said, yanking it from him, jamming the opener farther into the bottle, and pushing the cork inside.

"Shit." I wasn't bothering with a wineglass now. I filled a plastic water glass to the brim and chugged, daring O'Brien with a look to say another word.

"Hannah, you're being a jerk," he said.

He was right, but I wasn't about to admit it. I was angry, hurt, overwhelmed by the day, and now I was getting trashed too. Bad combination.

I refilled my glass, emptied it, slammed it on the counter, and headed upstairs. Before I realized where I was going or what I was doing, I found myself in the bedroom throwing clothes in a bag. I was forcing the thing closed when O'Brien came in.

"Hannah, for crissakes, this is silly," he said, grabbing my wrists.

"Let me go! I knew this would never work. You just keep wanting more. I can't do it!" I shouted, pulling out of his grip.

"Fine! Run away. Just know that I won't be coming after you."

O'Brien was in the kitchen scraping dinner into the trash when I stormed out the front door with Sadie on my heels.

It was late when I pulled into Pickering's Landing. I shouldn't have been driving, but by the time I eased into the gravel lot, the buzz was gone and a headache was taking its place. A light glowed from the office on the first floor; no doubt Calvin was still up.

I could see the silhouette of the *Sea Bird* at the end of the pier, the mast swaying gently in the glassy harbor. O'Brien had been the one who'd found the *Sea Bird* for me. A couple from California had bought it as a live-aboard. After six months in the confined quarters on the boat, they'd ended up divorcing. So much for retiring to paradise. O'Brien could think of no better place for me to make a home. I'd had in mind living in something a bit more solid, something with a foundation, maybe a little cottage up in the hills. But once I'd stepped on board the *Sea Bird,* my idea of home changed.

I liked waking up to the sound of water splashing against the hull, having breakfast with the gulls, and sitting at dusk watching pelicans dive. I liked the rhythm of the ocean, the way the water changed from deep indigo to the brilliant, sparkling shades of blue as the sun made its way across the sky, then set on the horizon, reflecting gold, tinged in sunset hues across the sea. Nights when I found sleep impossible, I'd sit on the transom dangling a toe in the water and stirring up the microscopic organisms that turned to luminescent diamonds.

I'd had the chance to call the boat my own when an uncle I hardly knew left my sister and me each some money. My sister had followed my father's advice and invested it in a mutual fund. I'd bought the *Sea Bird*. My father had been upset but not surprised. I'd quit doing what I was told at about sixteen. Back then, I had driven my parents, especially my father, crazy.

When I'd switched to criminology and a career in law enforcement instead of going on for a degree in literature, he'd been furious. He'd wanted me to follow in his footsteps, teaching. In spite of the futility of it, at seventy-seven he was still trying to direct my life. It's funny, though. We'd fought our way to being about as close as a father and daughter can be.

I'd missed the *Sea Bird* and living at Pickering's Landing. Calvin and Tilda Pickering were good friends. Calvin maintained the boats and ran a boat repair shop. Tilda tended a little grocery with the freshest fruit and vegetables in the islands. They had two daughters, Rebecca, seven, and Daisy, five. They'd become like family. Since I'd moved in with O'Brien, we were invited for the midday meal every Sunday.

Calvin was coming out the door, Tilda close behind, as I stumbled out of the car.

"Hannah, what you be doin' here dis fin evenin'?" Calvin asked, kind enough not to comment on my inebriated condition.

"O'Brien and I had a fight," I said. "I'm moving back onto the *Sea Bird*."

"You jus can't let dat man love you, can you?" Tilda asked, shaking her head. "When you gonna realize what you be havin'? He be one of a kind."

"He wants a kid, Tilda!"

"Dat such a bad idea?" she asked. Tilda was completely happy in her role as mother. Her girls were simply a part of her.

"Hannah needs to be makin' up her own mind about dat. Not everyone be suited to havin' kids, Tilda. Daisy and Becca will be real happy to be havin' you back, Hannah. Let's get dat boat unlocked," Calvin said, grabbing a key off a hook near the door.

"Have you eaten?" Tilda said.

"No." It was nine o'clock. I was famished and the headache had developed from a dull thud to a sharp pain behind my left eye. I could hardly remember breakfast. The day had started out as a leisurely Saturday morning diving session with Jimmy. Christ.

Tilda insisted on bringing me leftovers, as well as a few supplies from the store. She didn't come aboard. She simply handed them over the side of the boat, lecturing me the whole time about O'Brien.

"Tilda, you're supposed to be on my side," I said. "I knew you first."

"I am on your side. That's why I be tellin' you," she said. "Good night, Hannah."

I went below and dug out an unopened bag of dog food I'd left in a locker and fed Sadie. Then I took the casserole and a liter of water up to the cockpit to sit in the dark. The night was still, the ocean a smooth expanse disturbed only by the occasional fish breaking the surface.

A new boat was tied across the dock in the place that had once belonged to Elyse Henry. I didn't much like it, someone being in her slip. I knew it was silly, but Elyse and I had been close. Then she'd died. Elyse had been an environmentalist and worked for the Society of Conservation. This looked like her replacement. A new boat and a new environmentalist. I planned to stay clear.

Sadie and I walked down the dock to the beach. Along the water's edge, the sand was wet, cool, and hard-packed. My footprints disappeared behind me as waves washed the shore.

Sadie raced ahead, splashing in the water, then taking off up into the trees. Pretty soon she was back, a stick in her mouth. She dropped it at my feet and wagged her tail. No matter how far I threw it, she always brought it back. After a half hour, she was panting, wet, and ready for more.

"Enough, Sadie," I said, sitting down on a log. She lay down next to me and put her head in my lap.

I'd been trying to bury the fight with O'Brien in activity. Now it all came rushing in. What he'd said about my running, my fear. I knew he was right. Christ, I thought about the hurt on O'Brien's face when I'd walked out the door tonight. How could I be such an ass? I'd really blown it, overreacted. Hell, I admit it. I was scared, scared that I was giving up too much of myself to be with O'Brien.

And he was asking me to give up even more. Why couldn't he see how important it was for me to be who I was, do what I did? I wasn't asking him to give up his business. Why did he expect that I should be willing to give up what defined me?

This was the problem, the endless argument. As open-minded as O'Brien was, he was still a chauvinist when it got right down to it, when it came to his personal life. He was fine with having a mate who was a professional—but only to a point. He wanted a wife whose job didn't get in the way.

Once a part of me had wanted a family. I'd thought about it when I'd been with Jake. When he died, I'd left that dream behind. It was too late to go back.

I knew it wasn't just the fact that O'Brien wanted kids. He was worried about me too, about my dying on the job, either diving or chasing down a bad guy, and about the emotional impact of the kind of recovery I did today. But he'd known what I did when we met. I knew he loved me, but was it enough? Enough to let me be who I was?

I'd been so absorbed thinking about O'Brien that I didn't hear the man approach until he spoke.

"Hello," he said.

Some cop I was. I jumped and almost fell off the log.

I noticed his hands first—dinner plate–sized hands. The man was huge, but at least he was smiling. He was barefoot and wore only a pair of cut-off jeans that were wet and salt-stained. Loose threads fringed thighs the size of gumbo-limbo trees.

"I'm sorry I startled you. I'm Enok Kiersted. I'm on the boat down at the end of the pier," he said.

"Hannah Sampson. I'm on the *Sea Bird*."

"Sure. Tilda and Calvin have told me about you. You're a cop, huh? Mind if I sit?" he asked.

I didn't want the company but what could I say? I made room on the log.

"I heard what happened to Elyse Henry, the woman I've replaced," he said, sitting down beside me. "Guess you two were close. I'm sorry."

"Thanks," I said, thinking that no one could replace Elyse.

"How's it going with the new job?" I asked, changing the subject.

That's all it took. A half hour later, I had his life story and the feeling that he wouldn't last a month in the job. He said he was born on St. Thomas. His father had been Danish. The family was one of the few that had come to the islands when Denmark had colonized. His mother was from a generation of slaves who had worked on the sugar plantations. She'd been the one to instill his love of nature and the ocean. She'd taught him to snorkel and had known the name of every sea creature they ever encountered. He described his bedtime stories as treatises on the behavior of anything that swam, crawled, or grew on the ocean floor.

Kiersted had gone to school in California, earned a master's in ocean ecology, and learned about the Society of Conservation through a colleague. When he'd heard there was an opening for an environmentalist down here, he'd pushed hard for the job. Now his plan was to lobby every legislator in the BVI government to stop the dredging of beaches, the development of seaside property, and everything else that might threaten the ocean environment.

The problem was, he was an outsider, a non-belonger. You didn't just come charging into these islands and expect people to trust you. Elyse had been a zealot about the environment, but she had also been a BVIslander.

This guy was an extremist, a fanatic. Right now he was ranting about the boat he'd seen dumping garbage in Paraquita Bay. I'd tuned him out when he started talking about his research in the mangroves and the Woods Foundation. I recognized the name. It was the foundation where Simon's dad had been employed. Evidently the foundation had awarded Kiersted a big grant to finance his study and had sent a grants officer down to assess his progress on the project and determine future funding.

"That wouldn't have been Lawrence Redding, would it?" I asked.

"Yes. Do you know him?"

"I'm afraid he died in that airplane crash today."

"That's horrible," he said. "What about his kid?"

He was relieved when I told him Simon had made it out. Before I had the chance to quiz him about his ties to Redding, he got up, stretched, said good night, and walked down the beach to his boat.

I was left sitting on the log with Sadie's head still in my lap. Out over the water, I could see a thundercloud forming.

Chapter 10

At seven the next morning, I was standing at the sink, head pounding, trying to obliterate the foul taste in my mouth with toothpaste. It worked for about five minutes. I swallowed a couple of aspirin with a swig of coffee and headed into Road Town to check on Simon. The streets were lined with people walking to church, men in their Sunday suits, women in flowered dresses and straw hats, their children skipping behind.

I picked up an *Island News* at Wilson's Bakery on the way to the hospital. The airplane crash was spread all over the front page, along with a photo of Stewart and Debra Westbrook clinging to the yellow horseshoe and another of him helping her into the rescue boat. They'd also gotten one of Simon and me. You could see the shock in his eyes.

The headlines read, *Actor Saves Senator's Wife,* just as Lorenzo had predicted. The story read like a scene out of one of Stewart's movies.

Hollywood star Daniel Stewart risked his life to save the wife of Senator John Quincy Westbrook from a sinking airplane Saturday morning. With severe injuries to his shoulder and arm, he somehow managed to wrestle the aircraft door open. He jumped into the ocean with Debra Westbrook held fast just as the

*plane began its journey to Davy Jones's locker. In an
effort of extreme determination and heroism, he then
dragged her through the water to a life preserver and
clung to it, his broken arm dangling useless, until rescue boats arrived. Police divers Hannah Sampson
and Jimmy Snyder, who were in the vicinity training
when the plane went down, were able to rescue five
passengers.*

The article ended by listing the names and hometowns of
the dead. I could practically hear Sammy Lorenzo dictating
the text. It was fantastic hype for all those *Avenger* fans.

When I walked into his room, Simon was sitting up in
bed, dipping a spoon into what appeared to be oatmeal and
letting the pasty stuff dribble back into the bowl. He clearly
had no intention of eating it. I didn't blame him.

"Pretty bad, huh?" I said.

"Hannah! I'm glad you came," he said, his face breaking
into a smile.

"I brought you some donuts." I'd had the misfortune of
being confined in this hospital on a couple of occasions. I
knew what the food was like. Wilson's sold the best fresh
baked goods on the island. Simon stuck his hand in the bag,
pulled out a chocolate-covered specimen, and took a huge
bite.

"So, how are you doing, Simon?"

"I'm okay." I could see he wasn't though. The kid had to
be wondering what the heck was going to happen to him.

"No one has been able to reach your aunt yet. Is there
someone else we should be calling?"

His face crinkled in on itself, but he didn't cry. "I don't
have any other relatives. Just my friends at school."

He was quiet for a minute. Then he asked, "Where's my
dad, Hannah?"

Jeez, how was I supposed to answer that question? Tell
the kid his dad was in heaven? How were you supposed to

talk to kids about death? Myself, I was raised to confront death, to see it and accept it. We buried our pets in the backyard and had funerals for them. I realized later that my parents designed those ceremonies to teach us that death was an inevitable part of life.

Later, when grandparents died, we were part of the process. Our questions were answered honestly and we were never shut out. I've learned to hate euphemisms like "passed on" or, even worse, "sleeping with the angels." I believe in calling it like it is. Dead is "dead." Still, I was having a hard time knowing just what to say to Simon.

"What do you mean?" was all I could manage.

"I mean where is his body?" Christ, I'd been making it a whole lot harder than it was. Simon knew his father was dead as in "dead."

"Oh. Well, Simon, he's in the morgue. The hospital will keep him there until we get word from your aunt."

"Do you think I could see him?" he asked.

"I'll see what I can do, okay?" I had no idea what condition the body would be in. But the kid had the right to see his father.

About then Dr. Hall came in. He gave Simon a once-over and said he was fit to be released.

Christ. I pulled Hall out to the hallway and closed Simon's door.

"Doc, he doesn't have anyplace to go," I said. What was Hall thinking anyway?

"I know, Hannah, but I can't keep him in the hospital indefinitely," he said. "This is no place for a healthy boy. I've called Child Services."

"You can't just send him off to be with strangers after what he's been through. The kid just lost his father."

"What do you propose I do?" I knew Hall didn't like this any better than I did.

"What if you talk to Child Services and recommend that Simon be allowed to stay with me until his aunt shows up?"

I'd said it without thinking. I couldn't believe I was offering to take the kid.

"It can't be more than a day or two before she gets down here. Surely you can get them to agree. You are a doctor."

"How are you going to take care of a nine-year-old boy?" Hall asked. "What about your job?"

"I'm sure Tilda and Calvin will help and I've got plenty of room on the boat."

"What? You're back on the *Sea Bird*?" he asked. "What happened with O'Brien?"

Did everyone need to know the details of my love life? Jeez. "We're taking a break," was all I said. I wasn't about to stand in the hallway discussing it.

"Okay, Hannah. I'll arrange it because I happen to agree. He'll be much better off with you," Hall said.

It was a done deal, then. I knew whatever Hall recommended would fly. He was one of those doctors who always went above and beyond and his word was gospel in the islands.

"Thanks, Doc. I'll pick him up this afternoon."

Before we went back into Simon's room, I told him that Simon wanted to see his dad. Hall understood immediately and said he'd call the morgue to make sure everything was in order so I could take him down there this afternoon.

When I went back into his room, Simon had taken his digital camera out of the waterproof case it had been protected in when the plane went down, and he was snapping pictures of his feet. Typical kid.

"Hey, Simon, how about you come stay with me until we get in touch with your aunt?"

"Okay, Hannah," he said.

Hell, what else was he going to say? The kid didn't have a lot of options. He could go with me or stay with strangers until his aunt came. It was the pits, being a kid.

"I'll pick you up this afternoon. We'll go see your dad before we leave if you still want to."

*   *   *

When I got down to the *Wahoo*, Betty Welsh, the reporter from the *Island News,* was waiting for me. The first
time I'd met her, I'd wondered what she was doing working for a little island paper. She was a top-notch writer and
reporter. She always got the story right and she believed in
responsible journalism. Later, she told me that she'd tried
to work in the States, but no newspaper was interested in
hiring a five-foot-ten, 190-pound black Caribbean woman
whose cultural background differed so completely from an
American perspective.

She was pushing sixty, was a flamboyant dresser, and had
big hair that she pinned up in a nest at the top of her head.
She didn't take any flack from anyone. Today, she was
decked out in an orange and yellow African print that draped
loosely on her huge frame. She'd tied a matching scarf
around her head. Her photographer was with her. So were
Sammy Lorenzo and Daniel Stewart.

I knew what she was up to, and she knew me well
enough to know that I wouldn't like it. She also knew that
I owed her. The last time she'd had a story, she'd agreed to
hold it back when I asked because it would have jeopard-
ized a case. She wasn't above reminding me now.

"I told you I'd collect on the debt, Hannah," she said.
"This is the story of the year for our little islands. And Mr.
Lorenzo here is sure he can get it picked up in the States."

Sammy Lorenzo was standing behind her, gnawing on a
cigar and nodding enthusiastically. "This will be great!
Great!"

"Okay, Betty," I said, "but we need to make it quick. I've
got to get out to the crash site."

She spent ten minutes writing down the details about the
rescue and my take on Stewart's role. Then Sammy insisted
that Stewart and I stand together on the *Wahoo,* with all the
dive gear as the perfect backdrop. Stewart gave me an
apologetic look.

"It's okay, Daniel," I said. "If it will help your career, I'm glad to do it. I do appreciate your help out there yesterday."

Stewart followed me onto the boat. Sammy kept trying to position us so that it looked like we'd just come in from the crash. Stewart was used to this stuff. But me? I was working hard to keep a pained expression off my face. Though Sammy was clearly into it, this was not my idea of fun.

The photographer kept shooting. I was sure he was hoping for just one decent picture. He was snapping like crazy when a wave from the wake of the incoming ferry hit the *Wahoo*. Stewart lost his balance and I grabbed him. Damned if he didn't pull me into his arms and brush his lips against mine.

"Hannah, you are gorgeous," he whispered. I lingered an instant too long, stunned and gazing into those damn bedroom eyes. I mean, the guy was a movie star, a hunk with a voice like rounded pebbles and a day's perfect beard. Besides, I was still pissed at O'Brien.

"Perfect shot!" the photographer said.

"I do not want that photo to show up in the paper," I said, threatening Lorenzo. "This is supposed to be a story about Stewart's heroism, not some fictitious love affair."

Chief Dunn had been observing the entire encounter. I hadn't seen him arrive. He was standing in his shirtsleeves, watching, amused, his suit coat draped over his arm.

"Thanks again, Detective," Lorenzo waved as he ushered his companions to the car.

"Remember what I said, Sammy," I hollered.

"Hey, as they say in the islands, 'No problem, mon,'" he shouted as they pulled away.

Chapter 11

Dunn was helping Jimmy and me load dive tanks onto the *Wahoo* when Gilbert Dickson pulled up on his Harley. Gil was the one-man-lab guy in the department. He did everything from fingerprinting to the handling of DNA that was sent out for analysis. He was a stickler for detail and that made him good and reliable. Gil would oversee anything we brought up from the crash.

He'd been with the department for eight years. Today he wore a short-sleeved plaid shirt, polyester pants, and tennis shoes. His jet-black hair, which he slicked back over the crown of his head, barely covered the bald spot that was spreading across his skull. He had rolled his sleeves up. The only thing missing was the pack of cigarettes tucked in the fold. But James Dean he was not.

"Hey, Gil," I said as he hefted the bike onto its kickstand.

"Hi, Hannah. Hear we've got an interesting situation out there. I can't say I've ever worked on an airplane crash before." He was releasing a snarl of bungee cords from the back of the bike and unloading a tower of gear. I'd swear he'd brought his entire lab.

"Can't some of this stuff stay on shore?" I asked as he handed me a toolbox that had to weigh fifty pounds.

"Can't be too prepared," he said. "No telling what you

all will bring up out of that plane. The more I can do to preserve evidence out there, the better."

Gil spent the ride out to the site organizing all his equipment. By the time we dropped the anchor, he had every available surface covered—buckets for freshwater washes, containers of chemicals, his fingerprint kit.

I was arguing with him about giving us a little room to suit up when the salvage divers appeared. One was a white guy about twenty-five who looked cocky as hell. He stood in the stern of their vessel gazing out to sea, hands on his hips, one foot propped up on the rail. He wore a wet suit, zipped tight all the way up to his neck. He looked like he was posing for a *GQ* ad.

He was definitely modeling what was in the wet suit. It showed off every detail, wide shoulders, defined biceps and pecs, a tight butt, and washboard abs that offset a bulge that could only belong to a testosterone-overloaded twentysomething. Maybe by the time he was forty and things had started to sag a bit, he'd turn into someone you'd actually want to talk to. Right now, I figured, the only people who would be interested were twentysomething females inclined to the type—and maybe his mother.

The guy driving the boat was close to fifty, balding, his face a road map of deeply embedded wrinkles. He wore swim trunks that had probably once been red, but now they were a pinkish white, the waistband so stretched out that the suit barely covered his behind. He maneuvered their boat in next to ours, tossed a couple of bumpers over the side, and tied up to the *Wahoo*.

Mr. GQ stepped up on the rail and jumped onto our boat. "Trey Harper," he said, holding a hand out to Dickson, the only white male in the group. I guess to Harper, Dickson had to be the one in charge, given the fact that everyone else was black or female. Did this guy actually live in the twenty-first century? What an ass.

"This is my associate, Don Sturtevant," he said.

Dunn stepped up, his mass casting a shadow across Harper's face. "*Chief* of Police John Dunn," he said, emphasizing the *chief* part. Then he introduced Carmichael, Mason, Jimmy, Gil, and me. He made a point of telling Harper that I was the lead diver and heading up the underwater investigation. Harper almost choked at the prospect of diving with what he clearly thought was a substandard team. Me and Jimmy, a skinny kid with cornrows, wearing swim trunks that reached below his knees. Then there was Carmichael, in a wet suit as bleached and torn as Sturtevant's swim trunks. Mason was the only one who could compete in the cool category. His wet suit had bright orange accents down the sleeves.

"Sampson and Deputy Snyder were on the scene when the plane went under and were the first down there," Dunn explained. "They did the rescue and recovery yesterday, with help from Carmichael and Mason here."

"Jesus, I hope the hell you didn't disturb anything pulling those victims out," Harper said.

"Hey, what dey be doin' was savin' lives," Carmichael said, sneering at the guy. "Sampson here be an expert. If anything be disturbed down der, it be necessary. 'Sides, your job be salvage, not investigation. I be thinkin' you're not knowin' your ass from da hole in da ground. How long you be divin', Sonny?" Carmichael had moved into Harper's space and hovered over him, hands on his hips.

"Long enough," Harper said, holding his ground.

"We be seein' 'bout dat when you swim into dat wreck, Harper," Carmichael said, turning away and hefting a tank out of the rack.

"Okay," I interrupted, pleased that Carmichael had put Harper in his place but anxious to dispel the tension, "let's go over the dive plan."

Dunn had picked up the preliminary photos that I'd taken of the wreck yesterday. He spread them out and we spent the next half hour going over them. Sturtevant looked at each one carefully and took detailed notes.

"I want to make sure I know what we've got down there," he said when he saw me watching him. Those were the first words he'd uttered since he stepped on board.

"How long have you been doing salvage diving?" I asked.

"Too long," he said, glaring at Harper. "Started out as a navy diver. Dove out on the oil rigs after that. I'll be the one developing the salvage plan. It seems pretty straightforward, but I'll know better after I have a look."

I nodded and told them I intended to do the examination of the aircraft and recovery of material as efficiently as possible. I pulled out a schematic of the aircraft that Edith Leonard had given us. The Beech 99 had been configured to hold fifteen passengers, five rows with one seat on each side. Then in the back, two rows with two seats side by side and one extra seat across from the entry door. Small baggage compartments were in the long, pointed nose section, as well as in the belly.

In addition to the passenger door, which was in the rear of the aircraft on the left, there were emergency exits on either side of the cabin right behind the cockpit. That was where the Rileys had been sitting. No attempt had been made to open those exits. The tiny bathroom where I'd found Simon was in the tail section.

I would pair with Harper. I didn't trust the guy and did not want him diving with Jimmy. Harper and I would be examining the cockpit and the cabin for structural damage and I'd take more photos. Jimmy would accompany Sturtevant. They would do a visual check on the exterior, take photos, and comb the surrounding area for debris.

We'd carry grease markers and labels to record the location of each item we recovered. Jimmy and I would also carry containers to retrieve and store any items that needed to be protected from exposure to the air. That was standard procedure in an underwater crime scene and right now that was how we had to treat the aircraft. Anything that was significant would be placed in a watertight container along with the seawater to keep the object from corroding on contact with the air and to preserve fingerprints.

We'd be searching for any explosive devices or signs of explosion and taking more photos. We'd be looking for pieces of tape, wire, clock mechanisms, fuses, and battery parts. Any debris that was lying on the bottom or loose in the plane would be taken to the surface. We'd not be wasting our time looking for a black box or recorder. Sturtevant had spoken with the AAIB investigator and learned that this aircraft carried neither.

Carmichael and Mason were to stand by outside the plane to ferry items to the surface, where Gil would take possession of them. Harper's and Sturtevant's main tasks would be to assess the wreck for the best way to bring it up.

Once we'd labeled and collected the important evidentiary material, our final effort would be to recover the cargo in the holds. According to the records of Flight 45 that Edith Leonard provided, the cargo load was minimal and harmless. We would encounter no hazardous material, such as pesticides, chemicals, or explosives, but only luggage and a couple of boxes containing island goods being shipped to outlets in the States.

I knew Carmichael was secure enough about himself and his diving that he would have no problems being backup. Mason, though, like Harper, had things to prove. I could see that he'd identified Harper as competition.

Mason had just taken a job as dive master for Carmichael at Underwater Adventures. As a dive master, he was used to being in charge, supervising somewhere between ten and twenty recreational divers at a time. He would have been responsible for the safety of novices, some of whom would have a hard time emptying the air from their BCs or clearing their ears, and also keeping track of those who thought they were Jacques Cousteau and took off looking for an encounter with a man-eating shark.

Right now, Mason was standing on the deck with his hands on his hips, pissed. Harper was looking cocky, smug. I couldn't believe I was witnessing what threatened to turn into a battle for dominant male. Both would be willing to push the limits and take risks in order to prove themselves. Their attitudes were a formula for disaster under the water.

When a diver was encased in gear and swimming in tight, dark places, it was easy for panic to set in. If it got out of control, the diver would hyperventilate, cerebral arteries would constrict, heart rate would increase, blood pressure would drop or shoot up. The increased pressure of the underwater environment, the equipment, marine hazards, magnified everything. Stories were always circulating in the diving community about divers found lying on the bottom, regulators in their mouths and tanks full. I'd seen divers race to the surface, ending up with the bends and in a decompression chamber for days. Some could never dive again.

"Look, you two," I warned them, "save it for the bar. I don't want any problems."

There would be dangers down there, especially inside the wreck. We needed to know that if any of us got into trouble we could depend on the others. There was no room for animosity or for divers so concerned about outdoing one another that somebody, too worried about losing face to admit being in trouble, ended up dead.

We were quiet as we prepared our gear for the dive, all six of us intent on the task. I hefted a tank out of the rack and snapped it into my BC, then attached the regulator hose to the tank and the other hose to the vest. I turned the air on and checked my gauges—3,200 psi. Then I tested my regulator to make sure the air was flowing, taking a couple of short breaths. The others were following exactly the same procedure.

I spit in my mask, spread the saliva over the lens, and rinsed it in the sea to keep it from fogging. Then I put my weight belt on, with enough weight to carry me to the bottom when I was ready to go down. I remembered the first day I'd donned all the damn equipment and sat on the edge of the pool, ready to slip under the water for the first time. Had it really been more than fifteen years ago?

I'd gotten certified with a little dive shop in Denver. We'd spent some classroom time on theory. But when it came to getting in the water, hell, I couldn't understand why I'd need any weight. Didn't people always sink in the water? That's why they drowned. As a result, I'd ignored that part of the lesson and strapped on a weight belt with a token five pounds. I found myself fighting and using up air like crazy trying to get to the bottom of the pool. With all the equipment, my wet suit, and my BC, along with my body mass, I was a lot like a beach ball. That was the last time I ignored any rules when it came to diving. I'd become a stickler for correct procedures.

Now I sat on the back of the boat and pulled on my fins, and then Dunn held the BC with the tank attached as I slipped my arms into it, snapped it around my torso, and tightened it down. I snugged my mask in place and tumbled into the water.

Once in, I filled my BC with air, allowing me to float comfortably as I waited for the others. When we were all in the water, I gave the signal and we started down, releasing air from our BCs. We descended slowly, clearing our ears as we went. A school of yellow snappers followed us to the bottom.

The airplane was lying in the sand on its belly as though it belonged, somehow accepting its place in the ocean environment. The sharks were gone. There was nothing to draw them any longer, just a hard metal tube. If the plane remained on the bottom, it would turn into an artificial reef, accumulating sea life. Within the year, coral and sponges would attach to its shell and it would become home to hundreds of fish and other reef creatures. Divers would come to investigate the wreckage and marvel at the beauty of its transformation to something that belonged to the sea. The people who died here would be mostly forgotten, only mentioned in passing as part of the history and ghosts of the sea.

As we headed to the wreck, we scared up a flounder that had been perfectly disguised in the sand. It darted away, changing to blue, then gray, and back to tan as quickly as the bottom color changed. A school of squid was hovering in formation around the wreck, eight of them, moving forward then backward in the gentle current. They scattered as we approached and regrouped just yards away. Out where the water turned opaque, I could make out the shape of a ray flying through the water like a giant bird with a long tail.

I headed inside. Harper was right behind me. It was dark, eerie, and vacant, except for a few small fish. He followed as I swam forward to the cockpit. I paused and let him swim inside while I hovered in the doorway. The cockpit was too small for two divers to enter.

He was supposed to take a careful look around to determine the structural integrity of the nose section and take photos. He never even bothered to take his camera out of his bag. He was spending more time holding his regulator in his mouth and bumping his fins into instruments than he was spending on any assessment. I hoped he wasn't disturbing important evidence. I could see the signs. His movements were becoming frantic. He was beginning to freak out in the confined space and was trying to control it. Even worse, I was blocking the door and his access out. He had that look in his eyes—trapped and panicked. Suddenly he bolted, crashing past me and into the passenger cabin.

When he got to the cabin door, he stopped. I was right behind him. He hovered there, sweeping his arms in wide arcs. I knew he was coming back from the edge, regaining his machismo, no doubt because he could see sunlight streaming down from the surface. And because Mason and Carmichael were just outside the plane.

I signaled to him, asking if he was okay. He indicated that he was and pointed to his regulator. I knew it would be his way of blaming the entire incident on equipment malfunction when we got to the surface.

I figured he'd be fine outside the wreck, in open water. I pulled out my slate and indicated that Carmichael and Mason should start retrieving luggage from the nose section while I took a close look at the interior, retrieved what I could from inside, and handed it out to Harper. I'd help him save face by assigning him a task that would mean he didn't have to re-enter the aircraft.

I started in the cockpit, where I took detailed photos of the instrument panels. I shone my flashlight along the ceiling and interior walls. Moving from the cockpit all the way back to the tail, I examined every surface for signs of an explosion. I found nothing suspicious, but the final analysis would be in the investigator's hands when the plane was brought up.

Next, I did a careful search of the cabin, checking seat pockets and under seats. The plane was too small to have overhead compartments. I found a computer bag with a laptop in it jammed under the seat where Redding had been sitting. Across the way, I retrieved the Walkman that was sticking out of the seat pocket—no doubt Simon's. Farther up, I found a couple of handbags, and in the cockpit I retrieved the pilots' flight bags. I made several trips into the cabin, filling the evidence bags and handing them out to Harper, who swam them to the surface.

Finally, I took one last look around. Once the plane was lifted out of the water, anything loose could end up on the sea floor and be lost forever. I started back in, relieved that this would be the last time I would need to swim into this death scene. Seats were torn and empty now. The place where people had died was now just a shell filled with seawater and fish. I swam through the cabin, examining every cranny, under seats, in seat pockets.

I almost missed the gun. It was wedged between the wall and the seat where Debra Westbrook had been sitting before she moved to the back of the aircraft. I pulled another evidence container and a screwdriver from my mesh bag, slipped the screwdriver into the gun barrel, pried the gun out, and dropped it into the container, sealing it in seawater to preserve evidence. That was it. I swam out and toward the sunlight.

When I surfaced, Harper was in the boat, making a big deal about his regulator. I didn't say anything about what had happened below, but he knew he'd better tread lightly around me. I glared at him and he said no more.

Sturtevant and Jimmy were the next aboard. They'd taken more photographs of the engines, fuselage, wings, and tail section and had already brought up items that had been scattered in the sand—mostly contents from the interior, a few seat cushions, magazines.

Sturtevant was amazed at the integrity of the structure.

"The plane is pretty much intact," he said. "Usually the wings get torn off, maybe the engines, sometimes the nose section. This will be a textbook lift. I'll arrange for a barge with a crane. We should be able to have one out here in the morning."

We managed to retrieve the rest of the cargo from the hold in just one more dive. Harper insisted on leading—his strategy for recovering his reputation, I guess. It wasn't going to work with me. The thing was, I understood. He wasn't the first diver I'd seen panic like that. Hell, I'd felt the same way myself. I would never fault a diver for that.

The problem was that Harper couldn't acknowledge it,

be human about it. Now he needed more than ever to prove that he was a macho diver. It pissed me off. He went barging into the water as though it was his to own and every sea creature in his way better get the hell out of it.

When we got to the bottom, he had his knife out and was daring a barracuda to come any closer. I swam up next to him, shooed the fish away, and gave him the sternest look I could muster with a mask over my face. I don't think he got it. I was afraid Trey Harper wouldn't survive long as a diver if he didn't change his attitude. He'd end up dying under the water trying to prove how macho he was. We managed to finish the dive without incident though.

"Let's get this stuff to the warehouse," Dunn said when we'd all gotten back up top and into the boat. Gil was already at work on the gun.

"Harper's a flake," Carmichael said on the way back into Road Harbor. "I'm glad I won't be diving with him again. He's liable to get someone killed."

"Yeah," I said. "Like Sturtevant."

We dropped Mason and Carmichael off at Underwater Adventures, then tied up on the dock at the western end of the harbor, where Dunn had arranged for the warehouse. We would off-load everything we'd just collected and work out of the site. The airplane would be housed here also as soon as it was pulled off the ocean floor.

Stark was standing on the dock waiting for us. "How was the dive?" he asked, noticing the fact that I was pissed.

"Let's just say it was interesting," I said and left it at that.

Harper and Sturtevant had tied their boat up at the dock behind us and Harper was walking our way. He'd removed his wet suit and now wore only a skimpy spandex swimsuit.

I introduced them to Stark, who took an immediate dislike to Harper. No surprises there. After a quick handshake, Stark explained to Harper that in the islands, people were to come ashore fully clothed. Damned if Harper didn't go back to his boat and pull on a pair of shorts and a T-shirt.

"He part of the problem on the dive?" Stark asked.

"How did you guess?" I said.

"Good police work," he said.

Chapter 12

A speedboat followed the *Wahoo* into Road Harbor, keeping enough distance to ensure that the cops would not be suspicious. Two people were on board, one driving, the other holding a pair of binoculars.

They'd been out near the crash site all morning, baking in the sun and watching divers retrieve material from the wreck. They'd had no problem blending in with all the other gawkers out there hoping to see some gore. The cops hadn't let anyone get in close. The big black cop in the suit had made sure of that.

The taller of the two, the one with the binoculars, had had a hard time keeping his eyes off a woman in a nearby boat. She was topless and lying on her back on the bow. Every once in a while he let the binocs wander over her body, admiring the bare flesh. It was one of the things he liked about the islands—the women out on the water completely naked doing swan dives off their boats.

"Keep your eye on the police boat," his colleague had demanded, irritated.

They'd seen the divers go down once, finally surface, and hand some containers into the police boat. A while later, they'd gone back down to the wreck and brought up a bunch of suitcases and some boxes that disintegrated as they were lifted into the boat, spilling a lump of wet island clothes and some wooden carvings all over the deck.

"Chances are it's been ruined by salt water or was destroyed in the crash anyway," the man had said, peering through the binoculars again.

"Surely you've heard of waterproof? We can't assume anything. There's too much at stake. We need to know where they're taking all the cargo. Then we'll find our little item and get the hell out of here," the other said.

"It needs to be soon. That storm's moving in."

Finally, the police divers had pulled up anchor and headed into Road Harbor.

They'd followed and were watching now as the cops began unloading the cargo.

"We need to get that thing before the cops find it," the taller one said, clearly worried, binocs glued to the proceedings on shore. "You've got to learn to control that wild temper and not lash out at the slightest provocation."

"That's why we're together in this, isn't it? My violent streak?" the other said, steering the boat through the harbor while keeping an eye on the activity at the warehouse.

"Yeah, but killing, that's way over the top. All we needed was his signature and we were done. So it cost an extra half a million."

"He should never have threatened me. No one threatens me and gets away with it."

"Once things had been finalized we could have dealt with him. He was in way too deep to back out or go to the authorities. You knew that. It would have meant his ass too. Now what was supposed to be a simple business deal is completely down the tubes. I'll tell you what, if the cops find out what happened, we've got big problems." He cast a troubled glance at his hotheaded colleague. "You know that I don't want to see either one of us going to jail."

"I promise you. That's not going to happen," the one at the wheel said, gunning the boat and speeding out of the harbor.

Chapter 13

I was standing alongside the *Wahoo* when I heard the roar of boat engines out in the harbor. When I looked up, all I saw was the track of a wake leading around the point. If Jimmy hadn't been standing right beside me, I'd have been sure the kid was out there blasting the police boat through the waves.

Sturtevant went in to have a look around the warehouse while the others hefted suitcases, evidence bags, and boxes inside. He came out and gave Dunn the thumbs-up.

"This will work just fine," Sturtevant said. "No problem wheeling that plane in—plenty of clearance, big enough space to work, a clean, flat cement floor, running water, and good lighting. Harrigan will be pleased with the setup. You wouldn't believe some of the conditions he's had to work in."

"You've worked with him?" I asked.

"Yeah, probably close to twenty years. He's one of the best, extremely thorough. Believe me, he'll figure out what brought that plane down if it takes him a year."

"I hope it doesn't take a year," Dunn said. "The owner of the airline is looking for the right answer and she wants it fast."

"Harrigan won't bow to pressure from her or anyone else," Sturtevant said. "And if he can't find answers, he'll blame himself."

"Sounds like someone else I know," Dunn said, shooting a glance my way. "Let me know what you turn up here, Sampson."

Dunn went back to the office and left us to it. Sturtevant and Harper headed down to the shipyard to check on the equipment they'd need to bring the plane up. They planned to be out there at first light. If all went well, they'd have the plane in the warehouse well before noon tomorrow.

Stark and Jimmy had drawn an outline of the aircraft on the cement floor, marking the cockpit, each passenger seat and its occupant, the bathroom, and all of the exits. We spent the next couple of hours laying items out according to the place in the plane where we'd retrieved them and in the sand surrounding the wreck.

Dunn was insisting that we be thorough and treat this as a criminal investigation until we knew better. Between the water-soaked owners' address tags and the airline tags that we matched with the computer records provided by Leonard, we managed to put a name to every piece of luggage. Then we pulled on latex gloves and started the initial examination. I felt like a voyeur, invading people's personal belongings. But I knew it was necessary.

It was amazing what turned up in the suitcases. Gil had been going through the newlyweds' bags, making lewd comments as he worked. Evidently the couple had been well prepared for the honeymoon. The assortment of negligees and teddies was mundane next to the rest of the stuff.

"Nice," Dickson said, holding up a pair of crotchless panties that were tangled in plastic handcuffs.

"Jeez, Gil. How about you check out the weapon Sampson found wedged beside the seat while I finish up with that stuff?" Stark suggested.

"You get to have all the fun," Dickson said and went to work on the gun.

He pulled the weapon out of the salt water–filled evidence container as I watched over his shoulder. "This thing's a powerhouse," he said. "It's a 9 mm Beretta, automatic, fifteen rounds, muzzle velocity twelve hundred eighty feet per second. Very lethal."

Dickson was in his element. He was working fast to get prints and avoid any oxidation, which would occur quickly and would foul up subsequent ballistic tests. He air-dried the gun and examined it, exposing it for only a few minutes.

"We're not going to get any prints off of this thing," he said.

"Yeah. Not too surprising." We both knew that lifting impressions suitable for identification was a long shot when it involved salt water.

He'd immersed the gun in fresh water and gently swished it around to circulate water through the mechanism, careful with a gun he considered loaded. Then he dropped it into pure alcohol so that the water in the gun would be absorbed and oxidation prevented.

Finally, he checked it for a serial number and sealed it in an airtight container filled with diesel fuel to displace the remaining water and air bubbles. All this would keep the weapon from deteriorating any further.

"I'll run the number through the computer, see what comes up," he said.

"Sounds good," I said, as he made a notation for a ballistics test.

I started going through Debra Westbrook's belongings. There were two suitcases packed with expensive clothing and swimming apparel—enough for a different swimsuit every day. Debra's makeup case was filled with cosmetics. Buried at the very bottom was an intricately tooled leather address book. I opened it and fingered carefully through the wet pages trying to separate them without tearing them. It was crammed with names. I recognized some—a couple of senators, a Cabinet member or two.

In the back pocket I found a stack of business cards stuck together—one of them for a divorce attorney. I also found a hotel receipt for the Washington Arms in D.C. signed by Jack Westbrook, dated just a few weeks ago. I filed that piece of information in my "interesting, maybe significant" category. Since the Westbrooks had a home in D.C., I figured there was only one reason for that hotel stay. I was betting that Jack was fooling around and that he'd been careless enough to leave that receipt in the wrong place.

Stark had been examining the Rileys' bags.

"It doesn't look like Westbrook was exaggerating when he told you the Rileys were well off," he said, handing me the photos he'd pulled out of Louise Riley's wallet. One was an old shot of her and her husband with a girl and two boys standing in front of a mansion that rivaled the White House. In another, Riley was posed in the winner's circle, holding the halter of a sleek Thoroughbred. There were more of the same kids, now grown, with children of their own.

"One thing's for sure," Stark said, digging through Riley's leather suitcase. "William Riley never felt it when his legs were severed. He's got enough prescription painkillers and tranquilizers to stock a small pharmacy."

Lawrence Redding had checked a generic black suitcase on wheels, with nothing remarkable inside. The guy must not have owned a pair of shorts. It was all business casual—slacks, shirts, underwear, and socks. A Dopp kit held toothpaste, razor, shaving cream, and dental floss. The reading material matched the clothes—a book on grant evaluations, an annual report for the Woods Foundation. Redding had also carried the laptop that I'd retrieved from under his seat.

Simon traveled light. His green duffel contained a swim suit, a pair of baggy cargo shorts, two T-shirts, a stack of comic books, and a couple of pairs of underwear.

Daniel Stewart and Sammy Lorenzo had each checked a bag. Stewart's was filled with shorts, T-shirts, low-key vacation garb, an expensive Rolex, still running, and a couple of mystery novels. Sammy's contained gaudy shirts, a box of expensive cigars, and other basics.

Zora Gordon had not checked luggage but had only a backpack, which I'd found in the cabin. Maybe her luggage hadn't made the flight or maybe she traveled light too. We'd find out. Inside were her passport, a couple of granola bars, and her wallet. Her driver's license showed a Los Angeles address. A pouch in the wallet held several of her business cards. Zora Gordon was an attorney.

"Jesus, would you look at this," Stark said, pulling a clear plastic bag of white goo out of the copilot's flight bag. "Any bets on what this is?" He stuck his little finger into the paste and dabbed it on his tongue.

"Cocaine, pure," he said. Stark would know. He'd worked undercover narcotics in Miami for several years before deciding he'd had enough and returning home to the BVI.

Unfortunately, coming home didn't mean Stark had escaped the drug scene. Movement of drugs through the islands was always a problem, people looking for any way possible to transport them from South America, up through the islands to the States or Europe. Huge quantities came from Colombia, where drug syndicates refine eighty percent of the world's cocaine. Drugs went by boat and airplane, in the mail, in prostheses, and in people's stomachs.

A few months back, a woman had been apprehended with her baby's carrier filled with heroin, sewn in the blankets as well as stuffed inside the plastic frame. On top of it all was a screaming baby who needed his diaper changed. She got passed through customs quickly. No one wanted to deal with a screaming kid or the smell of a dirty diaper, until one brave customs woman who'd raised six kids of her own insisted on a closer look.

And last year, the coast guard sank a boat with three thousand pounds of cocaine hidden inside the hull. Another report detailed the interception of two tons of cocaine on a speedboat headed for a rendezvous with an accomplice on a cruise ship bound for the U.S.

The amount in the bag that Stark held was small by comparison, maybe two kilos. But multiply that by the number of flights that go out every day and it adds up, even if only ten percent of the flights have a crew member aboard transporting the drug.

"Could be a motive to bring down the plane," Stark said. "That copilot might have been causing someone trouble. It's usually what happens. The carrier gets greedy, wants a bigger share or starts cutting the coke and selling a little extra on the side. Or hell, maybe he was getting into the stash himself. We'll know when we get the tox screens back."

"Yeah, but why bring an entire plane down along with a couple of kilos of coke? There had to be other opportunities to get to the pilot," I said.

"I've seen it before. These people are ruthless," Stark said. "One high-end dealer in Miami blew up another dealer's house, wife and kids inside. It was a warning to every dealer on his payroll."

"Well, sabotage or not, it's pretty clear that we need to follow up on the drug angle," I said.

Stark was still holding up the bag of cocaine when a short, stocky guy wearing a pair of scuffed cowboy boots and a cowboy hat walked in. He wore a brown plaid shirt that looked like one Roy Rogers would have been proud to wear, right down to the mother-of-pearl buttons.

"Good day, gentlemen, ma'am. It appears that this crash may be solved before the week is out. I presume that powder is some sort of illicit material," he said, taking off his hat and running a kerchief over his forehead. "Pardon my manners. I should introduce myself. Joe Harrigan, AAIB."

Christ, this was our expert? Sturtevant's praise for the investigator didn't quite match the guy that stood before us.

His accent was pure Brit. A damn British cowboy? What the hell was that? He had ahold of the crown of the Stetson and was replacing the hat on his thinning brown hair. Then he hooked a thumb in his jeans. Nothing about him engendered any confidence that he was an expert at anything except impersonating Wild Bill Hickok.

"Mind if I take a look around?" he asked, and began strolling through the items laid out on the floor. He talked as he walked, his patter directed to no one in particular. It was clear that he was making a mental record of everything he saw—the location of all the passengers, which ones hadn't lived through the crash, where the cargo had been placed. I could see the wheels turning, assessments being made. He never touched a thing. He crouched, placed his arms on his knees, and took a hard look at the gun that was visible inside the clear plastic evidence container.

"You've recovered a weapon," he said.

"I found it wedged next to a seat," I said.

"I believe that someone slipped that gun onto the plane undetected," Harrigan said, stating the obvious. "I wonder how? More than likely it is not related to the crash, from what I have heard so far about how that plane went down. However, I will certainly be talking to airport security to find out how it could get through the metal detectors. I suppose it could have belonged to one of the pilots."

"We'll be running the serial numbers and see what comes up," Stark said.

I couldn't believe the stuff that was strewn all over the warehouse—a gun, sex toys, and cocaine, all on this little fifteen-passenger aircraft. God knows what ends up in a 747. If we needed a motive for murder, we'd found several, including an unfaithful husband and the threat of divorce and a 9 mm Beretta. The most likely was the cocaine smuggling. Stark and I would be following up on that immediately. Everything would remain in the warehouse until the investigation was complete, except for any items that Dickson or Harrigan might want to examine in the lab or send out for analysis.

We left the two of them standing side by side—a squat John Wayne and a Hell's Angel wannabe. They were surrounded by plaid boxers, T-shirts sporting Mickey Mouse, university, and sailing logos, cameras, film, toiletries, pocket calculators, and books.

"What do you think of Harrigan?" Stark asked on our way out.

"A cowboy? Jeez, Stark. Between Harrigan, Dickson, and Mr. GQ, I'd say we've got a cast for one of Stewart's movies."

Simon was perched on the edge of his bed ready to go when I got back to the hospital. He wore the same red hightops, baggy pants, and T-shirt that he'd had on when I pulled him out of the plane. The hospital had washed them. I realized it was all he had.

"Guess we'll need to get you some new clothes, huh?" I said, sitting next to him.

"Yeah, I guess."

"You ready to go?"

"Yeah," he said, sliding off the bed. "I still want to see my dad, though."

I called down to the morgue from the nurses' station and told them I was bringing the kid down. I didn't want Simon walking into a scene from *The Body Snatchers*. Dr. Hall had already talked to them and they understood what needed to be done. They said they would wheel the body to a room across the hall.

We were quiet in the elevator on the way down. Simon was nervous, shifting his weight from one foot to the other, one hand fingering the edge of his shirt, the other deep in a pocket.

When the elevator door opened, the same attendant that had been working yesterday when I brought Westbrook down was waiting for us, without the bloody lab coat. He led us past the morgue to a doorway on the right.

"You sure you're up to this?" I asked.

"Yeah. I just want to see him."

"Want me to come in with you or you want to go alone?" I asked.

"Maybe you could come with me."

The attendant opened the door and told us to take as long as we wanted. They'd done well. Simon's father was lying on a gurney that had been draped with white linen. His body was covered to the chin, his hands folded over his chest. Someone had actually put some blusher on his cheeks, trying to cover the waxlike countenance of death, and had placed island flowers in his hands. I owed these people big time.

Simon hesitated for a while, standing back. Then he stepped to the side of the gurney. He was barely tall enough to see over its edge. He stood there for a long time, just looking. Finally he touched his father's hand. He never shed a tear.

"I'm ready to go," he said finally.

The attendant was waiting outside. "I really appreciate your taking care of the body," I whispered to him as Simon went ahead to the elevator.

"No problem, mon. My wife be comin' by ta help out, brought da flowers. We got kids of our own. I jus be real sorry dat boy dun lost his daddy."

We were out in the hospital parking lot getting into the Rambler when I saw Jack Westbrook pull up to the entrance. I asked Simon to wait for me and went to talk to him. He was sitting in the car, tapping his fingers impatiently on the steering wheel, windows rolled up.

I knocked on the glass. When Westbrook rolled down the window a blast of cold hit me in the face.

"Detective Sampson. Hello. I'm just waiting for Debra. Doctor Hall said she was fine to go," he said, glancing over at Simon, near the Rambler.

"How's the boy?"

"Shaken, upset."

"He going home?" Westbrook asked. It seemed an odd question.

"Of course. He will be going home as soon as we get in touch with his family. Until then he'll be staying with me."

"Any word on why that plane went down?" he asked.

"It's way too soon to tell. The investigator from the AAIB just got in. They'll be bringing the plane up in the morning. We'll be needing to talk to all the other passengers, including your wife."

"She's in no shape for a lot of questions. I'd prefer you didn't bother her. Besides, what on earth could she tell you?"

"I'm afraid that no one is exempt, Senator." Somehow, I didn't see Westbrook as the concerned-husband type, but that was the card he was playing right now.

I told him I'd stop by their boat tomorrow and didn't give him the opportunity to come up with an excuse.

Chapter 14

Simon and I pulled away from the hospital and headed to the Tortola PD. I didn't want to leave the kid alone on the *Sea Bird,* so he was my companion for the rest of the day. He was quiet as we drove. He leaned on the window frame, head resting on his arms, gaze directed out at the ocean. I was guessing his mind was a long way from where we were right now. Probably still in the hospital morgue, looking at his father for the last time.

I didn't know what to say. I was no good at this. How could I possibly make it better? I couldn't. I pulled the Rambler over at a stretch of white beach at Paraquita Bay.

"How about a walk, Simon?"

"Okay," he said, coming back to the present.

We removed our shoes, left them near the car, and headed down to the edge of the water. I followed him into the gentle surf. He was up to his knees, arms raised, working to keep his balance against the periodic rush of waves that lapped against the bottom of his shorts. Water rushed around our feet and worked the sand from underneath them. As Simon began to topple into the water, I grabbed him under his arms and swung him around.

He laughed, a carefree kid's laugh. The first I'd heard. I kept him swinging, his heels brushing the tops of the waves. I twirled him until I was breathless. Then we splashed our way back to the shore.

"You know my dad and me, we weren't very close," Simon said as we walked down the beach. He had found a conch shell buried in the sand and had been holding it up to his ear, trying to listen to the ocean.

"Sometimes adults get wrapped up in things and forget what's important, Simon. I'm sure your dad loved you very much."

"Maybe, but ever since my mom died, he hadn't been the same. He used to come home from work and we'd play catch or he'd show me something neat on the computer till dinner. After she died, all he did was work. We got a housekeeper. He always said he'd be home for dinner, but he never was. When he did come home, he spent all his time in his den."

"Sounds like he was hurting, Simon."

"Yeah. I kept waiting for him to get back to the way he used to be," he said, regret filling the words.

I heard what he was saying, that now it would never happen. The father he had once had was lost to him forever. This kid was way too young to have to deal with that kind of regret. I found myself angry with Lawrence Redding for being so selfish, so unable to be there for his son. He hadn't been the only one suffering. Sure, he'd lost his wife, but Simon had lost his mother. I don't think I'd have liked Lawrence Redding much. He'd been self-involved and weak.

We kept walking, Simon darting in and out of the surf. In the distance I could see a man coming up the beach toward us. As he drew closer, the unmistakable bulk of Enok Kiersted, environmentalist and my new neighbor, took shape. He recognized Simon. Evidently the kid had been with his father when they'd met about the grant. He knelt and shook Simon's hand and then insisted we walk down

the beach to the mangroves. I had to give Kiersted credit.
He too recognized that the kid was hurting.

"Simon will love it. All kinds of cool stuff in there," he
said.

"Cool" would not have been the way I'd have described
it. As he led the way onto greasy mudbanks and into gnarled
and twisted branches and roots, my feet were sucked into a
foot of muck. God knows what I was stepping in. Every
once in a while I felt something hard poke into the sole of
my foot—some sort of shelled creature, no doubt. I tried
not to think about what else might be living in the stuff. I
was more troubled by what I couldn't feel—the soft, slimy
things that lived in the mud. The intensity of the slime was
outdone only by the putrid odor it emitted—that of rotten
eggs. I was about to suggest we head back to the beach.

"It's hydrogen sulfide," Kiersted said, noticing my discomfort. "There is very little oxygen in the mud.

"See these little holes in the prop roots above the
water?" he asked, crouching. "They lead to air passages
that carry oxygen down to the roots in the mud. That's how
the trees get oxygen."

Simon stooped next to him. He was fascinated. So much
for getting the hell out of there. We kept going, wending our
way through the tangled mass of roots as Kiersted, grateful
for an audience, gave Simon a lesson in mangroves.

Scores of fiddler crab holes dotted the banks. One crab
was industriously flicking mud out of its burrow until it saw
us approach and scrambled down its tunnel. Kiersted
picked up a stick and unearthed what he described as a bur-
rowing polychaete worm, fascinating to almost-ten-year-
old boys.

"The mangroves are loaded with nesting birds—egrets,
brown pelicans, cormorants, great blue herons, and even
bats," Kiersted explained. At the moment I could hear a
frigate bird clucking in the branches over our heads. The

mangrove was a canopy of waxy leaves and cigar-shaped seedlings decorated with intricate spiderwebs.

"All this muck? It's important in preserving the coral out there," Kiersted said, pointing out toward the reef. "The mangroves capture a lot of sediment and pollution that washes from the land and keeps it from settling on the coral and smothering it."

"Seems like a losing battle," I said. I knew that in many areas sediment and pollution were turning turquoise waters brown. Elyse had had a hand in preventing some of it when she'd convinced a local gravel pit operator to terrace the hillside and put in catchment ponds to keep the rain from washing sediment into the bay.

"People can be stupid," Kiersted said, his anger rising. "All they see is the muck and the smell and they tear these trees out. All over the world, the mangroves are being destroyed, replaced by fancy resorts, beaches, and shrimp farms. It's the same old story. A few come in and usurp the mangroves from the locals."

"What are shrimp farms?" Simon asked.

"They are football field–sized ponds constructed in the shallow water where the mangroves used to thrive. The operators use chemicals and nutrients as feed for the shrimp, turn the area into a toxic-waste dump, and then desert the farms when they no longer produce and simply move on to the next viable site. I call it rape-and-run agriculture, kind of like the slash and burn in the rain forests.

"Look at all the sailboats out there. They call Paraquita Bay a hurricane hole for good reason," he went on, pointing out into the lagoon.

I knew that if that storm continued on its path, O'Brien and the other charter company owners would be cramming as many boats as possible into the protected bay. The lagoon was about fifteen feet deep, surrounded by mangroves, and thus shielded from the wind and waves. There was only one opening wide enough to motor a boat through.

"Not only do these mangroves protect the sea from the pollution on land, they also protect the land from a violent sea," Kiersted explained. "Without them, regions which were protected from storms and tidal waves are now being destroyed, thousands killed in areas where few died when the mangroves were there to act as a buffer."

I thought about the 2004 tsunami that had killed hundreds of thousands and devastated entire villages in Indonesia and Thailand. I wondered how much of that region had once been guarded by mangroves. Suddenly the smell and the muck were tolerable.

"I am not going to let these mangroves or any others in the islands be destroyed if I can help it," he said, clenching his fists, his jaw set. "There are people down here who plan to convert the mangroves in Paraquita Bay into beachfront property. Just let them try."

I was glad that I was not a perpetrator of what he clearly considered the crimes of the century. Kiersted had no perspective. He was extremely angry and still ranting about the continued shortsightedness of government when I interrupted him.

"Who owns this land?" I asked.

"A local islander. He's given me permission to take samples here. I'm pretty sure that he's been approached by a developer. I've seen people wandering around on the property. He won't say who it is, but I'll find out and then I'll put a stop to it."

"How are you going to do that?" I asked. I wondered if Kiersted was crazy enough to resort to violence. He just shook his head, and didn't answer the question.

He was still standing in the mangroves, hands on hips, when Simon and I climbed back into the Rambler and continued to the office.

"What are you doing with the kid?" Stark asked, peering through the dirty window of the police department. I'd left Simon out front, where we'd run into Jimmy. The two of them were already heavy into a game of Hacky Sack in the parking lot. The kid had obviously played before. He balanced the little bag nimbly on the inside of his foot, then shot it toward Jimmy, who barely managed to capture it and send it back.

"He didn't have anyplace to go," I said as we headed down the hall to the chief's office.

"Jeez, Sampson, what is it with you and the abandoned?" He was talking about my cat, Nomad. I found her under a tree, trying to nurse kittens, though she was starving herself.

"You should talk, Stark," I said. He'd ended up with one of the kittens. "Besides, it will only be a couple days."

Stark and I stood outside of Dunn's office waiting for him to get off the phone. Finally he hung up and motioned us in. Stark had already given Dunn the rundown on what we'd found in the airplane, including the drugs.

"We got the autopsy results on the pilots. Both died of massive chest and head injuries. The preliminary toxicology tests indicate no cocaine, no alcohol present."

"So the copilot wasn't using," Stark said. "Still doesn't mean he wasn't cutting into profits somehow. Those drugs are our best bet if that plane was sabotaged."

"I agree," Dunn said. "I want you two on it. Get the records on the copilot from the airline. Find out where he lived, who his associates were. We'll need to talk to the passengers and the people at the airport as well. Maybe somebody saw someone around that plane who shouldn't have been there. We need to get on this as quickly as possible. All hell is going to break loose if that storm moves in."

Chapter 15

Simon and Jimmy were sitting under a tamarind tree, sweaty and drinking mango juice, when I went out to the parking lot. Stark was inside calling the airline to get the copilot's address.

"Looks like I could be a while," I said. "Stark and I need to do a couple of things."

"How 'bout Simon and me be headin' over to your place?" Jimmy suggested. "We be needin' a swim and I bet Tilda and da girls be home."

"You okay with that, Simon?" I asked.

"Sure." I could see that he and Jimmy were hitting it off. Figured. Jimmy was still just a kid himself.

"I'll pick up pizza on my way home," I said.

The two of them climbed into Jimmy's old Chevy. Fortunately, it wouldn't do much over forty. Jimmy was a speed demon who made up for his snail's pace behind the wheel of the Chevy when he got his hands on the throttle of the police boat. He floored the car and the thing rattled out of the parking lot.

The copilot lived over near Josiah's Bay on the north shore. Stark drove. He headed east along the waterfront on Blackburn Highway. You'd never know a storm was coming. Today the ocean was serene, gentle waves rolling across her surface. High above the water, a frigate bird soared. A pirate bird, it was zeroing in on an unsuspecting brown booby. It dove and chased and harassed until the booby dropped the fish it carried in its beak. Then the frigate swooped down and grabbed the fish in midair. I watched, staring blankly out the window.

I'd been running on adrenaline, charging from one situation to the next without much thought since that plane crashed into the ocean yesterday morning. I'd recovered the dead, left O'Brien, snooped through people's luggage and their lives, and stood by as Simon said goodbye to his father. And now the *Sea Bird*, my only place of refuge, was home for the kid. I was having trouble getting my bearings, seeing the horizon—the proverbial big picture, the damn forest. I was too caught up in events. The worst was the deep ache I felt for the kid and for O'Brien. What the hell was I doing?

"You okay, Sampson?" Stark asked.

"Sure," I said. "Just a lot going on."

"Yeah, well, you need to talk, I'm available."

"Thanks, Stark. Right now I just need to sort things out in my own head," I said.

We continued in silence. Stark drove like every other islander, honking at wayward goats and chickens that threatened to cross in front of him and at friends who lounged in doorways and at roadside bars. We zoomed through Kingstown, where the cottages of liberated slaves still stood almost two centuries later.

At Long Swamp, Stark took a hard left on Ridge Road and we headed into the hills through gumbo-limbo and frangipani trees. We passed a farmer, his mule laden with bundles of bananas, heading to the market in Road Town. In a nearby field, white egrets roamed among the cattle and foraged for insects.

As we drove higher, the air cooled and the roadside

turned to a jungle of heliconia, wild fuchsia, philodendron, and strangler figs.

At the top of the ridge, Stark pulled over and we looked down into Josiah's Bay. It lay at the foot of the valley where an isolated beach stretched along the shore, the only shade a few sea grape trees. Waves crashed on the rocks below, sending sprays of sparkling water into the sun. This was the wild side of the island, open to the fury of the Atlantic.

We found the copilot's house nestled in the hillside just above the bay. A woman was in the drive, struggling with groceries. A child of maybe two was trying to help. The woman looked up when she heard our car. She had the same look as Simon—shattered. She was maybe thirty, short hair tightly curled against her scalp. I was guessing she was the wife. The airline had notified her about her husband. She knew who we were when she saw us.

"Don't be wantin' to talk to you folks right now," she said, grabbing the child's hand and heading for the house.

I could think of only one reason that she'd avoid us. She knew about the drugs. Stark grabbed the last two sacks of groceries out of the car as well as the two she was trying to keep from dropping. She picked up the child and we followed her to the house.

"I'm sorry, but it can't wait," I said. "We have questions about why that plane crashed."

"My husband was a good man and good father," she said. "And he knew how to fly dat plane. That crash be no fault of his."

We followed her inside. Clearly her husband had done well. It was a well-kept bungalow, crowded with baby toys and furniture. Scribbled drawings were scattered on the table and a photograph held a central place above the couch. It was a family photo—the husband in his airline uniform, she in an ivory dress holding the baby. It was obvious they were proud of the child. Why the hell had he gotten involved in drug smuggling? It looked to me like he had it all. Had the drugs been so necessary in providing a home for his family? I doubted it. He had to make a good wage at the airline.

Stark put the grocery bags on the kitchen table. She set the child down in his playpen and busied herself putting milk in the cupboard and cereal in the refrigerator. She kept moving in fast, jerky motions, swiping at her eyes, clearly unaware of what she was doing and unwilling to face what she knew was coming.

I stopped her in midmotion, took the trash bags that she was about to place next to the corn flakes in the refrigerator, and led her to a kitchen chair. That's when she broke down completely.

"I tole him not ta do it," she said, covering her face in her hands and sobbing. "We had everything dat we be needin'. But for Jarvis it never be enough. He grew up real poor and scraped for everything he got. He didn't want his child to go without. He said we be needin' ta put money away to send da child to college. He be dreamin' of da boy becoming a doctor. He promised he'd be stoppin' when he had enough put away. I kept askin' him just how much be enough. Now look. I'll be lucky to keep food on da table."

"How long had he been transporting the drugs?" Stark asked.

"Since da boy was born. I didn't find out 'bout it till a few months ago. I was puttin' his lunch in his flight bag when I be seein' da bag of white powder. I knew what it was. I tole him I'd be leavin' him if he didn't stop, but he knew I'd never be doin' it. I loved dat man too much. Now I done lost him anyway." She looked at her son, fear for him marring her features.

"How did he get involved?" I asked. There was a drug connection out there somewhere. Just how extensive was yet to be determined.

She told us her husband had been approached by one of the mechanics for Island Air. It had started over drinks and talk about their child. The mechanic had been feeling him out and realized Jarvis would be a good bet because he was hungry for money.

"What about in the last month or so?" I asked. "Did your husband seem upset, worried?"

"No, just da opposite. He be relieved. You see I finally be convincin' him to stop. He promised this be his last time."

"Did your husband own a gun?" I asked, thinking about the Beretta that I'd pulled out of the airplane.

"No. I never be allowin' a weapon in dis house with da child and Jarvis agreed."

"Maybe he kept it in his locker at work," I suggested.

She just shook her head, exhausted. I knew we wouldn't get anything more from her today. She was devastated and stuck deep in her own pain and loss.

She was putting the child down for a nap when we left. I could hear her singing to him as we went out the door.

"This could be over fast," Stark said, as he maneuvered out of the driveway. "That mechanic may have wanted to ensure against others pulling out or keep that pilot from talking to anyone. He would have had access to that plane and he sure would have known how to bring it down. The loss of less than five pounds of coke would have been worth the message he'd be sending to the others."

"Yeah. Let's get over to the airport."

The terminal was deserted when we got there. It was well past seven and getting dark. We managed to find a janitor mopping the floor who directed us to a door marked "Island Air Operations. Authorized Personnel Only." No one paid a bit of attention when Stark and I walked in. A couple of pilots were standing at a counter, absorbed in weather maps. They didn't even look up.

Nearby, a guy was sitting at his desk examining the contents of a half-eaten sandwich. He looked up, smiled, and told us that any of the mechanics who weren't out on the tarmac would be hanging out in the lunchroom. He pointed down the hall.

We had no idea who we were looking for or whether the mechanic in question would even be around. The copilot's widow had never met the guy and did not know his name. It didn't matter though.

Three guys in blue grease-stained overalls were sitting around a table, smoking and playing cards. Another was standing at the vending machines. The minute we walked in, identified ourselves, and asked if anyone had been on duty yesterday, the guy at the vending machines slid out a side door and took off.

Stark and I were right behind him. By the time we got to the hallway, he was already heading out onto the tarmac. We followed him into the dark. The heat still stored in the pavement felt like a blast from a furnace. I could hear footsteps slapping against the concrete, then saw a shape disappear into a bunch of maintenance trucks and luggage carts that were parked around an airplane for the night.

Stark and I split up. We'd go in from opposite sides and try to corral him. I pulled my .38 out of the holster that was strapped around my waist and designed to look like an everyday fanny pack. Stark was doing the same. We had no idea whether the guy had a gun.

I could see Stark scurrying around to the left from one vehicle to the next, trying to keep low and out of sight. I was moving to the right. The mechanic would know his way around out here. I crouched behind a luggage carrier piled high with suitcases, fishing tackle, and boating gear. I waited, scanning, trying to figure out where the hell he'd gone. He had to be hiding somewhere, maybe in one of the vehicles, maybe in the plane. It was a fairly large turboprop that carried probably fifty or sixty passengers. Portable stairs were pushed up to an open cabin door, the only way in or out. If he'd gone inside, he'd be trapped but he'd have plenty of places for ambush, protected behind his choice of seats.

Stark was thinking the same thing. I saw him dart from behind a gas truck, run to the steps, and start to climb the stairs, crouched low. He was halfway up when I caught a slight movement on the other side of the luggage carrier. Then I saw the guy raise his arm, a gun in his hand, pointed right at Stark, fingers around the trigger.

"Stark! Gun!" I yelled. I heard two shots and registered the smell of gunpowder right before the baggage cart slammed into me and I was buried under a pile of luggage and gear. I was flat on my back, trying to figure out which way was up when the mechanic pounced and started tossing suitcases off me. Before I could figure out which end was up, he had his rough, stubby fingers wrapped around my neck and his full weight on me.

Somewhere in the mess of fishing gear and luggage, I'd lost the .38. I tried to knee him in the groin, but he had too much body weight on my legs. I could feel myself going, arms getting weak, darkness creeping into the edges of my vision. Then suddenly his grip relaxed and he fell away, stunned. Stark was standing there with an old hard-sided suitcase gripped in his hand and blood dripping down the side of his face.

Stark helped me out of the pile of luggage and then grabbed the guy by the collar.

"You okay, Sampson?" he asked.

"Yeah, but you're bleeding," I said, nodding toward his head. He touched his temple, flinched, and said it was just a scratch.

By the time we got to the police department and had the guy locked behind bars, it was past nine. Stark was sitting in the office dabbing the side of his head with gauze. The bleeding had stopped. The bullet had barely grazed him, just above the ear, lots of blood but no real damage. He'd been stunned for a minute on the airplane steps. When he'd

come around, he'd seen the guy trying to crush my wind-
pipe and hit him with the suitcase.

The mechanic wasn't saying a word except that he
wanted his lawyer.

"Let's get out of here, Sampson. We'll talk to his lawyer
in the morning. I'd like to see how he thinks he's going to
get away with trying to kill cops."

We headed to the parking lot, both of us more than ready
to call it a day.

"I guess you saved my butt out there," Stark said as I
was getting into my car. "Thanks."

"Hey, guess you did the same. Let's call it even," I said,
flashing him a grin. "See you tomorrow, Stark."

O'Brien's Jeep, a CJ5, was parked at Pickering's Landing. It didn't have a top or doors and was a primer rust
color. O'Brien could have afforded a Mercedes but much
preferred the old Jeep.

Simon was on the beach playing with Sadie. He came
running when he saw me. I could tell he was about to jump
into my arms and then thought better of it. I guess he realized we were really practically strangers. It didn't feel like
it though. I stooped and locked him in a bear hug that Sadie
got in the middle of. Heck, the kid and I had been through
a lot together in the last thirty-six hours.

"Hannah, you didn't tell me you lived on a boat and have
a dog!" he said. "It's so cool. I was playing with Rebecca
and Daisy, but they had to go in for dinner. Tilda asked if I
wanted to eat with them, but I told her we were waiting for
you."

"Well, you must be starved," I said, grabbing the pizzas
I'd picked up on the way home. I knew it was no match for
Tilda's Sunday meal. A good example of why I should
never be a parent.

Jimmy and O'Brien were sitting on the *Sea Bird* sipping
Caribs, the local brew. I was surprised O'Brien had come

here after our fight last night, but I was happy to see him—
too happy. He stood when he saw us coming, unsure just
how I was going to react to his being there.

"O'Brien, I'm glad you came," I said, stepping onto the
boat.

"I brought Nomad. She wasn't too happy at the villa
without you and Sadie."

"Oh," was all I could think to say. *Disappointment*
wasn't quite the right word for what I was feeling. O'Brien
wasn't there to try to patch things up. He was there to bring
me my cat. He didn't even accept my invitation to stay for
pizza. I walked him out to the Jeep, trying to figure out a
way to say I was sorry about last night.

Before I could find the right words, he took a jab. "Good
kid," he said, referring to Simon. "It's nice of you to take
him. But you'd better be careful, Hannah. It's pretty obvious he's getting attached. You wouldn't want anyone, especially a kid, getting too close or interfering with your job."

"Come on, O'Brien. Don't turn this into what's happened between us." I was angry now. "You've always
known how I've felt about my job. It's who I am. I thought
you'd accepted that when I moved into the villa. I guess
you really just hoped you'd find a way to change my
mind—change me. Chances are, if you did, you wouldn't
like me, O'Brien. Wouldn't like what I turned into. Can't
you understand that?"

"Maybe you're right. But I just can't stand by and watch
what it does to you, especially after a day like yesterday.
You try to hide it, but I know that the deaths affect you. You
blame yourself for every one of them—Jake, Elyse, and
every other person that you think you should have been
able to save. Each one takes a piece of you. I don't know,
maybe we simply can't be together, Hannah."

The way he said it, I could feel my heart drop, the anger
giving way to a horrible sense of loss and emptiness. I
loved O'Brien. He had always looked for ways to keep us

together. Until now. He sounded so resigned. But why the hell couldn't we find a way to be together and still be who we were? And why was I the one being asked to give up everything? Hell, I was just doing my job, just like he was.

Only a small part of me was willing to admit he was right. Sure, the job took its toll. It was the price I paid. I wanted O'Brien to stick with me, but maybe it was impossible. Maybe he needed to move on—find someone who wanted marriage, a family. It made me unbelievably sad to think of O'Brien with someone else.

"Let's just give it some time, " I said. "I don't want to lose you, O'Brien."

"Yeah, more time," he said, hopelessly. This wasn't the O'Brien I knew. I could see he was exhausted and I knew he had to be worried about the storm and his boats. I'd heard the weather report on the radio on the way home. In fact, it had been blaring from every vehicle and out of every doorway. Everyone on the island was on edge, listening and hoping to hear that the storm had died out somewhere in the Atlantic. Instead it had been upgraded to a tropical storm with a name—Felix—and it was still headed directly toward the BVI.

"Go home and get some sleep," I said as he climbed into the Jeep.

Then I changed my mind. "Peter," I called, needing to stay connected, wanting him to stay. But he gunned the engine and was gone before I could stop him.

I shuffled back down the dock to the *Sea Bird*. Jimmy and Simon were already halfway through one of the pizzas by the time I joined them. Between the two of them, they managed to consume two entire pizzas except for the slice I had. Then Jimmy went home. Calvin came down and helped us clear out the back cabin so Simon could have a place to sleep and call his own for a few days. I'd been using the space as storage with a little office at one end. We moved all my paraphernalia up to a locker at the marina that Calvin insisted I use.

Calvin showed Simon the men's side of the bathhouse. I got him a towel and we both headed to the showers. When I got back to the *Sea Bird,* Simon was sitting in the cockpit with Sadie's head in his lap. He was wearing one of Calvin's oversized shirts and a pair of flannel pajama pants, probably Tilda's—rolled several times at the ankles and adorned with penguins. I had forgotten all about the kid's clothes. Everything he had was now in the warehouse, being held until the investigation was complete.

"Jeez, Simon, I guess we need to get you some stuff."

"It's okay, Hannah. These are good and Tilda gave me a toothbrush." He smiled and held up a red toothbrush with Daffy Duck on the end.

"You doing okay?" I asked, sitting down next to him and putting an arm around his shoulders.

"Yeah. Thanks for letting me stay with you."

"I'm happy you're here," I said and realized I meant it. "Do you feel up to talking about your dad?"

At some point, we needed to know more about what his father had been doing in the islands and whether it could possibly be related to the crash. I figured it was better here than down at the office with Stark. Stark was a soft touch, but a first encounter with his shaved head, black muscle shirt, and six-five frame could be intimidating, especially to a nine-year-old.

Simon told me that he and his dad had been in the islands for the past week. His father was on business. He was in charge of the big grants at the Woods Foundation. His father had come to evaluate Enok Kiersted's project for a foundation grant. Simon thought a lot of money was at stake. He'd gone with his dad to look at Kiersted's lab in town.

"It was boring," Simon said. "They were looking at a bunch of stuff on the computer. I went out on the street and took a bunch of pictures. When I went back inside, I could hear them arguing. Mr. Kiersted was yelling at my dad. I got kind of scared."

"What was he yelling about?"

"Well, people got mad at my dad a lot," he said. "It seems like it was always about money. My dad never let people push him around, though."

The kid had slid farther and farther down in his chair as we'd talked and was having trouble keeping his eyes open.

"Let's get to bed, Simon," I said. "We'll talk more later."

I woke up confused. Something had jolted me out of a sound sleep. At first I thought I was in O'Brien's bed at the villa. I was out of bed and standing in the salon in T-shirt and cut-off sweats when I finally realized I was on the *Sea Bird*. Then I heard the screaming, terrified screaming. It was Simon.

"Simon, what is it?" I yelled, stumbling to his room and flipping on a light. The kid was sitting up in his bed, eyes wide, tears streaming down his face. I picked him up and carried him out to the salon.

"Hannah, they were chasing me, the dead people on the airplane. They were coming to get me. They were trying to pull me out to the sharks."

"It's okay, Simon. It was just a nightmare. There are no sharks and no dead people. You're safe." Of course, I was lying. There had been plenty of dead people and sharks, just not in this boat right now. It's no wonder the kid was having nightmares.

"I'm here, Simon. Me and Sadie, we're here." I sat rocking him until the shaking stopped.

"Hannah, can I sleep with you?" he asked, too scared to worry about being a baby.

By the time I fell asleep, I'd been forced to a small strip of mattress against the wall, with my arm around the kid and Sadie sprawled out at the foot of the bed.

Chapter 16

They were up in the bow, standing in the dark. Two of them were arguing. They always argued. They'd been arguing for years. The same argument. It was part of the game. It was all about the one's over-the-top violence and the other's need. It always reached the same conclusion. They were tied together in a way that would be considered warped by most.

The third guy stood back, muscular arms crossed on his chest, waiting for them to finish the debate they'd been engaged in since Friday and get on with it.

"I told you before," the smaller of the two was saying, "no one threatens me."

"That temper—it has cost us," the other said.

"You never complained before."

"You never went this far before. Now we need to cover ourselves."

"Don't worry, we'll handle it," the muscular guy finally said, interrupting the exchange. "There won't be any problems. I've already checked the building. It's locked and there's a cop out front—just one. Looks pretty casual. He'll be easy to deal with."

"I hope no one spots you. Neither of you look much like your average tourist." Both were dressed from head to toe in black. The smaller of the two, the one in charge, wore ugly purple running shoes.

"Did you ever think about wearing shorts and a T-shirt? If someone sees you, there won't be much doubt that you're trouble."

"No one's going to see us. That's the point. No one will ever know we were there. We'll send the cop on a wild-goose chase, get in, find the thing, lock back up, and we're out of there. This will be easy beyond belief."

They waited for several minutes in the dark near the warehouse. Finally, the kid showed up. He'd been a willing recruit, one of those kids hanging out in town, trying to look tough but actually looking desperate and hungry. All it took was a twenty. It would be more money than he'd ever had in his pocket in his young life. They told him to make sure the cop was gone for at least a half hour and then to ditch him.

The kid was a star. Even they would have fallen for his story. He ran to the cop, out of breath, real tears running down his face, and seemingly frantic. Seconds later, the cop took off, trying to keep up with the kid.

The two waited a couple of minutes, making sure that no one else was around. It was a deserted area of the water-front, commercial, the kind of place where everyone checked out by five, earlier if they could get away with it. Still, it paid to be careful. You just never knew who might wander by. Finally they crept across the open lot and pulled on gloves, quickly picked the lock, and slid the heavy door open just far enough so they could squeeze through. They didn't bother to close it. They planned to be in and out quickly. Once inside, they flicked on their flashlights and began the search.

Even though they'd leave nothing that would point to them, the cops would be determined to find out what had been so important on that plane. Especially Sampson. She and her partner had already been asking too many questions about the crash.

Now though, they'd get what they were after and get out of the islands before anyone was the wiser. Let them investigate all they wanted. They'd not find one shred of evidence of their involvement, even if they did find the body.

"Found your gun," the big guy said, shining his light on the Beretta that was lying on the cement floor in a liquid-filled container. He picked it up and looked at the label taped to the evidence tube.

"Interior cabin—against bulkhead on right, no prints, run ballistics," he read. "Guess you dropped your gun. Kinda careless, don't you think?"

"Give me that," Purple Shoes said, grabbing the container, emptying the fluid out, and stuffing the gun into a pocket. "They won't be getting any ballistics off this gun."

Fifteen minutes later they had been through everything and had not found what they'd come for.

"Dammit," Purple Shoes said. "It's got to be here somewhere."

Suddenly they heard a scraping sound, the door being slid open farther. They doused their lights and waited in the dark, listening. Someone was coming into the warehouse. If it was the cop, that kid would be in deep shit. Then they saw the dark figure of a man stop, lift a bottle to his lips, and take a swig. A bum who had no doubt seen the open door. He started singing an old whaler's song as he stumbled through the darkness.

> We'll drink tonight with hearts as light,
> To love, as gay and fleeting
> As bubbles that swim, on the beaker's brim,
> And break on the lips while meeting.

The drunk stepped inside and started filling his duffel bag, periodically stopping to swig from the bottle he grasped in his other hand. He looked through the luggage, examining and rejecting a pair of shorts, a watch, the glitter of a ring. Then he stuffed a pair of practically new sweatpants and a T-shirt that said, "Live slow, sail fast" into his duffel. When he came across a pair of woman's red crotchless underwear, he held them up, turning them inside out, seemingly trying to figure out how the hell they went on.

"My day, woman jus went without altogether," he muttered, shaking his head. He stuffed the panties in his pocket and kept rummaging.

He was putting a box of soggy cigars in his bag when Purple Shoes moved up behind him and smashed the butt of the gun into his skull. They left him in a pool of blood and got the hell out of there before the cop came back. They were empty-handed except for the Beretta.

Chapter 17

At six the next morning, I stepped off the *Sea Bird,* careful not to set her rocking in the water. Simon was still sound asleep. I didn't want to wake the kid. He'd had a rough night. Several times he'd startled in his sleep and mumbled, on the verge of terror. I'd tightened an arm around him and whispered him back from the edge.

The sun was just climbing past the palms and casting shadows on the sand. A gentle breeze swept down the shore. Tilda had shaken me awake at six. I felt a twinge of guilt that Dunn had been forced to call her to get me up. I had no phone on the boat.

When I'd left the States I'd made a big deal of crushing my cell phone in the garbage compactor and vowing never to have another. I'd had to carry one every waking hour on the job. I hated the damn things. And everyone had them. What was so important it couldn't wait? What really pissed me off was sitting in a restaurant, hearing a ring, and everyone within ten feet suddenly rummaging in pockets and purses, sure the call was for them. Then I'd have to listen to the person sitting at the table next to me talking for fifteen minutes. Ever notice how important things sound? Then you pick up the words. "Yeah, I'll buy milk and bread on the way home." I once saw a guy so engrossed in his phone conversation that he put butter in his coffee.

Besides, there are places that I count on to escape. The *Sea Bird* was one of them. I figured if it was important, whoever needed to talk to me would find a way. Dunn always did. Unfortunately, Tilda was the one who paid for my privacy. He'd called her at the marina and told her I needed to get over to the warehouse—now.

Tilda offered to keep an eye on Simon and get him breakfast when he got up. She was outside hanging laundry when I got up to the marina. Crisp sheets and little girls' dresses twisted and billowed in the morning breeze. I could hear Daisy and Rebecca chattering upstairs in their room. Rebecca would be getting dressed for school, second grade. Every morning Daisy would stand by the road, longing to go too, as her sister climbed on the bus.

I promised Tilda I'd be back before lunch and ten minutes later I pulled up in front of the warehouse. Dunn's car and a police vehicle were already there. Stark pulled up right behind me. I could hear sirens in the distance, coming closer.

"What happened?" Stark asked, unfolding himself from the car, a donut in one hand, coffee in the other, the morning paper under his arm.

"No idea. I just got the message to get over here," I said.

He handed me the coffee, then leaned into the car and grabbed another from the dash. "Want a donut?" he asked.

"No thanks."

"Nice likeness of you on the front page," he said, handing me the paper.

When I unfolded it, the headlines screamed *Police Detective Teams with Star. Will It Turn to Romance?* The picture was the one that Sammy Lorenzo had engineered yesterday on the *Wahoo*. It looked like Stewart and I were contemplating a sexual encounter right there on the boat.

"God dammit! I don't want to hear one word from you about this, Stark," I said, throwing the paper in a nearby trash can. "Let's get in there."

Dunn was inside, kneeling next to a body. "It's Capy," he said as we walked up.

"Christ," I muttered, trying to maintain my cool.

Everyone on the island knew Capy. He lived in a tumble-down structure in the trees. He had once been a skilled fisherman, operating one of the most profitable fishing boats in the islands. That ended the year his wife died of cancer and the big fish got scarce. He'd started drinking hard. Then he'd lost his boat one night in a storm. He'd told anyone that would listen that there'd been demons under the angry sea.

Folks watched out for him, made repairs to his shack, brought him supplies, and left him cigarettes when he wasn't around. Capy would not accept charity but often wandered the docks looking for the treasures that others considered trash—usually that amounted to discarded fishing gear, maybe an old blanket.

Now he was lying in a pool of sticky black stuff. His white hair was matted in it. His breathing was labored, raspy. I knelt next to him and took his wrist. His pulse was fluttering and skipping. I heard the ambulance screech to a halt outside and the siren go silent. About time.

Two medical techs rushed in and went to work trying to get him stable. He had lost a lot of blood. Whoever had hit him had not intended that he ever get up. When the medics placed him on the stretcher, he was muttering something about red underwear.

"Who would hurt Capy?" I asked after they loaded him in the ambulance and sped away, sirens again blaring.

"I don't know, but I intend to find out." Dunn was pissed about the old man, as angry as I'd ever seen him, fists knotted, his face set in hard lines.

Stark was standing nearby, running his hands over his bald head. "What about the guard who was supposed to be watching the place?"

"Seems some kid came yelling about a man attacking his mother," Dunn said.

"Where is the cop now?" I asked.

"Over there. His name's Sergeant Josephs." Dunn pointed to the uniformed officer sitting in a corner, hanging his head.

Stark and I went to talk with him. Josephs was beating himself up about what had happened.

"The kid rushed up all out of breath, said his mother's boyfriend had come home drunk and was threatening her with a butcher knife. Man, that kid was good. I never even questioned him. I followed him all the way down to the post office. About the time I realized he was leading me in circles, he disappeared around a corner.

"When I got back here," he continued, "it was just getting light. I saw the door was ajar. I came inside and found Capy. First, I figured he'd broken in and passed out. Then I saw all the blood and called it in right away."

"Did you touch anything?"

"Naw, I know better than that."

"What about this kid?" I asked. "Did you recognize him?"

"No. It was real dark. He was a skinny kid, all legs and arms, must have been around twelve. Had a baseball cap on, maybe black, dark blue with one of those Nike symbols on it. Wearing it sideways like the kids do. He wore baggy jeans that he had to keep pulling up, and a big shirt. He looked like half the kids in town—you know, the ones who are trying to look like rappers."

After Gil Dickson dusted for prints, we spent the next hour in the warehouse trying to re-create some sort of scenario. The lock had been picked. More than likely whoever had broken in had wanted it to go unnoticed. They'd probably planned to simply lock it back up and be long gone before Josephs got back.

But then Capy had gotten in the way. He'd probably found the door open and gone in, looking for more junk or maybe just a quiet place to finish his rum. He'd been unable to resist the stuff he discovered. In Capy's duffel we found Lorenzo's box of cigars and a couple of items of clothing that we knew had been in the luggage. Obviously he'd interrupted someone with more sinister intentions.

Burglary had not been the motive. Debra Westbrook's jewelry and the Rileys' expensive camera equipment were right where we'd left them. When we checked our list of the items we'd recovered, we found absolutely nothing missing—except for the gun.

"What do you think?" Stark asked as we walked out to our cars. "Was that gun what they were after?"

"God knows," I said. "We need to see if Dickson's gotten anything on those serial numbers."

When we got back to the office, the mechanic's lawyer was sitting outside Dunn's office waiting to pounce. He started making all sorts of demands, the most outlandish being that his client should be released immediately. Fat chance. The guy had tried to kill two police officers, namely Stark and me.

I had the feeling this was news to the lawyer. Finally, he agreed to let us talk to his client with him present.

We headed down to the cells. The mechanic was lying on his cot, feigning boredom until the lawyer clued him in about the charges. Then he got real talkative.

"Why did you bring down that plane?" Stark asked, going for the jugular.

"What?" he demanded, suddenly on his feet. "No way. Why would I want to do that?"

"We know about the drug running. We talked to the copilot's wife. She told us that her husband was getting out. Maybe you wanted to send a message to all the other runners in your little operation."

The guy spent a good ten minutes denying that he knew anything about drugs. Finally, his lawyer took him aside and explained the facts of life—those being that trying to kill cops was highly frowned on by the courts and that co-operating with us would be in his best interest.

"Hell, for all I knew you were sent by my connection when he heard about that plane. How was I supposed to know you were cops?"

"Hey, Stark, I distinctly remember identifying ourselves in that lunchroom, don't you?" I said, dripping sarcasm.

"Yes, I do believe we did," Stark said.

The mechanic scrambled for an excuse and finally said he thought it was a trick and that he never saw any IDs. "I mean, look at him," he said, indicating Stark. "Tell me he doesn't look like a dealer." He had a point.

Eventually, we agreed to back off on attempted-murder charges if he'd give us the information we wanted, but we weren't about to promise him he'd be walking out of jail anytime soon. He'd definitely be doing time for assaulting police officers and drug running. Still, he knew he was in no position to refuse the offer.

He couldn't turn his colleagues in fast enough. He told us he was just a middleman, had good contacts at the airport because he worked there, and got a couple of other pilots and flight attendants signed on. He swore up and down that he had not tampered with the plane. Why would he? His drugs were lost. Besides, Saturday was his day off, so he had been nowhere near the aircraft.

Dunn was hidden behind the newspaper when we walked into his office. "Interesting picture, Detective Sampson." That's all he said, but I knew he was perturbed. Dunn was a "keep a low profile" kind of chief and he didn't appreciate his people making headlines. Before this day was over, I planned on finding an opportunity to threaten Lorenzo's life if one more word appeared in the papers about me.

"What do you think about this mechanic?" Dunn asked after we'd given him the details about the interrogation.

"We'll check to see whether he was anywhere near the

plane while it was at the airport," I said. "I'm guessing he's off the hook in terms of sabotage and the break-in at the warehouse. It just doesn't fit, especially since he was in jail last night."

About that time Dickson knocked on Dunn's door. He'd run the serial numbers on the Beretta.

"I'm afraid I don't have good news," he said, holding a fax in his hand. "The gun was reported stolen last year from a pawnshop in California. It hadn't turned up since, until we recovered it from the plane."

"Another dead end." I could hear the frustration in Dunn's voice.

"What do you want to do about the drug running, Chief?" Stark asked.

"I'll call the coast guard and get them to start looking for the boat that the mechanic described. I wouldn't be surprised if word is already out that we've arrested this guy. Anyone involved is probably halfway back to South America by now. In the meantime, the mechanic stays in jail and you two stay focused on this plane crash."

Dunn was interrupted by the phone.

"Chief Dunn," he said, then listened for a good five minutes before he responded. "How long has he been gone?" He paused, then asked, "Does he miss work often?" Another pause. I could hear a woman's voice on the other end.

"All right," Dunn responded. "We'll look into it if he hasn't shown up in twenty-four hours. Please keep me informed." He paused again. "Yes, I know you're concerned, but chances are he'll be in his office in the morning. Call me if he's not."

Finally, he hung up. "That was a report about a missing person, a Conrad Frett," he said. "He's with the Department of Natural Resources. His secretary was calling to say Frett didn't show up for work today. When she phoned his home, his housekeeper said he wasn't there when she arrived this morning to get his breakfast."

"What's the big deal?" Stark said. "He probably decided to take the day off."

"Let's hope so," Dunn said. "If not, you two will have to get on that too."

The phone rang again. The longer Dunn talked, the more frustrated he got. After about ten minutes he hung up.

"You know, a couple of days ago," he said, "I was sitting here, caught up on all my paperwork, enjoying my view, and actually getting home in time for supper. Now it seems everyone in these islands has gone crazy. That was the manager of that dolphin park. He's been calling me at least twice a day because someone released his dolphins. He's worried about his job, I guess. Whoever it was swam in after dark and cut a huge opening in the netting. The manager wants the person caught and punished. We'll never catch him. Lot of folks on this island were up in arms about what was happening over at that park. Anyone could have decided to set them free. I have to admit I thought about it myself."

"What night did that happen?" I asked Dunn.

"Saturday night, sometime after the place closed."

I thought about Kiersted and his lecture to me about the dolphins that first night we'd talked on the beach at Pickering's Landing. He'd just been coming back to the marina, his clothes wet. That had been Saturday night. I decided I would talk to Kiersted myself about it.

Dunn's phone was ringing again as we headed out the door.

"We need to regroup," I said to Stark. We were sitting out in the central office on a couple of cracked vinyl chairs with wheels. "Nothing is making any sense here. Things just aren't connecting. The crash, the break-in, the stolen gun. Shit. Maybe nothing is connected."

Stark wheeled his chair over to an old blackboard that had been gathering dust in the corner. It was cracked and marred by use. He picked up a piece of chalk and we started trying to find some organization in the confusion. Stark and I both had thought that things would be solved quickly with the copilot and the mechanic and their involvement in drug running. It was the most straightforward scenario and more often than not the most obvious solution proved correct. Now we were starting all over.

The warehouse break-in was a red flag. We needed to look at everyone closely. Stark drew an airplane on the board and started filling in the details. *Why not?* I thought. Maybe something would shake loose. I sat with my elbow on my knee, knuckles propped under my chin, contemplating Stark's diagram:

LEFT SIDE	RIGHT SIDE
Row 1: William Riley (DOA)	Louise Riley (DOA)
Row 2: Vacant (Debra moved)	Vacant
Row 3: Newlywed husband	Newlywed wife
Row 4: Lawrence Redding (DOA)	Vacant (Simon Redding in bathroom)
Row 5: Sammy Lorenzo	Zora Gordon
Row 6: Debra Westbrook	Daniel Stewart

Finally, we started through the names. We knew little about the Rileys except what Senator Westbrook had told us. They'd been filthy rich. Their seats in the front row had pretty much ensured their deaths.

The second row of seats had been empty. Debra Westbrook had been lucky that she considered the back of the plane safer and moved to the rear section. All we'd learned about her was that there'd been trouble between her and Jack and that she might have hired a divorce attorney.

In the third row were the newlyweds. All we knew about them was that they were well prepared for their honeymoon.

On the left, behind the groom, was Lawrence Redding.

The fact that he had the power to give or withhold hundreds of thousands, if not a million, dollars meant he'd have enemies. But at the moment we were aware of only one person he'd had any contact with—Enok Kiersted. If Redding was recommending against the grant, Kiersted would not have wanted him to make his report to the foundation. Simon had said they'd had a fight.

Zora Gordon was seated behind Simon. Seemingly she was staying alone on a yacht. Until I'd seen her card, I never would have pegged her as a lawyer. She had the look of someone who spent all her time in gyms and health stores. I wondered what kind of law she practiced. It was possible that she'd made enemies along the way—some disgruntled client who'd just been released from jail or was pissed about her billing structure.

"What about Sammy Lorenzo and Daniel Stewart?" Stark asked.

"We know they were here on vacation. Stewart said he needed to get away. Sammy came down later to meet him. I suppose it's possible that Stewart has enemies. He's certainly well known, but it seems more likely that he'd be stalked by beautiful women than targeted for murder."

"They sure were able to turn the crash to their advantage." Stark was smiling now. "Looks like you're on the road to fame as the love interest of the stars." He had managed to resist the temptation to ride me about the morning headlines. Now he just couldn't stop himself.

"I told you, Stark, I don't want to hear it," I said. "Let's look at the warehouse. Why did someone break in?"

"Only one reason," Stark said. "They were after that gun."

"Why?" I asked, pushing him to figure this out.

"It would implicate them in something?" he suggested.

"Yeah, but how?" I asked. "Whoever lost it probably knows it can't be traced. Why risk it?"

"Let's think about it," Stark said. "The gun had to belong

to someone on the plane or someone who was on the plane while it was on the ground. We'll assume for now that it wasn't the mechanic."

"Okay. That leaves every one of the passengers and practically anyone who was working at the airport on Saturday morning. Hell, Stark, maybe the gun had been wedged in that seat for weeks."

"Yeah, maybe it's not related at all. Shit. What a mess. Maybe it was a random break-in. Whoever it was saw the gun and took it."

"But why not take the other stuff—like the jewelry?"

"Because Capy interrupted them," Stark said. "Let's hope he pulls through and can tell us something."

"Maybe they didn't find whatever they were looking for," I said, a random thought that took hold as soon as the words were out of my mouth.

"It's possible. Whoever broke into the warehouse might have been after something that would implicate them in the crash," Stark said.

The only items from the plane that had not been left in the warehouse were the coke and Redding's laptop. Dunn had wanted the coke locked up in the police department and Gil had taken the laptop to see if he could retrieve any data.

"Or they were looking for something else that was on that plane," I countered. "The gun? Possible. The coke? Maybe. The laptop? A stretch, but I'll ask Dickson to move it up on the priority list."

"Hell, it's feasible that the crash was an accident," Stark said, throwing the chalk into the trash.

"Yeah, it could be, but right now we need to assume it wasn't," I said. "We need to know more about these passengers. It's the most likely strategy for getting at what happened on the plane and in turn uncovering a motive for the break-in at the warehouse."

We divided the list. Stark would go out to the airport and interview airline personnel and check the mechanic's story, then head to the hospital to talk to the newlyweds. I needed to pick up Simon and get the kid something to wear. Then I'd go talk to Debra Westbrook.

"Parental responsibility? Could really cramp your style," Stark said as he banged out the door.

"That it could," I muttered to no one. "That it could."

Jean, Dunn's secretary, was hidden behind the front page of the damn *Island News* when I stopped at her desk.

"Wow, Hannah, you be one lucky lady. Dat Daniel Stewart is a hunk!" she said.

"Jean, it's not what it looks like," I said.

"Well, dat's a shame. Maybe you want to introduce me to him?"

"Do me a favor and don't be showing that paper to everyone in the office." I could tell by her expression that she already had.

"Has there been any word from Simon's aunt?" I asked.

"No. I called her office again this morning. Her secretary said she's left several messages with no response. Dat boy okay?"

"As good as he can be, I guess." Christ, was there anyone out there besides me who was concerned enough about the kid to take care of him?

Chapter 18

When I got back to Pickering's Landing, Tilda was just taking in the laundry. I saw Simon down the beach. He was holding Daisy's hand as they hurried toward me, each carrying a red plastic bucket. Daisy's was filled with shells. At five, Daisy could rarely be found without some sort of ocean artifact, usually deep inside one of her pockets. She and Rebecca had lived at the water's edge their whole short lives. It was their playground. When I knelt to inspect their treasures, she handed me a tiny hermit crab.

"This is Herman," she said. "Isn't he cute? I'm going to put him under my pillow."

"Maybe you should put him back where you found him," I suggested. "Remember how your mama said they didn't like being away from their own homes?" More than once, Tilda had found such creatures dead and smelling in Daisy's bed.

"But, Hannah, I don't want to take the crab back to his home," she said, sticking a finger in her mouth.

"Why not, Daisy?" I asked as she worried another finger into her mouth.

"It's scary up there," she said, nodding toward the brush at the edge of the trees, where the hermit crabs could be found hiding under palm leaves.

"What do you mean, Daisy?" I asked. "You've never

been scared of the trees. You went up there to get the crab, didn't you?" I figured this was a smart five-year-old's strategy for avoiding the directions of an adult, especially one who she knew damn well would never want her to be afraid.

"It's scary there now," she said. I could see the anxiety in the kid's eyes.

"Why, Daisy?" I asked, looking at Simon. He just shrugged his shoulders.

"When I went to find Herman I saw a man in the trees."

"A man? What man?" I was alarmed now.

"I don't know, but he looked mean and he didn't smile when I smiled at him. He just went away, but maybe he's hiding up there."

"Did you see anyone, Simon?" I asked.

"No. Daisy came running back saying there were monsters in the trees. I thought it was a game. I pretended to be a monster and chase her, but she started to cry and said she wanted her mom. I'm sorry I scared her."

"When did this happen?" I asked.

"Just a few minutes ago. Daisy didn't tell me anything about the man. She just said she was scared and didn't want to play anymore. We were on our way back to the marina to find Tilda."

I knew that Daisy wasn't normally frightened by monster games. She was at the age when she knew it was just pretend. "How about I go with you to put Herman back and you can show me where you saw the man?" I said, picking her up and holding her tight.

She pointed to the place and I carried her up to the trees. Simon followed with the buckets. Once in the palms, she insisted I put her down so she could release the hermit crab under what she seemed sure was exactly the right leaf.

"Where did you see the man?" I asked Daisy.

"He was standing right there near that big palm," she

said, indicating a tree a few feet away and then sticking her finger back in her mouth.

"Okay, you and Simon wait right here." I went up into the trees and crouched near the huge coconut palm. The sand looked disturbed at the base, but it was impossible to know whether anyone had actually been standing near the tree. The area was just too dry and disturbed by land crabs.

"Did you see where the man went?" I asked, returning to the kids. If someone had been there, it had to have been within the last ten minutes. Maybe I could find him. I didn't like the idea of some stranger watching the children from the trees. I was sure it wasn't someone who was there by accident. There just weren't that many people wandering around on this section of the beach unless they had business at Pickering's Landing. She pointed down the palm-lined beach.

"Okay, Simon will take you to your mother. I'll go have a look and be right back."

I watched the two of them until they'd made it back to the marina. Then I walked along the edge of the trees looking for any signs of the man. I imagined that I could see a trail of disturbed brush and leaves, but it was hard to tell. I walked around the point and was greeted by an empty beach that stretched for a mile. I headed up into the trees and out to the road, where the occasional car zipped past. There was no point in going farther. If Daisy had seen someone, he was long gone.

Daisy and Simon had already told Tilda about the man. By now, he'd turned into a troll with warts all over his face. Daisy was unable to give me even a semblance of a description except to say she was certain that the man was white. That was something, anyway.

Tilda was concerned. She could think of no one who would have been wandering around up there. "Do you think it be someone meanin' ta hurt da children?" she asked. "Dat sort a thing jus not be happenin' in des islands," she said. I could see her anxiety at the thought that someone might be intent on grabbing a child.

"I don't know why the man was there, Tilda. Maybe it was just someone who wandered down looking for a public beach and once he realized this was not one, went on down the road to the next likely spot. But I think it's a good idea to keep the children close to the house for a while."

I knew Tilda. She wouldn't be letting the girls out of her sight until she was sure it was safe. I wondered if the man had been watching and waiting for me. A lot of people knew I lived on a boat down at Pickering's Landing. But I couldn't think of anyone whom I'd pissed off lately.

"Do you think it's okay?" Simon asked as Tilda gathered Daisy and her shells and took her inside for her nap.

"Everything is fine, Simon." Just what the kid needed— another reason to have nightmares.

"Come on," I said. "Let's go get you some new clothes and then you can hang out with O'Brien." I hadn't checked with O'Brien, but I figured he'd be happy to have the kid around while I spent the afternoon talking to the passengers.

Simon and I headed for town. Our choices for clothes were limited. It was either one of the stores that catered to locals or the brightly colored cluster of shops down the street from the cruise ship dock. We started at Mitchell's, a store crammed with everything from wedding dresses to pots and pans. Shelves were piled with men's polyester pants, and racks of hangers displayed women's dresses, the most elaborate of which were brocade affairs adorned with rows of gold buttons down the front from neck to hemline. In the back of the store, lace doilies and embroidered baby blankets were neatly arranged under shelves overflowing with kitchen gadgets and auto supplies, all under a layer of dust.

We made our way to the boys' section, where Simon found several pairs of shorts, which he insisted were just the right size, though the waist was at least two sizes too big.

"This is the style, Hannah. All the cool kids wear these."

He scoffed at the suggestion of a belt, then found one so large it would barely keep the pants up on his bony hips. At least they wouldn't be falling down around his knees. He chose several T-shirts, one with Bob Marley plastered across the front. I liked it. When we got to the underwear, Simon launched into a dissertation about the attributes of boxers and grabbed a couple of packages.

The fundamentals taken care of, we walked over to the open market to check out the island apparel and crafts. It was teeming with people from the cruise ship that had just docked. Simon had brought his camera and he couldn't get enough pictures. The color in the market made a brilliant backdrop for all the tourists with their own cameras strapped around their necks, laden with purchases and wearing new straw hats that shaded their already sunburned faces.

He'd gotten one couple to pose and was showing them the results in his camera. It was a fantastic shot—the man with knobby knees protruding from his shorts, hairy legs ending at the ankles in a pair of plastic sandals. His wife wore a matching shorts and top outfit with ladybugs all over it. Both had on plastic visors. Hers said, "Sexy when wet." His read, "I'm up for anything!" Their eyes danced with mischief and I knew they were well aware of the implications of their hats.

Simon and I wandered through one tourist shop after another. Finally, he found a gaudy island shirt—bright blue with Rasta men dancing all over it—and a knit Rasta beret. He had the hat on and the T-shirt in hand when he stepped back out of the cottage to wait while I paid. I could see him outside talking to another kid, shoeless and in dirty shorts.

I'd just gotten my change when I heard Simon holler. By the time I got outside, he was halfway across the road, darting between moving cars. I went after him. The kid was fast. He raced down Main, waving his arms and shouting. By the time I got across Waterfront Drive, he was already three blocks down and still going.

When I caught up with him, he was standing in front of the library under a hibiscus bush.

"What happened?" I asked, bending over with my hands on my knees, trying to catch my breath.

"Some kid tried to grab my stuff," he said, on the edge of despair and hurt. "I kicked him and held on, but he grabbed the Rasta beret right off my head. I couldn't catch him, Hannah." I could see it was just one more affront.

"Come on. Let's go get another beret."

I'd be sure to report it to Dunn. At one time thievery on the islands was unheard of and it was still rare. If there was a kid targeting the tourists in the market, Dunn would add a patrol officer and put a quick end to it.

Christ. This day was turning to shit—Capy hurt, a strange man on the beach, now this. It seemed the whole island had gone crazy. I remembered the fire-and-brimstone preacher I'd heard on the radio this morning talking about the hurricane being God's punishment for man's sins. Jeez, it was a pressure change, a tropical depression—nothing more.

When we got to SeaSail, I went looking for O'Brien. The marina had been transformed since I'd been down there a couple of days ago. Now it looked like half the boats in O'Brien's fleet were in the harbor. Monohulls and catamarans ranging from twenty-eight to fifty feet filled every available slip. Between the docks, boats had been rafted together with tires tied between them. Still more boats were coming in and every available dockhand was at work, detaching biminis, pulling down sails, and lowering booms, which they were lashing to the boats.

O'Brien was at the end of B Dock, backing a huge cat into a slip that looked about two feet too narrow for the wide boat. He eased it into the slot, the bumpers squeezing between the dock and the boat rail. He jumped onto the dock before the dockhand had even cleated the lines.

"Hannah," he said, a wide smile crossing his face, that familiar open warmth that was O'Brien. Then he remembered his anger and he shut down.

"Hey, Simon," he said, shifting his attention and ruffling Simon's hair.

While Simon watched one of the riggers being hauled up to the top of a mast, I pulled O'Brien aside and told him about Capy and that Dr. Hall didn't know whether he would come around.

His reaction was identical to Dunn's. He was pissed. By this evening when the news had made its way around the island, the entire population would be fuming.

"He'll make it," O'Brien said. "That old guy is tough."

"I hope you're right. He's hurt pretty bad."

"You didn't come down here just to tell me about Capy, Hannah."

"I was hoping Simon could spend the afternoon with you. While I'm here, I need to talk with the Westbrooks."

"I'd love to have him. The Westbrooks' boat is over on C Dock. You can't miss it. It's the cat with the flags all over it. I've told them that they need to get off the boat today if they want it moved to the hurricane hole in Paraquita Bay, as Westbrook is so insistent that I do."

Then he called, "Hey, Simon, how about you stick with me? I'll show you the boats."

They were standing at the wheel of the *Katherine* when I headed over to C Dock. She was an old wooden two-masted boat that O'Brien's parents had restored. O'Brien had pulled Simon up into the captain's seat and was standing behind him, pointing to the rigging and explaining the intricacies of the sails.

I found Senator Westbrook and his wife, Debra, sitting on their boat, looking relaxed and tan.

"Detective, come aboard," Westbrook said.

While Debra went below to get iced tea, we made small talk. Westbrook was clearly uncomfortable and rambled on about the weather. It surprised me. After all, this was a guy who went toe to toe with the best. What was he so nervous about?

"Let's get to it," he said when his wife returned.

"I'd rather speak with Debra alone," I said. It was pretty much standard procedure. Whenever there was an observer things got skewed, especially when the observer was a spouse.

"I resent that," he said. "Debra can speak freely. We don't have secrets. Besides, I am a lawyer, though I don't practice anymore."

"Think Debra needs a lawyer?" What was Westbrook so worried that Debra might say if he weren't around to hear?

"Of course not," he said, "but she needs someone by her side. You know that this has been an extremely traumatic experience. She was almost killed. We lost close friends."

Somehow I didn't see Debra as being the dependent type, but she nodded and said she wanted her husband to stay.

"There's some question about why the plane went down. That means it is necessary that we talk with everyone connected to the flight. It's possible you saw something. Can you simply take me through it?"

As she started talking, it was clear that Debra was one of those people who got caught up in excruciating details and little side stories. I let her go. You just never knew when something important might be buried in the minutiae.

"That last day on the boat was a disaster. I was glad we were leaving in the morning. We were anchored over at Cooper Island. Jack left us there and took the dinghy into Road Town. While he was gone, a nearby boat's anchor dragged and they drifted right into us. Our anchor chains were all tangled. Jack's the expert on the boat. The Rileys and I didn't know how to handle it. Then Jack blamed me when the other boat gouged our gel coat." She glared at Jack, obviously angry that he'd deserted them out there.

"I told you I had to call the office to tell them I was going to be late returning," he said to Debra. "I couldn't get a signal on my cell phone at the anchorage," he explained to me.

"Jack decided to stay down here an extra day," she said. "He was supposed to fly home with me."

"So you canceled your reservation?" I asked. When I'd spoken to Westbrook Saturday at the hospital, he'd never said a word about it being a last-minute change in plans, only that he was scheduled to fly out later. The senator was supposed to have been on that plane with his wife. I considered that suspicious.

"Yes, I was worried about my boat with the storm moving in. I wasn't about to have it rafted out in the harbor with a bunch of others. I wanted to make sure that it was moved to the hurricane hole, where it would be secure. When we docked, I went straight to the top, the owner, O'Brien. He said he'd take care of it, but I told him I wasn't leaving the marina until I saw someone taking the boat over there." Westbrook was really on the defensive now.

"It seems as though you could have taken care of it before we went to the airport," Debra said. I was thinking the same thing. If O'Brien had said the boat would be moved to the protection of the mangroves in the hurricane hole, it would have been moved. As a boat owner, Westbrook should have had enough experience with SeaSail and O'Brien to know that.

"That morning we got up early and brought the boat in," Debra continued. "The taxi came about seven thirty. The flight was scheduled at nine."

"Did you notice anything unusual at all? In the airport or on the plane?" I asked.

Debra went through it, thinking out loud. The taxi had

dropped them off at the terminal. The driver handled the luggage. Five or six people were ahead of them at the Island Air counter. She'd noticed the newlyweds at the end of the line.

"They were so completely wrapped up in one another they hardly noticed anyone else. Jack and I had been like that once," she said.

"The little boy and his father were right behind us. We talked for a while. Mr. Redding was very aware of what happens on the Hill. He asked me what Jack's position was on some bill related to nonprofits. I'm afraid I was clueless. I didn't know anything about the issue."

"What about after you boarded the plane?" I asked, trying to nudge her back to the reason I was there questioning her.

"They were about to close the cabin door when another passenger came rushing onto the plane. She was an attractive woman with lots of curly red hair. Did she make it out?"

"Yes, she's fine. What happened then?" I asked.

She explained that she was supposed to be sitting right behind the Rileys but had moved to the back when the cabin door was closed. "I hate flying," she said. "I've heard that the tail section is the safest part of the plane and I always move as far back as I can and as close to the exit as possible."

"This may seem like an odd question," I said, trying to prepare her for something she might consider shocking, "but can you think of anyone who would want you dead, Debra?"

She was far from surprised by my question, but she didn't have time to reply. Westbrook didn't give her the chance.

"Don't be silly," he said, mortified. "No one would want to hurt Debra, for crissakes."

"What about you, Senator?" I asked.

"Me? Hurt Debra? Never!"

"I meant do you have any enemies?" I said, working to keep the sarcasm out of my voice and wondering why he was so defensive.

"I've got plenty," he said. "But I wasn't on the plane."

"But you were supposed to be," I said, stating the obvious.

"For God's sake, we've been down here on vacation. All my enemies are on Capitol Hill and they have other ways of threatening me."

"Like what?"

"It's all about killer politics. Not about taking lives," he said.

"What about your luggage or something you might have brought on the plane? Was there anything that someone might have been after?"

"Just my jewelry," Debra responded.

"That's an odd question," Westbrook said. "What does that have to do with the crash?"

"Someone broke into the warehouse where we've secured all the contents of the plane."

"Did they steal anything?" he asked.

"That's police business," I said. "What about the Rileys? How well did you know them?"

"Intimately. We've been friends for years. And no, they didn't have enemies," Westbrook said.

"What about a gun? Did you or the Rileys carry one on board?" I asked, turning to Debra.

"Goodness, no," Debra said, appalled at the suggestion. "I am opposed to firearms and so was Louise. Besides, how on earth would we get one through security?"

"I don't think we can tell you anything else, Detective," Westbrook said, standing. "I'm sure that when all is said and done, those investigators will find that the plane crashed due to the airline's negligence. When they do, I'll be considering a lawsuit."

I was being dismissed, but that was fine. I'd learned enough. I couldn't help wondering whether Westbrook was as concerned about his boat as he said or whether something else had kept him off of that flight. One thing was obvious. He'd been on edge and defensive the entire time I'd been talking to Debra.

I found O'Brien and Simon up at the marina restaurant having lunch at a table overlooking the harbor. Simon was intent on demolishing a burger and unconcerned about the catsup that was dripping all over his shirt. O'Brien was intent on the woman sitting next to him. He saw me coming and placed his hand over hers. He was clearly trying to make me jealous. It was working.

"Hi, guys. Claire," I said, pulling up a chair.

"Hannah," Claire said, abruptly pulling her hand from under O'Brien's. I knew her in passing and she knew that O'Brien and I were involved. If O'Brien were to move on, I could see it being to someone like Claire. She was a native BVIslander, an exotic beauty, with brown eyes shaped like almonds. She wore a tight, low-cut top and an island sarong tied around her waist—decorated with tangerine-colored hibiscus. No doubt the outfit was one of her own creations.

She'd started with a little shop in town that specialized in her island apparel. The clothing was stunning, but Claire was also good at the marketing end. She'd become the model for her fashions, savvy enough to know her island beauty would be part of the sell. The look had caught on and the business had grown into a lucrative operation. Her label could be found in some of the most upscale Paris boutiques and Fifth Avenue shops.

In between bites, Simon talked about the boats and scrolled through the pictures he'd taken. There must have been twenty, all of boats from every possible angle. Interesting abstract shots—all lines and angles of rigging and masts, a bow against turquoise water—not one typical photo of a pretty boat in the harbor.

"These are good," Claire said. "I've spent a lot of time wandering around the galleries in SoHo and near Greenwich Village. You are talented, Simon. You've got an eye for form and composition."

"It's my hobby," he said. "My dad promised he'd buy me a digital Nikon, one of those single-lens reflex cameras, if I keep at it." Then he realized his mistake. He'd forgotten for a moment that his father was dead.

"Quite a spread in today's *Island News*," O'Brien said, changing the subject. He handed me the newspaper he had folded on the table.

"Hey, he's a good-looking guy," I said, glaring at O'Brien. I wasn't about to defend myself to him while he sat there fondling Claire's perfectly painted fingertips. Two could play this game. And dammit, I was pissed.

Chapter 19

When I got down to the warehouse, Stark was leaning against a palm tree, arms crossed against his chest and sunglasses propped on his head, watching them unload the airplane. Harper and Sturtevant had gone out to the wreck with Harrigan before dawn. They'd managed to pull the entire plane up in one piece with a crane and set it down on a barge. Now it was being backed into the warehouse.

"I'm sorry I'm late, Stark. I got tied up talking with the Westbrooks."

Stark's response was exactly what I expected. "Hey, no problem, mon. I be enjoyin' dis fin day," he said in a casual island accent, one he resorted to only in such instances. Stark had a typical island mentality, one I envied and hoped someday to truly emulate. Though I was getting better, I still had a "hurry up, get it done, no time to linger" approach to life.

Harper and Sturtevant were standing with Joe Harrigan over near the warehouse door. Harper, still in his wet suit, looked humble for a change. Sturtevant was wearing the same faded swim trunks and a grease-stained T-shirt that looked like he'd used it to work on an engine.

"How'd it go?" I asked. Sturtevant just shook his head.

"That airplane wanted to fly out on the currents once we started to raise it. Then one of the straps around the right wing snapped," he said, glaring at Harper. "The plane was hanging in the water sideways with one of the wingtips buried in the sand. We're damn lucky we got the thing up in one piece."

"Anything apparent when you brought the plane up?" Stark asked as we walked Sturtevant out to the street to find a taxi. Harper was hanging back, shooting the shit with Harrigan. I could hear him making excuses about why that strap came loose and implying that it had to do with Sturtevant's carelessness.

"No, but I'm no expert. I just bring 'em up. Harrigan will take it from here. If there's something to be found, he'll find it. Harper and I are done here. We're heading back to the hotel to change and get our gear and then catching the next ferry back to Saint Thomas."

"Things were kind of rough out there?" I asked.

"You could say so. When that strap let loose, I was still in the water. It almost took my head off. I'll tell you one thing: Harper won't be contracted on another salvage operation if I've got anything to say about it. If I ever do another job here, I'll call you, Sampson, get you to help me."

I held up my hands. "Not on your life, Sturtevant. Sounds way too dangerous."

He was climbing into a taxi when Harper caught up with him. He had pulled his wet suit off his upper body. The arms dangled around his calves and he wore a T-shirt with a huge red and white dive flag plastered across the front, leaving no doubt that he was one macho diver.

Stark and I went into the warehouse. It was at least twenty degrees cooler inside. Harrigan was walking around the exterior of the plane, jotting notes on a clipboard. Edith Leonard had come by and was hovering, looking over his shoulder. He obviously didn't like the fact that she was interfering, and he was doing his best to let her know it. I could see him scowling under the brim of his Stetson.

"This airplane hasn't been made for almost twenty

years," he was explaining to Leonard. "That means the manufacturer is off the hook. So is the company that made the engine."

"Who is liable?" I asked. I could see Leonard's discomfort. She clearly knew the answer.

"That depends on what we find," Harrigan said. "Unless it's sabotage, it will fall on the airline's director of operations or on maintenance at the airport, maybe both."

"We are very thorough with our aircraft. I'm sure this will not be shown to be neglect on our part," Leonard said.

"In my experience, the airline is always more concerned about protecting itself from a lawsuit or having to make expensive fixes than about getting at the truth," Harrigan said. "Too many times I've seen companies trying to divert attention so that the investigation loses focus on what might be the true cause." He was clearly not going to let Leonard or anyone else interfere. I was beginning to think that the outfit was designed to throw people off guard, that he was really hardnosed, smart, and covering it under a cowboy hat.

"I'm sorry, ma'am, but not much of what you say will carry any weight with me," he continued. "I'll be examining your records along with every other piece of information that I can gather."

"You must have insurance," I said to Leonard.

"That's not the point. Our reputation is at stake." She was pissed that Harrigan wasn't going to be swayed by anything she said. And of course, the fact that the Leonard family had clout on the island meant nothing to him.

"Any speculation yet about what caused it to go down?" Stark asked.

"It could be any number of things," Harrigan said. "I pulled the records for these planes when I was asked to come down to investigate. The Beech 99 has had a few problems that have caused the plane to take a dive."

"We have never had an incident like that with one of our planes," Leonard said.

"Sometimes it's just a matter of time," Harrigan said, giving Leonard a disarming smile and hooking a thumb through a belt loop in his jeans. "All kinds of things can go wrong, and usually, sooner or later, they will. And sometimes it's simply not straightforward. A couple of years back, one of these ninety-nines stalled and crashed after it climbed steeply to four hundred feet after takeoff. All seventeen on board died. It turned out to be a combination of things: mis-trimmed horizontal stabilizer that caused trouble in the trim system. Other factors played in—the crew's inadequate training, deficient trim warning system check procedures, and insufficient maintenance procedures. But perhaps disaster would have been avoided, even with all the mechanical problems, if the crew had been quicker on the uptake. So what's the cause? The crew, the equipment, maintenance?

"We could have an engine failure here," he said to Leonard, "but if the pilots knew what they were doing they should have been able to bring her back into the airport on one engine—no problem."

"Believe me, my pilots knew what they were doing," Leonard said. She'd been told about the cocaine smuggling but had never conceded a thing about the copilot's competence. She knew that we'd found no alcohol or drugs in his system and argued that both he and the captain had done everything they could to bring that plane back to the runway.

"Maybe," Harrigan responded, "but sometimes even the best get careless. Pilots are no exception. A few years ago the National Transportation Safety Board investigated the crash of a plane that went down a few seconds after takeoff because the pilots forgot to set the flaps. It happens. I've known of pilots that have gotten lost or flown right into the side of a cliff because they weren't looking where they were going."

Harrigan continued walking around the plane. "I haven't

discovered any signs of fire or explosion on the exterior. It could be bad fuel, a broken fuel line. Christ, maybe someone left a rag in the fuel tank. Right now, I'm not ruling anything out. Including sabotage," he added, turning to Leonard.

"I'll want to see everything—the witness reports, passenger statements, and the autopsies. I intend to calculate the speed that this thing lifts off the runway and when it would stall and fall out of the sky, look at the engines, maintenance records, and the flight control system. I'll also be talking with air traffic control, and operations, which is responsible for fueling and cargo."

"How long will it take before you've got something definitive?" Leonard asked.

"That depends on what I find. Could be a matter of days, could be a matter of weeks, maybe months. I'll be sending some things out for analysis.

"In the meantime, I suppose you'll be carrying on your investigation of the passengers?" he asked, turning to Stark and me. "In my experience, if it's sabotage, it almost always involves someone who was targeted on the plane. Have you learned anything yet?"

"Things are very muddy at this point," I said. We'd told him about the break-in at the warehouse and the missing Beretta. Dunn had tightened the security as a result. Right now two officers were standing outside baking in the sun and no one without authorization was allowed inside.

Harrigan went through the same reasoning process that Stark and I had engaged in. "Why would someone break in and take nothing but the gun?" he asked, then answered his own question. "Maybe we are looking at sabotage. I'll let you know the minute I have anything at all."

Leonard followed us out. Evidently, no one had mentioned the break-in to her. We listened to her complain about not being kept in the loop all the way to her Lexus. After she pulled away, Stark and I went down to the waterfront for lunch. He had his mind set on a deep-fried fly-ing-fish. By the time we found a spot on a bench in the shade, Stark was consuming his second sandwich. He talked as he chewed, filling me in about his visit to the hospital to talk to the newlyweds. The bride was the only passenger who had not been released. She was still unconscious and in intensive care. Her parents had arrived late last night and were keeping a round-the-clock vigil in her room.

The new husband had been more than willing to talk with Stark. He said he and his bride had stayed on French-man's Cay and then gone over to the little cabanas on Cooper Island. They were supposed to have stayed only a week, but had prolonged their visit by three days. They both had demanding jobs in Silicon Valley. They knew that once they returned, they would be back in the rat race and so they were putting it off as long as they could. Though their jobs were high-powered, the work was not the kind that put them at risk. Besides, why would anyone go to the extreme of bringing down their plane as they returned from their honeymoon in the BVI?

"Maybe it was a jealous ex," I said. I knew it was a stretch.

"I thought about that," Stark said.

"Ah, great minds think alike. What did you find out?" I asked.

"The groom said they've been together since college. Neither was ever serious about anyone else. Thinking they had anything to do with the crash was a reach anyway. Hell, this whole investigation will probably turn out to be a wild-goose chase when Harrigan discovers the plane crash was accidental."

"Yeah, well, in the meantime, let's scratch the newly-weds off our list and focus on the others. Did you learn any-thing at the airport?" I asked.

"The mechanic's story held up. He'd been off all day Friday and Saturday. One of the other mechanics said that the two of them had been over at Long Beach drinking Friday night and stayed over there till the next afternoon with a couple of ladies. I verified it with the ground crew on duty on Saturday. No one saw him anywhere around the airport on that day and the plane had only been on the ground a couple of hours. It was the first plane in on Saturday morning. It came from Puerto Rico around seven, turned around, and was headed back at nine thirty," Stark said between mouthfuls of fish.

"No one saw anything out of the ordinary. Luggage was taken off the incoming flight, more put on, the plane refueled. A one-woman cleaning crew gave it a once-over inside. She was sure nothing, including a gun, had been left on the plane before passengers boarded."

"She could have missed it," I said.

"It's possible, but I don't think so. She seems like one of those anal-retentive types that doesn't let anything get past her."

"What else?" I asked.

"Everyone who was supposed to be on the flight was on it, except for Westbrook, who canceled the day before. The only passenger who didn't have a reservation was Zora Gordon. She came out and got on at the last minute."

"Guess that would mean she wasn't a target," I said.

"Yeah, unless someone followed her out there. No one at the Island Air ticket counter noticed anything unusual," he continued. "It was just a typical day—a bunch of sailboat charterers returning home, businessmen heading to San Juan or continuing on to the States, families visiting relatives.

"The flight was scheduled to be on the ground in Puerto Rico for a couple hours, then it was turning around and coming back. It was due to be on the ground in Tortola for the next twenty-four hours for routine maintenance."

"Did you find out anything about the flight back from San Juan?"

"Yeah, there was one thing. When Zora Gordon bought her ticket, she purchased a return on that flight coming right back."

"How long before the return?" I asked.

"Forty-five minutes."

"Let's go talk with Zora. She's the only one we haven't yet questioned."

Stark and I headed over to the marina in Brandywine Bay, where Zora had said the boat she was staying on was docked. On the way, I told him what I'd learned from Debra Westbrook. Then Stark got quiet. I could tell something was on his mind.

"What, Stark?" I demanded.

"Heard you moved back onto the *Sea Bird*," Stark said, getting right to the point. That was the thing about Stark. Once he decided to talk, he didn't ease into the conversation. It was pretty much the same technique he used with a suspect. I kept telling him he needed to use a little finesse. That, however, was not in Stark's repertoire.

"What's happening with you and O'Brien?" he asked.

"How did you hear I'd moved out?" I asked. A stupid question. Absolutely nothing stayed a secret on the island for long.

"Jimmy told me. He said he was on the *Sea Bird* last night waiting for you to bring pizza when O'Brien dropped your cat off. So what about it?"

"O'Brien keeps pressuring me to quit the job. I know he's scared. He thinks I'll get hurt or that all the violence will get to me."

"Maybe he's right."

"What does that mean?" I asked, on the defensive.

"You know you're worse than most, Hannah. You blame yourself every time something goes bad."

"Come on, Stark. I've been doing this for almost fifteen years now. I think I've learned to handle it." Christ, Stark was sounding just like O'Brien.

"Naw, you don't let anything go."

"And you do?" I asked.

"Yeah, I think I'm better at it than you are. I'm not saying that's necessarily a good thing, Hannah. I've learned to close down, find distance. You can't do that and it puts you in a lot of jeopardy. Someday you'll end up stepping in front of a bullet because you are too emotionally involved."

"Give me some credit, Stark. I can handle it."

"Maybe that's what O'Brien worries about the most. That you'll be so loaded down that eventually you'll stop caring at all about anything. We all saw how you beat yourself up about Elyse. You can't carry that kind of guilt around forever without it getting to you."

"I'm past that."

"Sure," he said and dropped it.

I leaned back in the seat, closed my eyes, and thought about what Stark had said. He was right about the guilt. But Elyse's death *was* my fault. I'd pulled her out of a fiery ocean after her boat exploded, only to fail her when the murderer had come back to finish the job. I'd failed as a cop and as her friend.

It had been six months now and I was still waking up with the same nightmare. In it, I was swimming through a viscous liquid, trying to get to Elyse before sea creatures consumed her.

O'Brien had sometimes diverted the dream before it was fully formed. He would recognize the signs while I slept, pull me in and hold me. In the morning, I'd wake up with my head on his chest and remember the half-formed images. He never asked me about the dream, but somehow he knew what it was about.

Chapter 20

Stark pulled the car into the marina lot. It was an exclusive facility, the equivalent of a high-end gated community in the States with million-dollar homes, except here they were million-dollar boats. The *Mystic* was among them. The guard saw us coming and spent several minutes ignoring us before he eventually turned to acknowledge the fact that we were standing in front of his guardhouse. Stark glared at the guy as he examined our IDs.

Finally, he opened the gate and pointed to the dock where the *Mystic* was tied. The hull had a navy blue sheen with "*Mystic*" etched on the back. She was huge, over a hundred feet long, sleek and modern, with windows that encircled the lower deck and reflected the sun. A satellite dish was perched on the top deck. On the back was an array of ocean toys—a Windsurfer, a couple of Jet Skis, and a Zodiac.

One of the crew was leaning over the side of the yacht's hull, cleaning it with a brush. She wore navy blue shorts and a yellow polo shirt with "*Mystic*" embroidered over a pocket. Her hair was pulled back in a ponytail. She stood and tucked a loose strand behind her ears.

About then a guy appeared in a matching outfit, biceps budging against the shirt, suspicion in his eyes. His hair was bleached blond, spiked, and cropped to an inch all the way around. He wore a gold hoop in one ear. His thighs bulged beneath the shorts. The clothes were out of place on the guy.

He looked like the guardian of the Grail. I guessed the crew had been instructed to keep all intruders at bay. He introduced himself as Burke, the captain, but he looked more like muscle for the Mob than the captain of a yacht. When we told them we were police, Burke reluctantly allowed us to board and showed us to the salon.

I'd been on some nice boats before, but this thing qualified as palatial. Pillows in earth tones accented plush carpeting, overstuffed chairs, and a couch in muted browns. A bronze sculpture took up a corner, an angular abstract figure, arms lifted to the ceiling. The blinds were down and soft lighting cast a glow. A vase filled with orchids decorated the coffee table. Another was placed on the marble top of a wet bar.

Through an open door, I could see the dining room. The table, polished to a fine sheen, was set for two, with crystal goblets, china, and an elaborate candelabra. A painting that I was sure was an original hung on the wall at the far end of the room.

Burke stepped to the wet bar, opened the refrigerator, and offered us drinks. I chose spring water. Stark took a beer. We settled on stools at the bar while he went to find Zora.

Five minutes later Burke reappeared and said she'd be along. She was down in the gym finishing her workout. A gym on board? Christ.

Burke propped himself at the end of the bar, his arms crossed, and glared at us in silence.

"Nice boat," Stark said, taking a swig from his beer.

"Isn't she." He beamed. Stark had obviously found something the guy wanted to talk about. "She's one hundred and twenty-three feet, made of aluminum, has teak decks, and only draws six feet. Her engines purr at top speed—eighteen knots. She has four cabins, each with its own head and sitting area. Of course the master cabin is huge, with a king bed, a private Jacuzzi, and a small office. The gym is on the lower level—even has a sauna."

"Must cost some money," Stark said, never one for subtlety.

"Several million," Burke said.

"Does Zora own the boat?" I asked.

"I guess you have to ask her about that. I just drive it." He didn't like the question.

"I see you've got a Key West hailing port." I'd seen it etched on the back and noticed that the boat flew a U.S. flag.

"That's right. We brought her down a couple of weeks ago."

Zora came in, wearing a tank top and tight Lycra workout pants, calf length, a towel draped around her neck.

"Detective Sampson. Any questions you have, you can ask me," she said, nodding to Burke, who headed out to the deck.

"This is Detective Stark," I said.

Zora gave Stark the once-over, her gaze drifting to his crotch. She smiled and wiped sweat from her forehead with the towel. Then she headed for the bar and proceeded to mix a bunch of stuff in a blender. As small as she was, no one would ever mistake Zora for weak. I watched her as she moved around the wet bar. Every inch of her exuded sexuality and power at the same time. I pegged her as someone who knew what she wanted and took it. Some men would find that very attractive, especially in bed.

Right now she was giving us a lecture about nutrition. "You know that I've never drunk anything brown?" she said over the noise of the blender.

I had to think about that. Was nothing brown a good thing or a bad thing? I could tell Zora considered it good. The stuff in the blender was looking a sickly green.

"I don't drink coffee or cola, don't eat chocolate. Never will."

"Too bad," Stark said. "I'd say you're missing out on some of the finer things in life."

She scowled at Stark and asked why we were there. So much for hospitality.

Stark took her through the questions. Had she noticed anything unusual in the airport or on the plane? She didn't tell us anything we hadn't already heard from the other passengers.

"How long have you been down here?" Stark asked.

"Almost two weeks now."

"This is a big boat for just one person. You own it?" Stark asked.

"No, I don't. It belongs to my employer. As it happens, I'm his lawyer. He's a very generous and wealthy man. I needed a vacation. He offered the boat."

"Does the crew come with the boat?"

"That's right," she said.

"Why were you on that plane to Puerto Rico?" I asked.

"Not that it's any of your business, but I was attending to some legal affairs for my boss."

"The airline records show you didn't have a reservation," Stark said.

"It came up unexpectedly. My employer called to ask for the favor. It was the least I could do. A day out of my vacation didn't bother me."

"How long were you staying in San Juan?"

"Why is any of this of concern to you?"

"You know that plane was scheduled to turn right around and return to Tortola. The passenger list has you on it," I said, hoping to catch her in a lie.

"That's a mistake. Typical island screwup. I was supposed to be scheduled on the last flight back that night."

That explained why she'd had no luggage.

"You didn't check your ticket?" Stark asked, pissed. "I mean, knowing how we islanders are always screwing up?"

Zora smirked and ignored the question.

"You made anyone but me angry lately? Someone who might not want to see you make it to Puerto Rico?" Stark prodded.

"Surely you don't think someone brought that plane down on purpose," she said, turning to me. She seemed truly shocked at the notion.

"It's still under investigation. We're just covering all the bases," I said.

"None of it has anything to do with me. Now, if there's nothing more, I've got a massage and God forbid I should keep the man waiting," she said, grabbing her drink.

"Just one more question," I said. "Did you bring a weapon on that flight, maybe lose it?"

"Don't be ridiculous. I know the consequences of bringing weapons onto airplanes. An oversight by island security, I assume?" she said, directing one last dig at Stark.

"I don't like that woman," Stark mumbled as we walked back to the car. "Did you notice her eyes—stone cold, if you ask me. She looks like she'd take out her mother if she had the slightest excuse. And man, what was that about not drinking anything brown?"

"You're just pissed about her remarks about island efficiency. It could have happened the way she said, with the ticket mix-up."

"Maybe," Stark said, "but it seems pretty darned strange that Zora's down here by herself on that yacht."

"Yeah, though not that strange if her boss has that kind of money and she wanted to get away," I said. "Let's get Jimmy to check the yacht registration and find out what we can about her boss and that captain."

"Sounds good. I'll talk to him when I get back to the office," Stark said, checking his watch. "I'm late. How about we call it a day?"

"Do you have a heavy date, Stark?" Stark was an item on the island, the strong, silent type that a lot of women saw as a challenge. He'd dated half the women over twenty-one on Tortola and was working his way through the other half. At thirty-five, he'd never been married.

"Yeah," he said. "I'm meeting Billy."

"Oh yeah? This must be a couple times just this week."

Billy Cooper was a BVIslander who ran her own tour business. She had a catamaran and took small groups out to snorkel or to visit the quiet bays in the islands. She was proud of the islands and loved being able to share the beauty with others. When she wasn't working, her passion was sailing, which was a real problem for Stark, whose idea of water sports revolved around a romp in his niece's wading pool.

"I'm supposed to meet her for dinner at her parents'," Stark said.

"Hey, that's great. Billy is one special woman," I said.

"Think so?"

"Come on. She's smart, beautiful, and one of the nicest people around. I don't know what you're going to do about the water thing though."

"Yeah, that's a problem," he said, then looked down the sidewalk and started laughing.

"What, Stark?" I asked. He was practically in tears now.

"You'd better watch out for that movie star," he said, nodding toward a vendor hawking the *Island News* on the corner.

The guy was working up sales by enticing prospective buyers with the front-page photo of Stewart with the woman police officer. A huge stack of papers lay at his feet.

A customer bought one and glanced my way, looked at the photo, looked back at me, back at the photo, and was finally sure it was me. Then he came over and started quizzing me about my status as the girlfriend to a star and proceeded to ask me for my autograph.

Stark was bent over now, laughing his head off. When he came up for breath, he handed me a damn pen.

"Here you go, Hannah," he said. "Sign the paper for this nice man."

"This is really not that funny, Stark," I said.

It was the last straw. I bought the remaining papers, tossed them in the Rambler, and headed straight to the Paradise Villas, leaving Stark standing on the sidewalk still laughing and the guy with the paper confused.

The hotel was a five-star resort with a spa, a pool, and views to die for. By the time I got there, I'd worked myself into a decent rage.

Stewart answered his door, looking tanned and relaxed. All he wore was a pair of shorts. His arm was still in a sling. It was obvious that he'd had no need for a double in his *Avenger* movies. He was perfectly sculpted, without the ugly bulk of a bodybuilder. He had the kind of body women wanted to touch. Shit.

His wide, boyish smile disappeared when he saw the look on my face and the stack of papers I carried. I was already through the door and dropping the papers on a chair by the time he invited me in.

"Hannah. I guess you're upset," he said.

"You could say that. Everyone on the island thinks I'm sleeping with you. I'm getting looks of pure envy from every woman I pass and lecherous stares from the men. And my reputation is shot."

"I'd wager you were getting looks like that before that article hit the paper. You just never noticed," he said.

"This is not funny. This kind of attention on a cop is not cool," I said.

"I am really sorry. I told Sammy I didn't want you exploited in his play for headlines. The thing is, Sammy doesn't consider it exploitation. He thinks any woman would want to be tied romantically to a movie star. He's been in Hollywood too long. Me too, I guess. What can I do to make it right?"

"Talk to Sammy. Make sure he drops it," I said, heading toward the door.

"Done," he said. "Hey, I was making a drink. Join me, please. I'd love a little company. You know, actors are really lonely people."

"That's hard to believe," I said.

"It's true. It's all surface stuff. People who want something, women who are attracted to the image. All the crap in the tabloids. People think they know you. The fact is they know everything but the truth. It would be nice to talk to someone who has just spent ten minutes chewing me out."

"Sure, a drink would be great," I said, realizing it was probably a big mistake.

While he made gin-and-tonics, I wandered out to the balcony. The sun was just about to drop behind Peter Island and the wind was picking up. I could see a sailboat out in the channel, heeling way over in the stiff breeze. I wondered if this was some warning wind, a precursor of things to come.

I could hear the TV inside. The weather forcaster was reporting that the hurricane was intensifying and still headed on a course to the BVI, but at least forty-eight hours out. "Anything could happen," he said. "God willing, it will not ravage our beautiful islands."

"These *are* unbelievable islands." Stewart handed me a drink and leaned on the railing next to me, gazing out to the ocean. "You know, I envy you, living here."

"That surprises me. It seems like you could live wherever you want."

"You'd think so, but I'm caught up in things."

"Like what?"

"The career."

"Surely you've made enough to quit if you want to."

"It's an addictive lifestyle. The fame, the luxury. Money in, money out. And I admit it—the women. It's probably an ego thing. I grew up a nobody in a hick town and got the hell out when I was seventeen. I don't ever want to end up back there."

"I'd say you've already left all that well behind." Stewart hardly had the look of a small-town boy.

"Maybe, but I've made a number of stupid choices. Someday I'll have to pay for all my mistakes." For a second his eyes reflected regret and something else, maybe desperation. Then it was gone.

He went inside to make another drink. I wondered about all his talk about mistakes. What could he have done that would have such dire consequences? I found myself feeling sorry for Stewart, apparently a nice guy whose life was spiraling out of control. I could relate to that. But he had choices. We all did, didn't we?

"Why don't you quit the acting?" I asked when he returned.

"Not a chance," he said, taking my hand. "I guess you could say I'm addicted. I love the fame."

We stood in silence for a moment, looking out to sea. Daniel's arm lightly brushed mine and my heart raced. *Damn,* I thought. *Not now.*

He took the drink out of my hand and led me inside. I knew better. Dammit, I *knew* better.

"Why don't we go ahead and make more headlines?" he said, pulling me to him with a wry grin.

Jeez, I was tempted, but I knew I'd regret it come dawn. *And what about O'Brien?* I thought as Daniel slid his hand down my neck and lightly ran a finger between my breasts. I closed my eyes and let the heat sweep through me. Then I held a gentle finger up to Daniel's lips and quietly exhaled. Quickly I turned around and headed to the door. I pulled it shut behind me as I used the last of my common sense to get the hell out of there.

*   *   *

O'Brien and Simon were sitting down on A Dock with their shoes beside them, their feet dangling in the water, when I got to SeaSail. Everyone else had already left for the day. The boats were ghostly silhouettes, the water still. In the west, a slash of pink still tinted the darkening sky. I could hear O'Brien talking. He was telling Simon the story of a famous clipper ship, the *Flying Cloud*.

"Hey, guys," I said and found a seat beside Simon while O'Brien finished the story. He had more seafaring stories than anyone I knew. I'd heard this one before. The *Flying Cloud* had been the fastest ship in her day. She'd held the record for more than a century for her run from New York around Cape Horn to San Francisco in eighty-nine days. The most compelling part of the story was that the *Flying Cloud* was navigated by a woman in a era when women stayed home waiting for their men to return from the sea.

I found myself drifting with the sound of O'Brien's voice mixing with the crickets, tree frogs, and an occasional plop as a fish jumped. I leaned back and breathed the cooling night air, felt the day's tension loosen.

"Hannah?" O'Brien was looking at me. It was that look. The one that turned my insides out. I could see that he wanted to say more but couldn't find the words that would get past the turmoil we were both feeling.

"Jeez, O'Brien, listen . . ."

"Hannah. You'd better take Simon home now."

When we pulled into the lot at Pickering's Landing, Enok Kiersted was down on the beach tossing a stick for Sadie. She saw the Rambler and came running, tongue hanging out the side of her mouth. She couldn't decide who she was happier to see—Simon or me. What had happened to loyalty? I guess I couldn't blame her. The kid had spent more time with her in the past couple days than I had all month. The two of them dashed down the beach.

"How you doing, Enok?" I asked.

"I'm good," he said.

"Did you hear about those dolphins being released over at Dolphin World? The manager is after Dunn to find out who's responsible."

"Yeah, I heard," he said.

"You wouldn't know anything about it, would you?"

"Sure wouldn't, but I'd say it was the best thing that happened here all week. Next time they bring dolphins in I hope someone tears the whole place apart."

"Sounds kind of extreme, Enok. Someone could get hurt."

"No one who didn't deserve it," he said.

"You think people should die over it?" I asked.

"Of course not," he said, but I wondered how far Enok would go to save a dolphin.

Chapter 21

The sun wasn't even up when Sadie came bounding onto my bed, Simon right behind her.

"Simon," I said, pulling the covers over my head, "it's not even light yet."

"Come on, Hannah. Get up!" He yanked the blanket off my face.

"Jeez, it can't be even six," I moaned.

"It's five. We need to get going so I can get back in time for school," he said.

"Don't worry, Simon. I'll have you back in plenty of time."

I couldn't believe any kid could be this excited about going to school. I'd promised to take him snorkeling over at the Indians this morning and get him back in time to catch the bus with Rebecca before I met up with Stark.

I'd been in touch with the school and arranged for him to attend for a few days. I figured the kid needed some structure until his aunt could get down here, which in the eyes of Child Services needed to be soon. Simon had been with me since Sunday. Today was only Tuesday and they'd already called Dr. Hall to find out what the plan was and when the aunt was taking custody. So far, Hall had kept them at bay by explaining that the aunt was in Europe and no one had been able to reach her. He kept reassuring them that Simon was in good hands, but I figured school was a good idea. Besides, I was concerned about the man who had been standing in the trees yesterday. Until I knew who he was and what he'd been doing, I didn't want Simon roaming the beach alone all day.

"Come on. I'll make some breakfast," I said, crawling out of bed.

We borrowed Calvin's speedboat and were out at the Indians by six thirty. We had the place to ourselves. Every mooring ball was empty. People were getting more and more nervous about being out on an ocean that could turn deadly. But it wasn't going to happen today. It was the perfect morning—absolutely no wind and no current. Four rocky pinnacles jutted out of the sea here, surrounded by coral heads that darkened the blue-green water. Underneath, the ocean teemed with reef fish.

Simon had his snorkeling gear on by the time I'd picked up a mooring and cut the engine. He'd brought his camera and was clamping it into the waterproof case. I wondered if this kid went anywhere without the thing. I knew he was hooked on capturing his surroundings in digital images, but I had the feeling that right now the camera was also an important connection to his father.

I gave Simon the standard spiel: "It's not your world, be respectful of the creatures that inhabit it. Look, don't touch. Watch your fins so you don't kick against the coral and break it off. It's a fragile place down there. And for God sakes watch out for fire coral."

"Will it kill me, Hannah?"

"No, Simon, but it will sting you and it will burn for the rest of the day."

"What about sharks?"

"Sharks don't sting," I joked.

He didn't find it funny. "Yeah, they just bite your leg off." I could hear something between fear and the utter excitement of a nine-year-old boy ready for adventure. I guess fear was part of what defined the adventure.

"Don't worry about sharks. Maybe we'll get lucky and see some nurse sharks. A couple of them sometimes hang out at the bottom in the rocks. They won't bother us."

We jumped in and immediately our world turned blue and magical. I gave Simon a chance to acclimate and stayed beside him. He was taking pictures like crazy, afraid that something might escape the indelible record he was storing in that camera. Blue tangs, yellow snappers, a pair of French angels, rock beauties, blue chromis, a passel of sergeant majors, sea fans—Simon was skimming over the surface, trying to take it all in at once.

Finally he stopped and lifted his head out of the water.

"Hannah, this is totally cool!" he said. "Did you see that big fish over there? It's just hovering. It looks kind of mean."

"That's a barracuda. Follow me and I'll show you some other stuff," I said. "Sometimes you have to look real carefully."

We headed over to the rocks and swam along the edge. I spotted a golden-tailed moray eel peering out from a colony of fire coral. Simon came up sputtering.

"He looks mean too!"

"I guess it's the teeth, but isn't he gorgeous? Look right next to him on that piece of brain coral. That's a flatworm, the green and purple thing that looks like a pretty piece of spotted lettuce."

We stuck our heads back under and I pointed. It took him a minute, but finally he saw it. We kept going and I kept pointing to the little things that are easily missed—the Christmas tree worm that flicked closed when I touched it gently with the tip of my finger, the flamingo tongue snail that was eating a sea fan, a porcupine fish under a ledge of brilliant red sponges. Simon came up laughing when it puffed to twice its size like a prickly balloon.

On the way back to the boat, we got lucky. We saw the sharks, two gray, ghostly shapes lying on the bottom in the sand between colonies of elkhorn and star corals. The sharks were still except for the movement of their gills and the occasional flip of a tail.

Simon spent the ride back looking at his photos. He'd gotten several shots of parrotfish tails as they swam out of the frame and dozens more of dark schools of blurry fish. But a couple were outstanding, a streak of sunlight turning a staghorn golden, a French angel perfectly posed, its yellow flecks electric against a blue-black backdrop.

Calvin was down in the shed when we got back, pulling out old sheets of plywood.

"Hey dar, Hannah, Simon. How was da snorklin'?" he asked.

"You wouldn't believe what we saw!" Simon said. "I can't believe what's under the water. We saw sharks! And worms! And all kinds of fish and stuff."

"Hannah's a good guide," he said. "She be learnin' a lot 'bout da ocean since she be comin' to des beautiful islands."

"Yeah, thanks for taking me, Hannah," he said. He hugged me fiercely for a second, then ran to the *Sea Bird* to get ready to go to school.

"Dat be a good boy," Calvin said. "He sure be likin' you. Be hard when dat aunt finally be showin' up and takin' him away."

Calvin was right. It was going to be hard. I was getting used to having the kid around, rattling dishes in the galley, running on the beach with Sadie, sleeping in the aft cabin. He was an amazing kid—a survivor. Even at nine it was obvious he was one of those people who would embrace life—unless someone wore him down, burdened him with obligations or whatever it was that adults thought important. I wondered what his aunt was like and if she'd nurture his spirit or smother it.

"Some folk still not believin' a storm be brewin' out dar," Calvin said, wiping his face with his sleeve. It was not even nine o'clock and already the thermometer on the shed was pushing ninety. I was guessing the humidity was the same.

"Do you think it will hit us, Calvin?" I knew he'd been through his share of hurricanes. Most of the islanders had. The last one that came through had been Wrong Way Lenny. No one had expected that one. It had built up in the western Caribbean and moved east, glancing off the BVI, sweeping down on St. Martin, and causing damage all the way along the island chain to Martinique.

"Sure be lookin' like it," he said. "I be goin' to act like it will. I be needin' to protect da marina and get da boats tied down real good. What you be wantin' to do 'bout da *Sea Bird*? We be well protected here in da harbor. Mos likely da wind will come over da hills dar. We'll be gettin' a lot of water comin' in. I plans to move da boats off da docks and raft 'em together. Put dos big moorings out dar for just des occasions. God willin' they be holdin'. Better for da boats to be out in da deep water dan smashing 'round here on da docks and gettin' blown onto shore."

"I'll leave the *Sea Bird* in your hands, Calvin. You know what you're doing." I hadn't really thought about losing the boat. Maybe my father had been right—bad investment,—easily destroyed by a swipe from Mother Nature.

Simon and Rebecca were standing by the road waiting for the bus when I pulled out of Pickering's Landing and headed into Road Town. Simon waved and gave me a quick smile.

In town, people were mimicking Calvin's preparations, anticipating the worst and hoping for the best. They were not really engaged in a full-out effort yet, but gathering materials—plywood, boards, hammers.

I stopped for coffee at Wilson's Bakery and picked up

donuts for Stark. Next door, the hardware store was crowded with people buying nails, tarps, and staple guns.

"How you doin' dis fin day?" Marie Wilson asked as she poured me a coffee to go.

"I'm good, Marie. Are you ready for bad weather?" I asked.

"Yea. I be feelin' it comin'. Da air, it be swellin' like a woman ready for childbirth. Pray dat baby not some devil be comin' ta send us all ta hell." She was shaking some kind of dried plant around the store when I left.

"Crazy Marie," I muttered to myself as I headed to the car. Still, a knife of anxiety caught me off guard. I wondered what kind of precautions were being taken at the school. Jeez, I was thinking like my mother, who had always been unreasonable when it came to worrying about her two daughters. Nothing was going to happen at the school today.

I drove past the hospital and took a quick turn into the lot. I had just enough time to check on Capy before meeting Stark over at the warehouse. When I walked into his room, a nurse was trying to coax gooey oatmeal down his throat.

"Dat stuff looks like da trail of slime from a sea slug," he said. "What I be needin' is a good drink of rum."

"It is not yet ten a.m. and we do not provide alcohol for our patients no matter the time," the nurse said, indignant. No doubt she was a God-fearing woman who forbade anything stronger than cider in her own home. I'd seen her husband staggering home from the Doubloon more than once though.

"Why if it don't be my friend Hannah!" he said. "Ain't you lookin' pretty. I hope you not be here ta arrest me. Dat warehouse door be open. Figured nobody be missin' a old T-shirt, a coupla soggy cigars."

"I'm not here to arrest you. I'm glad to see that you're okay. The whole island has been worried about you, Capy."

"Well, I be too hardheaded to kill," he said. His head was wrapped in a bunch of gauze and one of his eyes was swollen shut.

"Can you tell me what happened?"

"Like I said, dat door be open. I jus thought I'd be havin' a look around. It be real dark in dar. I be rummagin' through all dat junk. Come across some strange stuff, I tell you. Der be a pair of red ladies' unmentionables. Well, guess I be gettin' old."

"Did you see anyone at all? Hear anything?"

"Naw, but I be seein' da nicest purple shoes I ever did see. Gonna try dem on when all of a sudden, I be seein' stars. Next thing I know, I be layin' here with dat Doc Hall standin' over me. Don't like dat man one bit."

"What kind of shoes?" I was sure there had been no purple shoes in any of the passengers' luggage. More than likely, Capy had been having the delusions of the alcohol-saturated. Christ, for years he'd been telling anyone who would listen about the sea monsters that had taken his boat to Davy Jones's locker. He'd been out on the boat completely trashed when a squall had come up. He'd clung to a piece of debris and drifted for hours out there until one of the fishermen spotted him.

He gave me a detailed description of the shoes though—purple with purple laces, rubber soles, and a yellow lightning bolt down each side. Either Capy had vivid delusions or he really had seen something.

"Do you think they were athletic shoes?" I asked.

"Yeah, dat be what dey were. Probably wouldn't a fit anyways. Dey be lookin' kinda small."

It wasn't much, but maybe it was something. Capy gave me a little salute on my way out and told me to bring a bottle of island rum the next time I visited.

* * *

Stark didn't see me walk up. He was leaning on his car in front of the warehouse, looking smug. "Hey, Stark, how was dinner last night?" I asked, handing him the donuts.

"Horrible," he said.

"You don't have the look of a man who spent a horrible evening."

"It was the after-dinner part that I was thinking about. I tell you though, Billy's mother is better than any interrogator I ever met. Jeez. By the time Billy and I left her parents, her mother knew what vegetables I ate as a kid."

"Really? What kind?"

"Funny, Sampson."

He was relieved when I told him that Capy had been sitting up in bed giving the nurse trouble this morning. "Weird about those shoes. Do you think he actually saw something?" Stark asked. He knew Capy's reputation for drunken exaggeration.

"God knows. I think we should check to see if any of the stores carry anything like them."

"Yeah, I can see purple running shoes being a big seller down here. We'll probably find out that half the ladies over sixty consider them a fashion statement. Of course, you know most of the stores won't have any records."

"You know, Capy did say the shoes were small."

"Well, small to Capy might mean no bigger than those huge rubber boots he flops around in. Come on, let's go in and see what Harrigan has found."

Several guys were inside dissecting airplane parts, which were scattered all over the floor. Harrigan was standing with his sleeves rolled up, holding a clipboard and talking to one of them.

"Here's what we know so far," he said, getting right down to business. "There are no signs of a bomb. Expanding gases would have deformed every surface that they touched. "There would be signs of pitting—a bunch of craterlike holes and black streaks that radiate from the blast site. There are no burn patterns that indicate fire either."

"What about the report that smoke was coming from an engine and that there was an explosion?" Stark asked.

"Some witness reports remind me of the fairy tales my mother told me. Pure fantasy. Too many movies. One of the accounts said a witness reported an engine falling off! Hardly the case, as you can see. We'll keep looking, but nothing at all indicates engine fire or any explosion. In fact, I don't think that either engine was running when the plane hit. If they had been, the props would have been twisted. That agree with what you remember, Hannah?"

Jimmy and I had already told Harrigan what we'd seen that morning, which had included none of the drama that the other witnesses had reported. "Like I said, the thing just fell from the sky. I remember how silent it was until the plane smashed into the sea."

"That matches what I'm finding," he said.

"So what do you think?" I asked.

"Could be a fuel problem, though the gauges show both tanks were almost full. They had seawater in them, but that's not surprising. Salt water would have seeped in after the plane went under."

"Would salt water have been enough to bring the plane down if it was mixed in with the fuel before takeoff?" I asked.

"Absolutely. The engines would have sputtered a few times and quit. That would mesh with what you saw—that the plane just turned into the sea. The thing is, it would take a whole lot of salt water. I've already checked with the airport. No other plane has had problems with contaminated fuel."

"It's really the perfect ploy—contaminating the tanks with salt water. Who'd know once the plane went into the ocean?" I asked.

"I will know. I sent the fuel controls out for analysis.

There's one mounted on each engine. They meter the fuel into the engine. It's a closed system. They will have fuel trapped inside, along with any contaminants. We will know precisely what was going into those engines."

"Do you have any educated guesses?" I asked.

"I know better than to guess. I've been at this business for almost twenty years. Half the time I'm just about sure it's one thing and it turns out to be something else altogether. Last year I investigated the wreck of a little plane that slammed into the side of a hill. Everyone was sure a bomb had exploded. The news media turned it into a big story about gangsters because they heard there was a guy who had been approached to testify against some Mob figures. Everyone was screaming sabotage. We took samples from the debris in the engine and sent them to an expert at the Smithsonian. She found feathers—Canada geese."

On the way into the office, I told Stark of my conversation with Kiersted about the dolphins last night.

"Sounds like he's over the edge," Stark said.

"Probably," I said. "How the heck do people turn into such extremists?" I wondered out loud.

I didn't expect an answer, but Stark provided one anyway. "Maybe it comes from too many failures," he said.

"Yeah, or from going unheard."

Chapter 22

Stark, pull over," I said. Debra Westbrook was sitting alone at a sidewalk café. I insisted he drop me off at the curb and go away. It was an opportunity to talk to Debra without the senator around and I certainly didn't think Stark's presence would enhance the conversation. He actually looked hurt when I told him so.

"Hello, Mrs. Westbrook," I said as I approached her table.

"Detective Sampson, good to see you," she said, smiling. Not a bad start. Unlike her husband, she didn't seem to think she needed a lawyer to talk with me.

"Mind if I join you?"

"Please do. I was about to order lunch. I would love the company. Please call me Deb."

"And call me Hannah," I said, pulling out a chair as the waiter appeared. She ordered a salad with fresh lobster. If it was fresh it would be spiny lobster, the only species found in the Caribbean. I was disturbed to see that turtle was on the menu. When I asked the waiter about it, he said it was excellent. I skipped giving him a lecture about the fact that turtles were endangered. There was nothing he could do about it. I ordered jerk chicken.

"Did the senator desert you?" I asked after the waiter headed to the kitchen.

"I'm afraid so. He's off looking at a big house on the point near Soper's Hole."

"Really? Are you thinking of buying a home down here?" I knew the house. It was more like a mansion.

"Oh, Jack has this idea about retiring in the islands. Until then he wants to have a place to spend a couple of weeks. It's not that straightforward though. He's got to apply for some sort of Non-Belonger Land Holding License before he can buy property in the BVI. He's supposed to gather financial references, character references, and a police certificate. He's sure that he'll get permission. He hasn't bothered with all the references. He says all it ever takes is money to the right person."

"I'm surprised you aren't looking with him," I said as the waiter appeared with our lunch.

"Actually, I'm not interested in owning a place here. I don't like the idea of being so far away from the children. And someday there will be grandkids. Jack knows how I feel. We argued about it this morning. I told him I didn't want to look at any property and that he was on his own." She emptied her wineglass and signaled the waiter for another.

"I'm sorry," she said. "I don't mean to bring you into my personal affairs. I'm just upset that he is completely ignoring my wishes."

I could see that Debra needed to talk. "It's okay. You're pretty alone down here right now," I said. "I'm sorry about the Rileys."

"Louise and I were close. Jack has hardly given it a thought—the fact that we've lost good friends. He can be a very indifferent and insensitive man. Very self-centered. Now that the kids are all grown, perhaps I'll let Jack live down here by himself."

"Are you thinking about leaving Jack?" I asked. It was none of my business, but I wanted to know what the relationship between them was.

"I'm considering it very seriously," she said. "I've suspected for a long time that he's been seeing other women."

I couldn't believe she was willing to have this conversation with a stranger. "You could be mistaken. Why not ask him?"

She just laughed, a bitter laugh, filled with something else—hurt maybe.

"Don't be silly. Jack would deny it. You see, he can't afford to have me leave him."

"What do you mean?"

"I'm the one with the money. When we married, Jack was a struggling attorney with few clients and no reputation. Our marriage changed all that. Jack likes to think that he's the one in control, but if I leave him, the money goes with me. My father made sure of that when we married. I guess he saw right through Jack."

"Do you think he knows what you're considering?"

"Probably. You see, Jack got careless. When I was packing for this trip, I found a hotel receipt in his shirt pocket. Since I had not been with Jack, it was pretty obvious he'd been with someone else."

That explained the receipt I'd found in her address book.

"So you asked him about it?"

"I did. He came up with some ridiculous story about his charge card being taken. This whole trip has been a disaster because of it. I am so angry. I told Louise about it. She thought I should file for divorce and gave me the name of a divorce attorney."

"Surely your husband has money of his own by now."

"He would, but he has expensive tastes and no control. And as long as we are together he has an endless supply."

So, if Debra were to leave Jack, he'd have big financial problems. I wondered if he'd have resorted to bringing down that plane if he knew she was contemplating divorce. "What would happen if you were to die?" I asked.

"I know what you're thinking. And yes, he'd inherit half

of it. The rest goes to the kids. I admit I've considered the fact that Jack's best option is for me to be dead. I've thought about it a lot. But I just don't think he'd kill me for it. And to bring down an entire plane? As little respect as I have for the man, I don't think he'd stoop that low."

"Why are you telling me all this, Debra?"

"Insurance," she said. "I'm not stupid. If Jack is involved, he'll think twice before he tries it again, especially when he realizes we've spoken."

"So you'll tell him about our conversation?" I asked.

"I won't have to say a word." She looked past me and smiled. "Hello, darling," she said.

Westbrook walked up and pecked Debra on the cheek.

"Hello, Detective Sampson. I'm so glad that Debra had company at lunch."

"I asked Hannah to join me. We've had quite a nice woman-to-woman chat," she said.

Westbrook didn't have any trouble understanding what Debra meant. He signaled to the waiter and ordered a double martini.

"How was the house?" she asked after the waiter scurried off.

"It's beautiful. But the deal is complicated." He didn't explain why and Debra clearly didn't want to know. Westbrook insisted on paying for my lunch and was ordering another martini when I left.

I knew the Realtor who was listing the house Jack was looking at and I walked straight to her office over on Wickham's Cay. The streets were empty at this time of day. It was just too hot to be out on the pavement. Storekeepers sat under awnings, fanning themselves. A couple of tourists were carefully examining a saber as I walked past the Pirate's Bounty. Down the sidewalk I could hear music blaring from one of the bars above the grocery store. It was a local hangout. Several men were gathered around a table outside, sipping Heinekens and playing dominoes.

The realty office door was shut, but the "Open" sign dangled in the window. I walked into a blast of cold. Terry Brackwell was sitting behind her desk thumbing through the real estate ads in the newspaper. She looked up when she heard me enter and was about to make a remark I knew I didn't want to hear about yesterday's headlines. I'd been relieved to find that in today's paper Stewart and the news about the crash had been relegated to page three and the only photo was one of Daniel Stewart resting near the pool.

"None of it's true," I said and held my hands up, warding off any comment from the Realtor about a romance with Stewart. I asked her about Westbrook.

I had to trade what I knew about Westbrook's finances— that they were tied to Debra's and that she was against the purchase of a house—for what she knew about the "complications" Westbrook had mentioned. It turned out that getting a non-belonger's license wasn't as easy as Westbrook had thought.

"Westbrook is in a big hurry to buy that house," Brackwell said. "From what you just told me it's probably because his wife is about to cut him off. But he's taken the licensing requirements way too casually. I told him he needed to get down to the government offices and get things resolved with Conrad Frett. Frett's in charge of all the licensing when it comes to the transfer of property and development by outsiders."

Stark was in his office, sitting with his legs propped up on his desk, arms behind his head, gazing at the ceiling. Anyone who didn't know him would think he was still daydreaming about his evening with Billy. But I knew the look.

"What's the problem, Stark?"

"You realize we are nowhere on this crash or the break-in at the warehouse."

"Come on, Stark. We know a lot."

"Like what?"

"We know it wasn't about the drugs and that the mechanic was not involved," I said. "Unless we've missed something, I think we agree that neither the Rileys nor those newlyweds were targets."

"Yeah, we agree. What about Debra Westbrook?"

I told him about our conversation over lunch and about Jack Westbrook's trying to buy the house near Soper's Hole. "If Debra had died in that crash, Jack wouldn't have to worry about ending up in divorce court and broke. He'd be able to afford that beautiful house and be dreaming about lounging around the pool with a couple of island beauties."

"Maybe. It seems extreme though," he said.

"What about those shoes?" I asked.

"We've got a couple of officers checking the stores. It's a stretch, but you never know."

"Let's go through the other passengers. We're reasonably sure the Rileys and the newlyweds weren't targets," I said. "Debra Westbrook is a possibility. Who else?"

"There's still Zora Gordon. We don't know enough about her, that's for sure," Stark said, swinging his legs off the desk. "She's hostile, but it's no crime to dislike the police."

"Maybe someone didn't want her making it to San Juan to take care of her boss's legal affairs," I said.

"Hell, maybe they didn't want anyone in Puerto Rico who had never drunk anything brown," Stark said, throwing the pencil he had propped behind his ear across his desk. "I know I wouldn't."

"Anything on her boss?" I asked.

"Snyder checked the registration for the *Mystic*. It turns out it belongs to a guy named Leo Poltolski. He lives in L.A. I called my old partner in Miami. He's using his contacts in California to check on the guy."

"Then there's Redding," I said, "and his connection to Enok Kiersted and the fact that Kiersted is such a fanatic.

Let's go see if Gil came up with anything on Redding's computer or those disks."

Gil had his eyes glued to a microscope when we walked in. He didn't bother to look up.

"Detectives, what a pleasure to have you visit." How he knew who it was I didn't bother trying to determine.

"Just one little adjustment," he said. "There. Take a look at this." He waved us over but was reluctant to tear himself away.

Finally, he stepped back so I could take a look. All I saw was a black glob with something dead in it.

"What is this and where did it come from?" I asked.

"It's oil. One of the guys helping with that plane dropped it off. That Harrigan is really thorough. He sent over several samples and asked me if I'd take a quick look, see if there were any unusual particles in any of the samples. He said it was a whole lot faster and easier to have me check out the stuff than to send it out. I told him that was cool and to send over anything he wanted."

"What's the dead stuff in it?" I asked.

"Plankton. Amazingly little creatures, aren't they?" Gil said. "They turn up in most of the ocean samples I look at."

"That's it? Plankton? Nothing else?" I asked, still hoping that Gil's excitement had been about something more than dead microscopic organisms.

"Nope, just oil. Too bad. It would have been nice to find something definitive."

"Jeez, Gil. Were you able to retrieve anything from Lawrence Redding's laptop?" I asked, stuffing my frustration.

"No. Not too surprising. The machine is completely ruined. Salt water and computer chips just don't mix. I was able to read the disks though. Those cases were watertight. The files were standard Word and Excel spreadsheets. I don't know if any of it will mean anything. It's a bunch of reports, financial stuff, and data. Let's see, what did I do with those disks?"

I never could figure out how Gil found anything in his lab. He was good at conveying the illusion that he knew exactly where everything was. But anyone who had been exposed to the massive disarray more than once knew better. Every time I came in, I expected to hear that some vital piece of evidence had somehow ended up in the trash. It had never happened though. I could only hope that now would not be the exception.

"Here they are. You can use the computer on my desk," he said, brushing a stack of papers into a pile on the floor.

There were three disks, all labeled "Kiersted Grant" followed by a number. We started with the first. It contained a bunch of data and reports about Kiersted's research in the mangroves and several dozen tables of data about the sediment content, the species in each location, and genetic sampling of the trees. The second disk contained a spreadsheet with Kiersted's expenses, including everything from test tubes to centrifuges to chemicals.

The third disk contained Redding's draft detailing his recommendations about renewing the grant. He was recommending that Kiersted's grant be terminated. He wrote at length about the value of the research but concluded that Kiersted was too involved in political issues and too much of an extremist when it came to the environment. He had heard that Kiersted had threatened people in the government. Redding was concerned about the reputation of the foundation if Kiersted were to become too volatile.

"That's a motive," Stark said. He'd been reading over my shoulder for the past half hour.

"It would all fit," I said. "Kiersted figured Redding was going to pull his grant. He didn't want him to make that report, so he sabotaged the plane to stop him. Kiersted is extreme enough to do it. When he found out that we'd brought up all the contents from the plane, he'd been worried. He couldn't be sure that Redding's files wouldn't survive. What if we linked him to the crash because of the report?"

"So he broke into the warehouse looking for Redding's reports," Stark said, filling in the rest. "He would have been unable to find the laptop and disks because Gil had brought them here. Then Capy ended up walking in on him. I wonder if Kiersted owns a pair of purple running shoes."

"The thing is, I can't believe he'd be willing to sacrifice all those passengers, Stark, especially the kid. And for what? To keep his research going on the mangroves?"

"He's probably done a lot of rationalizing about the 'greater good' or some kind of bullshit like that," Stark said.

"Okay," I said. "Let's go talk to him."

Chapter 23

The Society of Conservation office was over on Main Street. Enok was in the back in his makeshift lab. Clippings of mangroves sprouted in glass vials on every free surface. The walls looked like the back of a Ken Kesey bus, except these weren't of the "Make Love Not War" variety. Rather they were messages of despair: A backhoe crashing through the rain forest, a pelican covered in oil and floundering on the beach, a satellite view of Earth with detailed graphs and tables about global warming, a bumper sticker that said, "If You're Not Outraged, You're Not Paying Attention."

Enok was in the back pouring chemicals into a pitcher of liquid that was turning the color of pee.

"Hi, Hannah," he said, turning. He was wearing shorts and flip-flops. A pair of muddy athletic shoes sat near the back door. Once they'd been white, not purple.

I introduced him to Stark, who had picked up a vial filled with liquid and was shaking it.

Kiersted scowled, took it from Stark, and placed it back in the rack.

Stark just shrugged. I knew what he was doing. He was applying pressure and watching Kiersted's response.

I was studying every inch of the lab, looking for anything that could implicate Kiersted. In contrast to the chaos on the walls, the room was neat to the point of obsession. The bookshelf above the desk held a couple hundred books, alphabetically ordered by author.

Several dozen chemicals filled another shelf, every jar and container labeled in precise block letters and again organized alphabetically. Pencils were lying in a box in a neat row from long to short. Another held pens sorted by color. Every surface was spotless. There weren't even any water spots around the stainless-steel sink.

The room had all the signs of a control freak. It fit the profile of a man who might kill to command his destiny. But then, what did I know? Maybe this was how good scientists worked.

"I hope you're not here to arrest me for those dolphins," he said. "I hear they're talking about bringing another pair in at Dolphin World."

"It's about Lawrence Redding," I said.

"What about him?"

"Simon told me he heard you two arguing. What was that about?"

"He was not happy about my involvement in the political issues down here. I got kind of upset with him, I guess. I mean, my politics and beliefs are my business."

"What about the grant?"

"What about it?"

"He was down here assessing your study, wasn't he?"

"That's right. I think he found things in order."

"We found his notes," I said and waited.

Kiersted thought about it for several minutes, trying to decide how to respond. Finally the dam burst. "I'm sick to death of these so-called environmentally concerned foundations who back off the minute things get one bit political. Don't they know that it's all political? So ludicrously shortsighted. They have to play it safe. Don't want to make too many waves. Hell with 'em."

"Did you get that pissed at Redding?" Stark asked.

"Don't be ridiculous. I had to go along. It's the money I need to do the research. I told him I'd back off. He seemed satisfied."

"Did you know that he was recommending against further support from the foundation?" I asked. I didn't catch a speck of surprise on Kiersted's face.

"You knew that, didn't you?" Stark said. "Were you intent on keeping him from making that report? Maybe planning to get your act together before the next grants examiner came down?"

"Surely you aren't thinking I had anything to do with that crash!" he said. "I would never resort to that."

"What would happen if the grant were suspended?" I asked.

"I'd write another proposal, go looking for other sources of funds. I've been living on this kind of soft money for years. I know how it's done."

"Were you in the warehouse on Sunday night, snooping around the evidence from that crash?" Stark demanded. "Maybe picked up a 9 mm Beretta while you were there?"

"This is the first I've heard of any evidence in a warehouse, and I have never handled a gun. This idea that people have the right to carry guns is abhorrent in our modern society. And believe it or not, I would never resort to violence as a solution."

"Right," Stark said, eyeing a newspaper article tacked to the wall detailing the torching of a beach resort where leatherbacks were known to nest.

Just then, Stark's cell phone rang.

"Stark," he answered. He listened for a moment, then said, "Okay, we're on the way."

"Are you going to tell me what's happened?" I asked when we got outside.

"Someone found a body."

*　　*　　*

It was tangled in the mangrove roots. One of O'Brien's boat handlers had come across it. He'd been nudging a forty-two-foot sloop in between two other boats in Paraquita Bay when he'd managed to get the anchor chain wrapped around some roots. He'd gone into the water with snorkel and mask to free it. At first, he thought what he'd found was just trash—until he realized an arm was dangling out of the black plastic garbage bag.

When we got out to the lagoon, O'Brien and six or seven other SeaSail employees were waiting in speedboats near shore. Paraquita Bay was crammed with boats, many of them with the SeaSail logo. Unfortunately, the protected mangrove bay had room for only a fraction of all the boats seeking refuge from the hurricane. Stark and I had driven by the SeaSail marina on the way. Close to two hundred boats were sandwiched into the marina docks and more were coming in.

The storm had picked up speed and was on its way to being classified a category four, with winds from 131 to 155 miles per hour. That meant major damage. It was on a direct course for St. Martin and the BVI. Some still held out hope that it would change directions, or that the winds would lessen, but if it didn't, it would hit sometime late to-morrow or in the early hours of the next day.

Stark had not been at all happy about having to go out in the *Wahoo*. He'd strapped on a life vest before he even set foot on the boat.

"How can anyone give the impression of a macho cop looking like an orange marshmallow? You definitely need therapy, Stark," I said.

"Who said I need to look macho? Besides, it's not fear. It's respect. Human beings should know where they be-long—that's on terra firma. The ocean is for creatures with fins and gills. You're the one who needs therapy, strapping on air and pretending like you're a fish. It's unnatural, a death wish, if you ask me."

Stark was probably right and today I was going to have to dive alone. Jimmy had been helping with the search for the purple shoes in shops over near West End and was out of reach when the call had come in about the body.

I eased the *Wahoo* next to O'Brien's boat and he threw us a line. God, he looked good, hair tousled, arms tanned, sunglasses dangling around his neck.

He gave me a quick smile, then got down to business. Not even a hello. Stark saw it—O'Brien's calculated coolness and my forced nonchalance. He just shook his head and muttered under his breath.

When O'Brien realized I planned to dive alone, he insisted on going down with me.

"Come on, it's all of what—ten, maybe fifteen feet? I think I can handle this alone," I said.

"Maybe you ought to review the safety procedures for diving, Hannah. Like the one that says never dive without a buddy. You just can't stand the idea of needing someone beside you, can you?" He had stepped onto the *Wahoo* and was pulling Jimmy's gear out of the locker.

I didn't want O'Brien with me, but I wasn't about to get into an argument, not with half a dozen guys standing around and a body down there. I could see that O'Brien was coming along whether I liked it or not. "Fine," I said.

We finished getting into our gear in silence. No one else was saying anything either. Stark handed me my camera and I splashed into the water. O'Brien was right behind me.

It wasn't the first time we'd dived together. In the past, we'd gone diving and sailing almost every weekend, taking the *Katherine* to some secluded anchorage. I never tired of the beauty of the coral reef. Neither did O'Brien.

But I was uncomfortable with his being with me now. This was not going to be beautiful. This was going to be ugly. This was O'Brien really seeing what I did. All his concern about the effects my job had on me, until now, had been only theoretical.

I didn't want him to swim into a crime scene, into a dead body. It wasn't just that everything he thought about my diving would turn to hard fact. I didn't want O'Brien to have to experience it too. I didn't want him to know the horror. But there'd been no way to stop him.

We released the air from our BCs and descended the short distance to the muddy bottom. I could see the sloop's anchor chain lying in the muck. I signaled to O'Brien and we began to follow it toward the mangroves. A tangle of roots materialized in the gloom of darkness under branches that kept the sun from penetrating the water. We swam along the edge of the root system following the anchor chain, careful to keep our fins from brushing the thick sediment that the trees had trapped.

The mangroves were magical in their own way—in a shadowy, mysterious, frightening way. Deep in the dark roots, barnacles, tunicates, and oysters made their homes. Baby shrimp and small reef fish hid in the tangles, protected from predators as they foraged in the thick black mud for tiny organisms.

Farther out, urchins, queen conch, and starfish littered the sandy bottom. Scores of Cassiopeiae, upside-down jellyfish, undulated in the water, their lacy tentacles loaded with algae and soaking up sunlight. The brownish-yellow jellyfish were named after the mythical queen who was banished by the gods to the northern constellation for her vanity. There she is doomed to reside upside down for most of the year. But for these jellyfish, upside down is right side up.

I was swimming over patches of manatee grass, O'Brien behind me, when I saw the dark mass take shape in the gloom. I signaled him to stop and hang back. I'd told him before we went down to stay away in order to avoid any unnecessary disturbance of the fine sediments on the bottom. I was protecting him too. I wanted him as far away as I could keep him. I swam toward the shape, looking back once to make sure O'Brien was staying put. He was.

The body was wrapped in what looked like a couple of black plastic garbage bags that had been tied with rope. The plastic had been ripped and mangled by tree roots and water action, exposing the corpse, an adult black male. His shirt-sleeves were rolled up and a tie dangled from his neck. The tie clip, a gold circle enclosing a BVI flag, indicated that he worked in government.

I swam around him, shooting pictures as I went. By the condition of the body, I knew it had been in the water for several days, maybe a week.

I moved in for close-up shots, taking a dozen pictures. Once the body was disturbed, critical evidence could be washed away. I needed to make sure everything was documented and on film.

Rigor mortis was gone. Worse though was the damage that sea life had done. In this area rich in crustaceans and feeding fish, any flesh not protected by clothing had been eaten away. Much of the soft tissue from the face, hands, and arms was gone. I looked at a face with eyes bulging from sockets, teeth bared in a lipless grin, and a hollow indentation where the nose had been. Sea creatures were still nibbling on the bony remains.

I was working in automatic now, immune to the carnage, objectifying the human being, and intent on photographing. I hadn't realized that O'Brien was by my side until he touched my shoulder.

I swung around and glared at him. He just shook his head and hovered there, watching me do my job and backing me up if I needed help. Christ, I hadn't wanted O'Brien to see this.

I signaled that I was going to check the surrounding area and swam away from the body. O'Brien stuck with me as I searched for evidence—anything that might have been dumped here with the body. I swam in ever-increasing arcs, scanning the bottom.

I retrieved a couple of rusted beer cans and a glass bottle and put them in my mesh evidence bag. This felt more like litter removal than evidence retrieval, but I kept at it. Finally, I signaled to O'Brien that I was ready to head up.

We swam to the *Wahoo* and I handed Stark my camera and the evidence bags and climbed in. O'Brien followed me aboard.

"It's a black male," I told Stark. "But the body is in bad shape."

A half hour later, O'Brien and I were back in the water with a body bag. Again, O'Brien hung back, but was ready to assist. I went to work. The head was first. I covered it in a plastic bag to preserve any evidence that might be present. Next, I secured a bag over each of his hands, one clenched in a tight fist, even in death. Then I released the body, along with the remnants of the trash bags, from the grip of the mangroves.

O'Brien, who had been hovering nearby with the body bag, swam over now. Again, I regretted the fact that he'd come with me, but I needed the help. Bagging a body underwater is no simple task. O'Brien held the body bag open as I lifted the legs in, then the torso, and head, and zipped it up. That was that—gore hidden.

I swam to the surface with the victim while O'Brien set about freeing the anchor that had led to the discovery of the body.

"Sorry you had to see it," I said when we were both back in the boat. O'Brien was standing behind me, helping me pull my BC and tank off.

"I'm the one who's sorry. Sorry that you feel that you need to keep doing this job," he said as I turned toward him. I was ready for the argument until I saw the look on his face. Regret, sadness maybe. He wasn't looking for a fight.

"Come over tonight, O'Brien," I said. "Simon and I will

make dinner. No talk about our jobs or brewing storms. Just dinner. Okay?"

"I'd like that, Hannah."

After O'Brien and the boat handlers left the lagoon, Stark and I took a few minutes to examine the body before the air began to do its work. I took more photos. Stark found a government ID in the shirt pocket—"Conrad Frett, Minister of Natural Resources and Labor."

The coroner was waiting for us when Stark and I tied the *Wahoo* up to the dock. "Are you thinking what I am?" Stark asked as we followed the van over to the morgue.

"Depends, Stark. What are you thinking?"

"I'm thinking that this is all tied together—Frett's murder, the crash. I'm thinking about that report that Redding had written. Chances are Kiersted was going to lose his grant because of it. And then according to Redding's report there was all Kiersted's ranting about government giving way to developers. Frett had a lot to do with that. Things are starting to stack up here. We know that Kiersted is a fanatic. That's what it would take to bring down a plane. Next to that, killing Frett would have been nothing."

"Let's see what the coroner finds," I said.

What he found was a 9 mm slug in Frett's chest, fired at close range. Same caliber as the gun that had been lost on the airplane and then stolen at the warehouse. Coincidence? Not a chance. That gun had been used to kill Frett sometime before the plane ever ended up in the water.

Frett's wallet with almost a hundred dollars in it was still in his pocket, his watch still on his wrist.

The coroner estimated that he'd been in the water for at least four days, maybe five. We needed to find out who had last seen Frett and what he'd been involved in.

Chapter 24

Conrad Frett had been living way beyond his salary as a government official. He owned a lavish home up in the hills above Road Town. The housekeeper let us in. She told us she hadn't seen Frett since Friday morning, when she arrived at seven to make him breakfast as she did every morning before he went to work. She left dinner for him in the oven before she went home at five, as usual.

She had weekends off and had returned Monday to find the house empty. She assumed that he'd left for the office early and had gone about her chores, wondering briefly why his bed was made, something he never did himself. She always took care of it after he left for work each day, had done it Friday, and expected to do so on Monday. She didn't give it another thought until his secretary called around one o'clock, asking if he was home, sick perhaps. That was when the maid started to get concerned. She checked and found the dinner she'd made still in the oven and the mail still in the box. Even so, she figured he had just gone away for a long weekend without telling anyone.

His secretary thought differently though. She was sure he would have called the office. She said she was going to call the police. That would have been one of the calls Dunn got yesterday while we were in his office.

"How long have you worked for Frett?" I asked.

"Almost two years now. He jus be buyin' dis big ole house. Way too big for jus one man, you ask me. I be thinkin' he like showin' off for da women," she said. She was ready to gossip.

"Did he see many women?" I asked. "Maybe have them up here for the weekend?"

"Not too often," she said. "I have to admit I be hopin' he be gettin' lucky dis past weekend. Da man was not da type dat women would be wantin' to spend da time with. He be almost forty and never be married. Guess he be thinkin' dis here house and da nice car be changin' dat."

"Do you think it did?" I asked.

"Oh, sure. Like I said, he be havin' a few women here. Da man was kinda whiny, timid, you know what dey say— no balls. But for some dat not be da important thing—nice house, new clothes—dos be da things dat count. I can't say I be envyin' him. I be glad he had dat money. He be real alone without it."

"Do you know where he got his money?" I asked.

"No, maybe a rich relation in da UK or something. Sure weren't from anyone in da islands. He don't have no family here."

"Did he see anyone on a regular basis?" I asked.

"Not dat I be knowin'. He not be confidin' in me," she said, dying to say more.

All it took was some minor prodding. "Surely you heard rumors," I said.

"I not be one to gossip, but his secretary be known ta visit."

"Did you ever see a man named Enok Kiersted here?" Stark asked.

"Nobody by dat name ever come by when I be here," she said.

We told her we might have more questions but right now she was free to head home.

"You think one of dos women done murdered him?" she

asked as I walked her to the door. "Maybe he be havin' someone here for da weekend and dat secretary got jealous," she said.

She was hoping for some juicy tidbit that she could spread around the island and was disappointed when I told her we didn't know enough but that I didn't think the secretary was involved.

I figured that Frett's secretary deserved the benefit of the doubt and did not need her reputation bloodied by his housekeeper. Besides, the circumstances of Frett's death didn't seem like the act of a jealous woman. However, we did need to meet the secretary.

After the housekeeper left, Stark and I took a look around the house. Everything smelled new—like the plastic wrapping had just been removed. A stereo system took up one whole wall, the shelves nearby loaded with CDs. Plush furniture, Oriental rugs, and mahogany tables filled the room. Everything was perfectly coordinated. It was not an eclectic mix collected over a lifetime. It looked like Frett had simply had a furniture showroom moved into his house when he bought it.

The bedroom was as sterile as the living room—no family photographs, no pictures with friends or photo albums on bedside tables. I rummaged through the rolltop desk that was nestled in the bay window on the other side of the bedroom. The letters were all business, except for one of those birthday postcards from his dentist. Not one personal letter or card or any indication that he had anyone who cared about him.

In the bathroom, I found an unopened box of condoms. One can always hope. I felt sorry for the guy. And I could see how coming into money might change things. People always said "You can't buy happiness"—but when you were this alone? If you had to buy love, it was something anyway. The question was where had he gotten the money? We'd talk to Frett's secretary first thing in the morning.

*   *   *

The lights on the *Sea Bird* reflected into the still water. I
pulled my shoes off and dug my feet in the cool sand. The
moon was a sliver of yellow in a black sky. I could hardly
tell where the water ended and shore began except for the
thin strip of white bubbles that lapped the sand. The only
lights were from the *Sea Bird*. Kiersted's boat was a dark
shadow across the way. I wondered briefly where he was.

As I stepped onto the dock, I heard a splash under my
feet. Then a dark shape darted out from under the boards
and disappeared into deep water, more than likely spooked
by a bigger fish.

A burst of laughter echoed from the *Sea Bird*. Simon and
O'Brien. It was good to hear the kid laughing. Sadie had
heard me coming. She jumped off the boat and raced down
the dock to greet me. I stooped and let her nuzzle my face,
then followed her back to the *Sea Bird*.

Even though I'd planned on cooking, O'Brien had already started dinner. He knew I was always happy to relinquish my spot at the stove, and was in the galley, stirring
and tasting. I tried to ignore the vivid image of the night
we'd fought. I was determined that we would simply enjoy
a meal and escape the tension we were both feeling. Simon
was sitting at the table with a knife and chopping board,
carefully removing every seed from a green pepper. Nomad
was curled on his lap.

"Hi, Hannah!" he said, a huge smile spreading over his
face. Nice, I thought, to have someone besides Sadie so
glad to see me. Make it one more—O'Brien. He left the
spoon in the pot, wrapped an arm around my waist, and
pressed his body into mine. God, it felt good. I could feel
the heat starting deep in my belly and spreading.

We took dinner up to the cockpit and settled under the
circle of light that glowed from the overhead lamp. We
were quiet as we ate, enjoying the silence and the calm

night. Then Simon started to chatter about his day at school and told O'Brien about the snorkeling.

"I got some awesome pictures. Want to see them?" He scrambled down the steps and I could hear him rummaging around in his cabin. Finally he emerged with his camera and settled in between O'Brien and me. O'Brien draped his arm over him and rested his hand on my shoulder.

An hour later, we had seen every photo that Simon had taken since he'd arrived in the islands. Evidently, his camera had extra memory. Even on the tiny one-by-two-inch digital screen, the beauty of the photos was evident. We saw his underwater photos, the boats at SeaSail, then the photos he'd taken with his father.

I'd been about to suggest we look at the rest later, when I saw O'Brien shaking his head. I knew what he was thinking. The kid needed to go through them, mourn some. What better place to do it than on a quiet boat, in safe harbor, with people who cared about him?

"There's my dad," Simon said, his voice catching. The photo was a close-up of Redding standing in the water, drenched, having just come out of the ocean. There was another of the two of them standing on the beach and scores of pictures that Simon had taken out on the water.

"We rented a motorboat and went all over the place," Simon said. "My dad even let me drive." He scrolled through them quickly now, clearly feeling overwhelmed but needing to come to the end. There were pictures of islands and harbors, boats anchored in them with tiny sticklike figures that I assumed were people standing on decks.

Simon and his father had taken a swing through Paraquita Bay, a contrast to the look of the place now with all the boats jammed into the lagoon. It had been nearly deserted when Simon had snapped his pictures, with only a couple of empty boats on moorings. The last photos were a gorgeous series of shots of a white egret high in a mangrove, silhouetted by the sun, marred only by the shape of a motor boat in the water.

"These are wonderful, Simon. Would it be okay if I had a couple enlarged and printed?"

"Sure, Hannah."

"What about any of the others? Maybe the one of you and your dad?"

"I guess that would be okay." I could tell he wasn't sure. Maybe it would hurt too much. But he needed something of his dad to hang on to.

"We'll go by the camera shop before school," I said.

By the time O'Brien and I had done the dishes and wiped down the galley, Simon was asleep in his cabin, his body curled around Nomad.

We headed up top and walked down to the beach, Sadie on our heels. I could feel the tension building between us. It was called forced avoidance.

"Simon is a really good kid," O'Brien said. I knew he was looking for some neutral ground.

"Yeah. I don't know what's going to happen. I'm scared for him. He's not connected to his aunt in any important way. And I have a feeling she's not going to be excited about taking him in. It will probably be about duty rather than love. That's a bad way for a kid to have to grow up."

"Is there no one else?" he asked.

"No."

We were shuffling barefoot through the sand, hand in hand. "He's obviously happy with you, Hannah," O'Brien said.

"What are you suggesting, O'Brien?"

"Maybe you should take him for a while, see how it goes."

"Me? How can I take care of a kid? I've had to leave him with Tilda every day."

"Is that so bad? He'd have lots of extended family with Tilda, Calvin, the girls, Jimmy Snyder, Stark. And he'd be with people who truly care about him."

"What about you, O'Brien?"

"Definitely me. As I said, he's a good kid."

"I don't think I'm cut out for it."

"I'd be willing to help you parent."

"Are you talking about being a family, O'Brien?"

"Maybe." I could see that we were moving into dangerous territory and the same fight we'd had a couple nights ago. A variation on the "quit the job, have kids" conversation. I was not going to go there.

I spread the blanket that I carried under my arm on the sand and pulled O'Brien down next to me. I pushed him back, pressed my body into his, and felt his heart thumping. Mine fluttered as I flicked my tongue in his ear, then across his lips. He grabbed my arms and rolled over on top of me. He ran a hand inside my shirt and slowly and meticulously unbuttoned it. I pulled his shirt over his head and drew him into me. The rest of our clothes followed.

God, I thought, *how could I not be with this man*.

Afterward, we lay together looking up at the stars.

"You know, sometimes I wish life were simpler. Just you and me, an island somewhere," I said.

He stood, pulled me up, and pressed his body into mine in a tight embrace. Then we waded into the ocean and floated under a million stars. I lay my head back, closed my eyes, and let the sea block out sound.

I don't know how long I'd been drifting there when suddenly O'Brien was yanking me above the surface.

"What, O'Brien?"

"It's Simon," he said, splashing to shore. That's when I heard it too. Simon's horrifying screams. Another nightmare. Sadie ran ahead as we raced down the dock to the *Sea Bird*, pulling on clothes as we ran. By the time we got there, Simon was standing in the cockpit.

"Hannah," he cried, "I couldn't find you. I got so scared."

"It's okay," I said, jumping onto the boat, O'Brien right

behind me. "We were down on the beach. We're here now. You're okay."

O'Brien picked him up and carried him down to the salon and sat with him while I heated some cocoa. He was still trembling when I sat down next to him. O'Brien had him wrapped up like a burrito.

"Did you have another nightmare?" I asked as he managed to extract a hand and take a sip from the cup.

"I guess, but this one was different. I was dreaming about someone moving around on the *Sea Bird*. I remember in the dream I thought it was you. Then a man came and stood in my doorway. I was so scared. It felt like I was awake. I called out for you, and then I started screaming and screaming and the man disappeared."

"It's okay, Simon. You stay with O'Brien and I'll have a look around." I didn't expect to find anything, but the kid needed to be reassured.

I headed up top. The moon was barely visible behind heavy clouds that were moving fast across the sky. I felt that same unease I'd felt at the market yesterday. Everything felt off—heavy, foreboding. The air was leaden, swelling with moisture. The wind had picked up and was blowing through the palms on shore. I shone a flashlight in the water, the light bouncing off choppy wave crests and casting eerie shadows onto the shore. I saw a mongoose dart across the sand and run into the brush, but there wasn't a soul around.

By the time I went back below, Simon was already asleep. O'Brien was sitting in the salon with the kid cradled in his lap. He carried him back to my cabin and laid him in my bed.

O'Brien took Simon's bed. He didn't want to leave. He wanted to be there if Simon woke up again.

I lay there for a long time, Simon cuddled near me, listening to the wind moaning in the dark.

Chapter 25

Enok Kiersted was in his lab testing some of the hundreds of samples he'd collected in the mangroves in the past month when he heard the door bang open in the front office. At first he thought it was the wind. Then he heard it click shut. He never bothered to lock up, not in the islands. A stab of apprehension twisted in his gut. It was well past midnight. Too late for anyone to be conducting business.

He hadn't meant to stay so late, but he'd lost track of the time. He'd gotten wrapped up in his samples. It happened often. For Kiersted there was nothing more important than his research. He'd been worried about his grant and what was going to happen to his funding once Redding got back to the States and reported to the foundation. Now that was not going to occur.

And he'd be smarter next time someone from the foundation came down. He'd be savvy enough to cover his ass. It wouldn't be hard. He'd back off about the politics and the corruption he was sure was taking place on the island. He'd never needed to give Redding that information. He'd been mistaken to think Redding or the foundation would care, maybe even increase the grant money so that Kiersted could counteract what was happening. The next foundation officer who came down would get the revised version.

He'd heard that the cops had found Conrad Frett dead

that afternoon. Good riddance was how Kiersted looked at it. He had seen Frett in the mangroves with the owner of the property, checking out boundaries. Kiersted didn't believe for one minute that they'd simply been trying to firm up property lines for the records. That's what Frett had said.

Kiersted worried about what might happen to the mangroves. Something had been going on there. He'd seen Frett back later with some other people, drifting in the lagoon on a motorboat, looking at the property. He'd recognized the boat. It was the same one he'd seen Friday dumping garbage over the side.

When he'd spotted it tied to the dock in Road Town, he'd confronted the boat owners about the garbage. Then he'd gotten into it with them about the damage that would be done if the mangroves were bought for development.

They'd laughed in his face. "Do you think we really care about a few fish and coral?" they'd asked.

He'd threatened them, told them he'd expose them, go to the papers and to the charter companies' owners. Those owners would be up in arms when they learned that Paraquita Bay was about to be sold for development. They depended on the mangroves in the bay to protect their boats during hurricane season, and they had a lot of clout in the islands.

Now Kiersted realized he'd made a huge mistake when he'd threatened the two boaters. They were standing at the lab door and he knew it was not a friendly visit.

"What are you doing here?" he asked.

The big muscular guy held a gun.

"You're just too environmentally conscious for your own good, and you've seen too much. Besides, I don't like being threatened," the other said.

Kiersted had been so distracted by his grant and Redding's recommendations that he hadn't taken the time to think it through—Frett's death, the fact that they'd been out in the mangroves with him. Now he put it all together.

The garbage he'd seen being thrown over the side had been a body—Frett's body.

"That's right," the other said, seeing understanding and then fear cross Kiersted's face.

Of all things, Kiersted found himself distracted by the shoes, wondering why anyone would wear purple shoes. He started to laugh. He knew he was losing it. Near hysterics. There wasn't much question about what was going to happen.

"Think something's funny?" the big guy asked, moving toward Kiersted.

"Don't mark him up," the other said. "We need this to look right."

The big guy pushed Kiersted to the front office and into his desk chair. Then he handed Kiersted a pen and paper and told him exactly what to write.

"Not a chance," Kiersted said. The words were hardly out of his mouth when the guy grabbed him and held him down while the other jammed fingers under his ribs and twisted. Searing pain shot through his body. It felt like every organ was on fire.

By the time they were finished, Kiersted was begging for the pen.

Chapter 26

O'Brien was gone when I woke up. I lay there for a while trying to figure out what last night on the beach had meant. Where did it leave us in terms of our relationship? Had it just been an intermission in the boxing match we'd been having, a truce because we were so attracted to each other? Neither one of us had conceded defeat or shown any willingness to make compromises. We'd made physical contact without ever moving out of our corners.

O'Brien had left coffee on the stove. I poured myself a cup and went up top to a day that was gray and overcast, the sun a blurry white disk behind slate clouds. The wind whistled through the boat's rigging and raised whitecaps in the harbor. On the shore, coconut palms clattered and bowed in the gusts.

Simon was already up, running into the wind with Sadie at his heels. Nothing like the resilience of a kid. I was tired and edgy. When I'd stood in the galley a moment before, things had felt off, slightly out of sync—a book not exactly where I'd left it, my Birkenstocks kicked under the table. I'd shaken it off, reasoned that both O'Brien and Simon had been up before me, rummaging around the boat.

Simon and Rebecca were waiting for me when I got to the car. Simon had told the teacher about his photography and today he was doing a "show-and-tell" about digital technology. I'd agreed to take them to school so we could stop at the camera shop. Simon talked all the way into town about how he was going to take pictures of the kids in his class and then show them the photos on the little camera screen.

I'd been working with Gus's Camera Shop since I'd started at the Tortola PD. Gus was the best in town and he did all my developing and printing. He'd learned to steel himself against the grizzly images that emerged on the prints. He was way up to speed in terms of digital technology and sold the newest and fanciest in his shop.

Simon showed him the camera. I told Gus we wanted a couple of the photos enlarged and printed but that we couldn't leave the camera. Simon needed to be able to show the photos at school today.

"No problem, mon," Gus said, popping the card out of the camera. "Give me ten minutes." We watched as he downloaded Simon's photos onto his computer. He snapped the card back into the camera, explaining that he had copied all of the photos and that he'd save them onto a CD as well.

"It be a good idea to have dem stored on a disk," he said. "Dat way you be havin' a backup. And den you can be deletin' all dem photos from da camera and be makin' room for more. And you can be fixin' and changin' da photos on da computer with Photoshop. You come by sometime dis week, I be showin' you," he said to Simon.

I described which photos we wanted printed and we were out of there with a promise from Gus that he'd have the prints done this afternoon.

We were just in time for the school bell. Simon and Rebecca tumbled out of the car, raced across the playground, and disappeared behind the front door. Suddenly the Rambler felt empty. The two of them had been jabbering all the way, Rebecca giving Simon a lesson in Creole.

"If you be hearin' a man say 'de longes' prayer got

amen,' he be meanin' dat nothin' last forever," she explained.

"What's a 'jump-up'?" Simon asked. I wondered where
he'd heard that in his short time in the islands.

"Dat be one big party da folks drinkin' plenty of rum,"
Rebecca said knowingly. "Dey say, 'We be jammin', mon.' "

I could just hear Simon telling his aunt what he'd learned
while in my care.

Conrad Frett's office was in the government building
next to the courthouse. His secretary was going through his
desk and filling cardboard boxes.

When Stark tapped on the open door, she looked up,
startled. Blotches of mascara marred her high cheekbones,
a sure sign that she'd been crying. I wondered if Frett's
housekeeper had been right—that Frett and his secretary
had been romantically involved.

While she went to get us coffee, Stark and I snooped,
looking for anything that might tell us more about the man
or why he had been murdered. His office was like his
home—no personal photos on the desk. A framed diploma
from the Grenada School of Business and a certificate from
the governor for ten years of government service broke an
otherwise long expanse of empty wall space.

"Can you tell us what Mr. Frett's job entailed?" I asked
when his secretary returned.

"He was responsible for all the land-use issues related to
development in the islands. He made recommendations for
building and approved land transfers and applications for
landholding licenses from non-belongers."

"Sounds like a huge responsibility," Stark said as he
dumped half a bowl of sugar into his coffee.

"It is, but day to day it's a lot of red tape and paperwork.
He used to complain about too many people with their
hands in his work, looking over his shoulder. He didn't like
it. Wanted to be autonomous."

"Was he?" I asked, eyeing Stark as he added just one more heaping spoonful of sugar into his cup.

"For the most part, yes," she said. "Though I've taken a couple of messages from the chief minister in the past week. He'd been going over the quarterly report and was upset about the increased number of land purchases by non-residents. Mr. Frett was avoiding his calls."

"Do you know what Frett was working on lately?" Stark asked.

"Same as always. Nothing unusual, if that's what you're asking."

"Was he having any trouble with anyone besides the chief minister?"

"People are always coming in here mad because Mr. Frett rejected a transfer or mad because he approved one. No matter what, someone was unhappy."

"What about Enok Kiersted?" I asked. "He's the new environmentalist working for the Society of Conservation."

She knew exactly who Kiersted was. "He's been here several times in the past couple of weeks. The last time he was extremely angry, started arguing and accusing Mr. Frett."

"What about?" Stark asked.

"Oh, you name it—the approval of condos over on Scrub Island, the destruction of seabeds, turning mangroves into beachfront property. There wasn't much that man wasn't angry about. Mr. Frett actually called security and had him escorted out."

"Did you see him again after that?" I asked.

"No. I think he knew better than to show his face in this office again. Mr. Frett said he'd have him arrested."

"When did you see Frett last?"

"It was Friday. He had an appointment to meet that senator, Westbrook. Then he said he had some personal business to attend to."

"What time did he leave?" Stark asked, tipping back the last of what had to be all sugar from the bottom of his cup.

"Right after lunch. He said he'd be back in a couple of hours."

"So he never came back to the office?" I asked, thinking that Frett was probably dead in the mangroves that afternoon.

"That's right. When he wasn't back by five, I locked up and went home. He had his own key if he came back to the office. But he never did."

"How do you know?" Stark asked.

"I'd left some papers on his desk to sign. They were still there Monday morning. When he wasn't in by ten, I called his house. The housekeeper said he wasn't there and then she realized he may not have been home since Friday morning. That's when I got worried. Mr. Frett never missed work. The one time he did, he called in with the flu. I waited till noon, then called the police."

She shuddered as she thought about it. "I can't believe he was dead all that time and laying in those nasty mangroves."

"Were you involved with Frett socially?" I asked, seeing the emotional opening I needed.

"No," she said, glaring now. "I would never consider getting involved with my boss. You must have been talking to that maid. I'd dropped some documents off at his house. I saw the look. That woman is always searching for something to talk about.

"Look, Mr. Frett was a nice man and a good boss, but not particularly my type, if you know what I mean." I figured she meant a guy with just a tad of sex appeal. That definitely wasn't Frett.

"Why all the tears then?"

"I've worked with him for five years. He was a good boss, fair. Wouldn't anyone be upset to learn someone you work with every day has been murdered?"

She had a point.

"We'll be in touch if we need to talk with you again," I said as I headed out the door, Stark right behind me.

Outside, I ran right into Westbrook, who was just about to come through the door. The papers he'd been holding ended up scattered all over the hallway.

"Detective Sampson, Stark. I'm surprised to see you two here," he said, annoyed.

I knelt and helped him scoop up the paperwork. He obviously didn't want me to see the stuff and tried to pull it out of my hands before I had a chance to look at it. He was too late though. It was copies of his application for the transfer of the property near Soper's Hole.

"So, you decided to go ahead on that house after all," I probed, wondering why he should care whether I saw the application.

"Nothing is definite yet. I just want to make sure that the license is in order if I do decide to buy. Now, if you'll excuse me, I've got business to conduct." He yanked the documents out of my hand and went into Frett's office. I could hear him giving Frett's secretary grief when we left.

"What do you make of that?" Stark said as we headed back to the car. "He sure didn't want you to see that application."

"Yeah. When I spoke with his wife, she said he'd been looking for a place to retire but that he could only afford to buy a place because of her money. Maybe he doesn't want her to find out he's going ahead without her. That guy's a jerk. It's possible that he's involved in all this."

"My money's on Kiersted," Stark said. "I think he brought down the plane because Redding was going to ruin his research. And according to the secretary, he threatened Frett. I think we get him, we get both—the man responsible for the crash and for Frett's murder. Let's go back over there and invite him down to the office for a few questions."

When we got to Kiersted's office, the door was open. You know how you get that feeling right away that something's not right? I had it now. So did Stark. We pulled our guns. Stark toed the door open and we waited. Nothing happened. No flurry of bullets zinged past. No one charged us. Finally, we went in. Stark moved right. I went left. I guess what we'd felt was death. Enok Kiersted was lying on his desk in a pool of blood. He held a 9 mm Beretta in his right hand. The entire side of his face was missing. All that remained was a mass of bone fragments and brain tissue.

The place felt empty, but Stark checked the bathroom as I moved toward the back room and into Kiersted's lab, gun raised. It looked like he'd been working in the lab. Specimens were spread out all over the table in petri dishes. A slide was under the microscope. The microscope light was still on. I took a look through the lens. Just a lot of brown specks as far as I could tell, but then I'd been more interested in the hunk who taught my college chemistry course than in anything under a microscope.

Stark was standing over the body when I went back up front. "Sure looks like the gun that was stolen from the warehouse. I put odds on it being the same gun that killed Frett," Stark said.

In the out basket at the edge of his desk, right on top, nicely placed out of the way of all the gore was a note—a full confession about how Kiersted had killed Frett and how he'd brought down the plane to save the environment from the likes of people like Lawrence Redding. All nice and tidy, practically wrapped up with a bow.

We called Dunn and Dickson and then waited outside for them to arrive. The longer we stood around out there, the more I thought about it. I was having a hard time buying the whole scenario. From the looks of the back room, Kiersted had been in the middle of lab work. Given his obsessive neatness, I couldn't believe he'd kill himself before cleaning up the lab.

When I mentioned my skepticism, Stark got pissed.

"Come on, Sampson, can't you just accept the fact that we solved this whole thing—the crash, Frett's death, the break-in? Dunn will be ecstatic. So will Leonard when she learns the airline is off the hook. I swear, you do this every time. You're never satisfied."

"Admit it, Stark. I'm right a lot of the time. Besides, why would Kiersted be working in his lab one minute and the next decide it was time to end his life? He hadn't even turned the microscope light off."

"Maybe something happened. Maybe he saw something under that microscope that he didn't like."

"You're reaching here, Stark."

"He could have heard we'd found Frett's body. He knew we'd connect it to him. Just like we did."

"Yeah, but how did that gun end up in that plane in the first place if it belonged to Kiersted? It just doesn't make sense."

"Maybe he dropped it when he was out there sabotaging the plane. Somehow he sneaked on board that morning, tampered with something, dropped the gun, and couldn't take the time to find it because maintenance or someone was coming to service the plane."

"Except that we already established that no one suspicious was seen anywhere near that plane."

"He could have gotten himself a pair of coveralls, blended in with everyone else."

"You really want this to work, huh, Stark?"

"It does work, Sampson."

Chapter 27

When I left Kiersted's office, Dunn, Dickson, and Stark were in the back checking Kiersted's lab for anything that might provide evidence to corroborate what they already believed.

I told Dunn that I'd head over to Pickering's Landing, have a look around Kiersted's boat, and secure it, then meet them at the warehouse to talk with Harrigan.

When I got there, Calvin was tying tires around the rails of the *Sea Bird*.

"Yours be da last, Hannah. I be movin' dem out to the moorings and start raftin' dem together late dis afternoon. Looks like dat storm goin' to be hittin' sometime in da early mornin' hours."

Calvin had already boarded up all the windows at the marina and had all of his vehicles nudged up along the leeward side of the building. "I be sendin' Tilda and da girls inland to stay at Tilda's sister's. You and Simon be welcome dar too."

"What about you, Calvin? Where will you be?"

"I be ridin' things out here," he said.

"O'Brien offered to let us stay at his place. I'll take Simon and the animals there and I'll stay here. You may need some help."

"Hannah, I been through 'bout four or five of des storms.

Now sometimes dey don' amount to nothin' but sometimes dey be real nasty. I don' think you be needin' to be down here."

"We'll see, Calvin."

I told him about Enok Kiersted.

"Dat be a damn shame. I liked dat boy even if he be a little bit of a loose cannon," he said.

"What do you mean?"

"Folks in town talkin'. Guess Derrick Johnson be seein' him down at da cruise ship docks threatenin' a steward 'cause he done found some bottles washed up on shore with da ship's logos on dem. Everyone knows dat boy be da one let dem dolphins go. Good thing he did it, you ast me."

"Did you ever notice anyone coming around to visit him, Calvin?"

"Nah. You know he only be down here a month. Mostly, he come home late, leave early. Didn't see too much of him."

I told Calvin I wanted to have a look around Kirsted's boat.

"I think it be open," he said. "Never did see dat boy lockin' dat boat. I be goin' into town for more supplies, den I be back to start movin' da boats. Best be gettin' Sadie and Nomad, some of your stuff after you finish."

I walked down to the end of the dock, jumped aboard Kiersted's boat, and went inside. Enok's compulsive neatness was as obvious here as it had been in his lab. The bunk was made, his clothes were hung in a closet—all the shirts together, long-sleeved at one end, short-sleeved in the middle. They were also organized by color. There wasn't even a dirty coffee cup in the galley sink.

So what was with the stacks of papers that were scattered all over the salon table? Like the mess he'd left in his lab, this clutter was out of character. I sat down and started looking through the material. Most of it was about the mangroves, articles about birds that inhabited them, and reports on the possible effects of the trees' being torn out.

On the top of one stack was an article that Kiersted had cut out of the _Island News_ about development, with a quote from Conrad Frett about how important the development of ocean property was for the economy. Someone, seemingly Kiersted, had underlined the quote with an angry red pen that had torn the paper.

Nothing about Kiersted's rage surprised me. Frett's secretary had confirmed that Kiersted had confronted Frett about his approvals for development. This was probably just one more indication of how pissed Kiersted had been. But it was almost too pat. Like someone had placed it there to be found. I knew what Stark and Dunn would be saying though. I hadn't found one thing that vindicated Kiersted.

Kiersted had kept a key for the boat on a hook by the door. I left things as they were, tightened down all the hatches, grabbed the key, and locked up.

I was surprised to see Daniel Stewart coming up from below deck on the _Sea Bird_ as I stepped off Kiersted's boat. I caught him by surprise. He looked like a teenager sneaking into his parents' liquor cabinet.

"Sorry, Hannah. I was looking for you. I thought you might be down below. I can't believe you live on this thing. Don't get me wrong—it's nice but pretty darned small," he said, covering his discomfort with a lopsided smile.

"Why were you looking for me?" I asked. I could feel heat rising in my face, the result of something between embarrassment and desire. The last time I'd seen Stewart, I'd been hightailing it out of his hotel room before I got involved in an act that required I take my clothes off. Now though, I was irritated. I didn't like people going aboard my boat when I wasn't home.

"I thought I might take you to lunch. Simon too. Maybe go up to the greenhouse at the botanical gardens. I figure the kid could take some pictures while we find a quiet place to talk," he said, his tone suggesting that he wanted to do more than simply converse.

"Simon's at school," I said.

"That's too bad," he said. "It would be a shame if we had to have a romantic lunch alone."

"I can't, Daniel. I'm working. In fact, it's amazing that you happened to find me here."

"I just took a chance. Figured I'd at least find Simon. How about dinner?"

"This is a bad time. Just too much going on and that storm's moving in. I've got to get some clothes together and then head over to the warehouse."

"That investigator find out what brought the plane down?"

"Not that I know of, but it's possible we know who did it."

"Really? That's good."

"Yes, it is," I said, glad that he didn't ask for details that I wasn't about to share anyway.

He followed me below and watched as I threw some clothes together. I handed him Simon's camera bag and a duffel, then grabbed the animals' food and gathered Nomad. Sadie followed me to the car and jumped into the passenger seat.

"You know you've got to eat," he said as we stood next to the Rambler. "Why don't you meet me at my hotel for dinner?"

"That's going to be hard, Daniel. No telling what the rest of the day will bring."

"Look, I'll be there. If you can make it, great. Around seven," he said and headed toward his rental car.

"Daniel, the camera bag," I yelled. He still had it slung over his shoulder.

"See what you do to me, Hannah?" he said as he walked to the Rambler and tossed the bag in the back. "Guess Simon would be lost without his camera."

"It's just the underwater case, some other gadgets.

Simon's doing show-and-tell about his camera at school today," I said as I got into the car.

"Come tonight," Stewart said, leaning into the open window and brushing his lips against my cheek.

I stopped at O'Brien's to drop off the animals. The gardener and several other men were outside boarding up the windows. Claire answered the door, gorgeous as always in a sarong the color of an ocean sunset—no doubt another one of her own designs.

God, I felt like a fool, standing there with my bags, my cat, and Sadie, like a repentant girlfriend. Shit! I tried to cover my stupidity, telling Claire that O'Brien had offered to have Simon and the animals till the danger of the hurricane was over. I walked through the door in a flurry and threw the bags in the foyer. She just stood there, her hand on the doorknob, trying to figure out what to say. Finally, Marta, O'Brien's cook, saved us.

"Hannah, I'm glad to see you!" she said, giving Claire a sideways glance. "Let me take your things."

"I'm sorry to invade, Marta. Do you mind if Simon and the animals stay here till the storm passes? It's not safe down at Pickering's Landing."

"'Course not," she said. "Dis place be battened down tight in no time. "And you know dat Peter done love dis dog! I be partial to cats myself," she said, taking Nomad.

"I'll drop Simon off after school," I said.

"What about you? You know you be welcome to stay too." Marta was definitely stepping over the boundaries here, but it had always been clear that she was in charge at O'Brien's.

Claire still stood in the doorway with a smile hardened on her face.

"I'm sorry, Claire. I'm not here to interfere. I'll be staying at Pickering's Landing and helping Calvin out."

"Don't worry. It's not what you think, Hannah. If I could

take O'Brien away from you, believe me, I'd do it. It's just not going to happen."

I didn't believe a word she said. Maybe I would reconsider Daniel's invitation for dinner.

By the time I got to the warehouse, Dunn and Stark had already been there and left. They had told Harrigan about Kiersted's confession.

"It fits," he said. He'd gotten the results from the fuel controls he'd sent out for examination. The fuel had been contaminated with salt water before the plane ever left the ground.

"The analysis came back with more salt water than jet fuel in the tanks," he said. "No wonder those engines quit. Your Chief Dunn is convinced that Kiersted found a way to foul that fuel."

"Do I hear a 'but' in there somewhere?" I asked.

"I won't consider this investigation complete until I determine how this Kiersted managed to contaminate that fuel. In other words, it's not over yet. I get the feeling you're thinking the same way."

"Yeah. Nothing feels quite right." I told him about Kiersted's obsessive neatness and the state he'd left his lab in before he supposedly killed himself.

"How about we mosey out to the airport? I want to check the fueling procedures," he said.

"Mosey?" I asked, grinning. I'd never heard anyone attempt cowboy with a British accent.

"I'm practicing." He laughed.

It was noon when Harrigan and I walked across the tarmac to the area where the fuel trucks were parked. The sky was leaden, the ocean at the end of the runway an angry swirl of confusion. The last flight was taxiing out. Every other plane had already left for the safety of the airport in San Juan.

We found a fueler who was put out by the fact that we were bothering him. I couldn't blame him. Every employee had been enlisted to secure vehicles, luggage carts, and anything else that could be nailed down or moved.

"All da trucks be in dis here hangar," he said. "What you be needin' ta look at?"

"I need to check the fuel in the trucks," Harrigan said, walking over to the fuel trucks and pulling vials from the shoulder bag he carried. He drained samples from each of the trucks into glass containers, held them up to the light, and shook them.

"Nothing in here but jet fuel," he said. "Not surprising. Let's go check the underground tanks. I've seen it before at airports that are at the edge of the ocean. All it takes is a small crack in the tank and seawater seeping in."

"But there should be indications in the fuel trucks and other planes would have been affected," I said.

"You're right. That was one of the first things I checked when I began my investigation. No other aircraft have reported engine trouble and plenty have been fueled since Saturday morning. Still, stranger things have happened."

We got the fueler to take us out to the underground tanks. There were two of them a couple hundred feet from the shore. Harrigan sampled them both. The fuel was clean. Then he walked toward the ocean, kicking his boots through the brush and debris as he went.

"What are you looking for, Harrigan?" I asked, following. The fueler trailed slowly behind, wanting nothing more than to get back to the hangar.

"Just checking," Harrigan said. "Some of these island airports have old tanks buried closer to the ocean's edge that they sealed up when they put in better and larger ones."

He kept walking, stirring up dust that was being blown away by the swift wind. It was beginning to drizzle and massive clouds were piling up on the horizon.

"Looks like this is a waste of time," he said. "Let's get out of this weather."

"Wait a minute," the fueler said when he finally caught

up. "Der be a ole tank right around here somewhere. Done forgot it even be out here."

Just then Harrigan's boot struck something hard.

"Dat's probably it. It be out of service for a coupla years."

"The top's loose," Harrigan said, crouching. He opened it and peered inside with his flashlight.

The guy just shrugged.

"There's still fuel in here," he observed. "Do you think someone could have used this by mistake?"

"All da men know dat tank's no good. It be all corroded inside. New guys don't even know it be out here."

"This could be a problem," Harrigan said.

It didn't take long to find out what had happened. A few questions to the right fueler had done it. The guy had worked at the airport for almost fifteen years. He'd been hungover, maybe still a little drunk, when he'd come in on Saturday morning. He'd mistakenly filled his truck from the bad tank. When the Island Air plane had gone down, he'd realized what he'd done. He'd flushed out his truck and had been covering his ass ever since. He couldn't 'fess up fast enough. It had obviously been eating at the guy.

"I can't be affordin' ta lose dis job, mon," he said. "Hell, it not be my fault dat tank be contaminated. I done filled my truck from dat tank for years, den all of a sudden we sposed to remembers dat we not be usin' it."

It was obvious that the guy had been so alcohol sodden, he'd been on automatic Saturday morning, unwittingly filling his truck from the same tank he'd been using for years until the new ones had been installed.

"If it's any comfort," Harrigan said, "you won't be the only one whose head will roll. Airport operations will be liable big time."

We walked to the car and started back to town. Harrigan was anxious get to the warehouse and let the local mechanics who'd assisted with the wreckage go home to their families and get their houses secured before the storm hit. He would tie up loose ends, fill out final reports, and head back to the UK as soon as the weather cleared.

"Doesn't that just take the cake?" he said as we drove.

"Yeah," was all I could manage at the moment. Christ, Kiersted had confessed to sabotaging a plane that had not been sabotaged at all. And Stark and I had been looking for a perpetrator and a motive that didn't exist. None of the passengers had been targeted to die. It had all been an accident.

"Guess that puts a whole new light on things," Harrigan said. An understatement, to say the least.

"Like why was Frett killed, who broke into the warehouse, and who framed and killed Kiersted," I said.

All along, Stark and I had ruled out any of the passengers as perps because we'd been proceeding with the sabotage theory. Now? It could be someone on that plane, someone who carried that gun on board, something that person wanted on that plane and was looking for in the warehouse. Somehow Kiersted had been a threat to be eliminated. It had to connect to Frett's death. What the hell was going on?

Chapter 28

I'd called the office from the airport to tell Stark and Dunn that nothing was as it seemed—that the crash had been an accident. Dunn's secretary told me that Dunn had gone home for the day to secure his house against the storm and that Stark had gone to help Billy with her place. He was out of reach by phone. I called Dunn's. No answer. Shit.

I left Harrigan standing in the rain at the door of the warehouse. He nodded, water dripping from the brim of his Stetson, and then disappeared inside. I headed over to Sea-Sail. The best lead I had in Frett's murder was the owner of the mangroves at Paraquita Bay, where Frett's body had been found. O'Brien would know the owner and where I could find him. I wondered if O'Brien or any of the other charter owners had heard rumors about the bay.

I also wanted to check on O'Brien. When it came to his boats, he would lose all judgment. I wanted to make sure he didn't do anything stupid with the storm approaching.

When I got to the SeaSail marina, every slip was full. Between each pier and the next one, at least a dozen boats were rafted together with tires tied between them to keep them from smashing into one another when hurricane winds blasted into the shore. Booms were down and lashed to decks and the marina was alive with people, charterers unloading gear in the rain and dockhands carting equipment through increasingly deep puddles and into storerooms.

It had been even worse when I'd driven through town. People were scurrying to board up the windows of their businesses and homes. The grocery stores had sold out of bottled water and canned goods and every hotel on the island was filling up with sailors taking refuge on land.

I found O'Brien on C Dock, fueling up one of his speedboats. He saw me coming. I knew by the look in his eyes that last night had not been just an intermission from the fight.

"Let's talk when this storm is over," he said.

"Yes, after it's over and everyone is safe," I agreed.

When I asked him about the owners of the mangroves, O'Brien knew exactly where I could find them.

"They live just around the breakwater there." He pointed. "Can't see the house from here. It's an old stone structure back behind the mangroves. Why?"

I told O'Brien about the bad gas, that the crash had been accidental, that Kiersted did not bring the plane down, that his confession was bogus, and that I didn't believe he'd had anything to do with Frett's murder. "The property owners are a lead," I said. "They knew Enok Kiersted, and Frett's body was found over there. I need to talk with them."

"That old couple. I doubt that they know anything," O'Brien said as he finished topping off the boat's gas tank and placed the nozzle on the pump. Then he started throwing gear into the boat.

"What are you doing, O'Brien?" I asked, realizing that he was getting ready to take the speedboat out.

"Not all the boats have made it in. I've got one stranded out there. They were up in the Spanish Virgin Islands and sailed out of the anchorage at Culebra early this morning for Tortola. Culebra is not the place to be in hurricane winds and even though they were sailing against the wind and wave, they should have been able to make it into Road Harbor by noon."

"So what happened?" I asked.

"They radioed in. They lost their engine. They'll never make it in with just the sails. They were too far out to radio SeaSail, so they called Saint Thomas on their VHF. Saint Thomas relayed the call to me. There's no one else that can go. Besides, they're my responsibility. I've got their GPS coordinates. The chase boat is fast. I can make it out there in a couple of hours. I'll be back by six, seven at the latest."

This was sounding all too familiar. O'Brien's parents had died rescuing some charterers who had gotten caught out in a hurricane. They'd motored out with one of their boat handlers, gotten the people off the chartered sailboat and into O'Brien's parents' speedboat, and had the boat handler hand-motor the characters into the nearest harbor. His parents had tried to weather it out on the sailboat. They were never found.

"Jeez, O'Brien. You think my job puts me in harm's way. What about you? I don't want you to end up like your parents."

"I'll be fine. I can't leave them out there. Besides, they've got kids on board. I'll be out and back long before the storm hits. If it continues on its projected path with the current wind speeds, it will be another twelve hours— sometime around midnight."

"Don't go out there, O'Brien," I said, even though I knew I was wasting my breath.

I found the house at Paraquita Bay right where O'Brien said it would be, hidden at the edge of the trees. The old man was on a ladder, nailing boards to the roof. He saw me coming, stood, and brushed off his gray coveralls. He was shirtless and thin rivers of water streamed down his chest and left streaks of dirt. He had to be seventy, his hair a coarse white. The garden was small, probably just large enough to feed him and his wife, who was working to protect a row of beans. I introduced myself and told him I was with the Tortola PD.

"Come in outta dis rain," his wife insisted and led the way into the house, a tumbledown structure that had to be a hundred years old. I wondered how many hurricanes it had survived and whether it could possibly withstand the next.

Inside was damp, dark, and old, but spotless. The floor was linoleum and worn by scrubbing, the pattern cleaned right out in places. A green sofa with delicate embroidered doilies on the arms graced one wall under a print of *The Last Supper.* A TV with rabbit ears was situated in the corner on one of those wooden spools that most people replaced by the time they reached thirty and could afford real furniture.

The kitchen spanned the other wall, with an old electric stove, a refrigerator, and white metal cabinets decorated with aged stickers of roses. There was another room in the back behind a curtain. I assumed it was the bedroom. I'd seen an outhouse out beyond the bean rows.

The old woman was tiny, with skin like cracked leather, fingers bent and arthritic, a smile I was betting was the same as it had been at eighteen.

There were signs that kids had once inhabited the house—family photos, a dusty plastic trophy, a faded red rocking horse. Clearly, it had been decades since a kid had lived here. The house and the people in it had an abandoned feel. For some reason, it made me think of Simon and my heart sank a little.

They handed me a towel to dry my face and directed me to a chair at the kitchen table. The old woman poured iced tea and placed cookies neatly on a chipped china plate.

Finally, everything in order, they joined me at the table.

When I asked them about the property, I got the entire history. They told me the house and the mangroves had been in the family for generations. Their kids had spent hours playing among the trees and the muck. "Come home caked with mud and smelling like yesterday's garbage," the woman said, smiling at the memory. "One of da kids died when he be jus a little one. Other two be livin' in New York City."

"When Conrad Frett come by askin' us if we be wantin' to sell da land, we be real surprised," the old man said. "Ain't nobody never showed no interest in dat swamp. Me and da wife, we talked it over. Why we be wantin' to keep dis here tumbledown house and a tangle of trees, I be askin' her. She not be likin' da idea, but I tole her we be gettin' too old to tend da garden and keep da house. Kids won't never be back, so we decide okay.

"Right away Frett be sayin' he have some foreigner wants ta buy. He said he be makin' sure da deal would be approved. But he done tole me not to be mentionin' it to anyone. Said if word be gettin' out dat he be approvin' da sale, da charter folks be puttin' da pressure on to stop it. Dey like havin' dat lagoon during hurricanes."

"Do you know who was interested in buying or why they wanted to buy?"

"Frett didn't say. Was keepin' it a big secret. Can't see why anyone be wantin' dat property though."

I could. It was a prime location. Right on the edge of Road Town, right on the water. They'd tear out the mangroves, bring in a bunch of sand, and it would be considered prime real estate. I was surprised that O'Brien or some of the other charter company owners hadn't gotten wind of it.

"Dat Enok Kiersted came by askin' 'bout who dos folks be out in da lagoon. I be lettin' Enok into da mangroves whenever he be wantin' to do dat research of his. He sometimes be out dar from dawn to dark."

"He be a nice boy," the old woman said. "Always be bringin' something—fruit, flowers. Brought dem pretty doilies for my birthday."

"Enok, he be seein' Frett and some other folks out in the mangroves a coupla times over da past weeks," the old man said. "He be askin' if I knew what dey be up to. I sure didn't like lyin' to dat boy, but I did like Frett said. I didn't say nothin'."

"When did you see Frett last?"

"Dat woulda been da day I showed him da boundaries of da land. Met him at da fancy new café on Wickham's Cay. He be der with a American."

"You remember what day that was?"

"Dat be Friday afternoon."

"Did you know the American?"

"Think he be some kinda politician. Heard Frett call him Senator."

"The senator didn't go with you?"

"Nope. He be sittin' at da café drinkin' some kinda foamy coffee, espresso dey be callin' it, when we be leavin'. Frett said he'd be callin' da senator and dat he should be gettin' the application in order."

"So it was just you and Frett checking out your property?"

"Yeah, but der be a boat out driftin' in the lagoon. Got da feelin' dey be watchin'."

"Could you see who was on the boat?"

"Not really. It be kinda far out."

"Were they islanders?"

"Naw, white folks for sure."

"What did they look like?"

"You know, like all da rest. One of 'em had a baseball cap pulled down over his eyes, wearin' shorts, a T-shirt. He be taller dan da other one. Dat coulda been a woman."

"What about the boat? Do you know what kind it was? Did you see a name on it?"

"Dat be one fancy speedboat, dat for sure. Couldn't see no name."

"Did you notice anything else at all about the boat. Color? Markings?"

He described it as sleek and expensive with two huge engines, dark with a yellow stripe on each side.

"Do you think they were with Frett?" I asked.

"Dat one thing I be sure of. Frett done rode over here with me from da café. When we be done lookin' at da property, he said he be goin' to look around a bit. I be walkin' back to da house when I see dat boat pull up to shore. Frett be gettin' in."

"Did you see where they went?"

"Dey be cruisin' da shoreline along da mangroves. Last time I be seein' dem, dey be turnin' into one of da little inlets. Don't know why dey go in dar. Place got lotsa roots ta catch a propeller on. Lotsa bugs."

"What time was that?"

"'Bout three in da afternoon."

"Did you see Frett again?"

"Nope. Seems like he be satisfied 'bout dem boundaries. He be sayin' he call about signin' da papers. We be goin' to meet sometime on Saturday. He never be callin'. Now I be hearin' he dead."

I was sure that Frett had never left the lagoon until I'd pulled him out of the mangroves yesterday.

"You think dat sale be off?" the old man asked. "Keep hopin' dat buyer be gettin' in touch. Frett said all da licenses done be approved. Just need ta be signin'."

"I don't know," I said, hesitant to destroy hope.

"Dat be jus fine with me," the old woman said, walking me to the door. "I be livin' here mos my life. Don't know where be any better."

Good, I thought as I walked to the car. I was glad the old woman was just as happy not to sell because I was sure that whoever had been interested in that land would not be calling. Things had gotten way out of control and they had killed Frett, probably Kiersted too. The airplane crash had complicated things somehow. I had no idea how it figured in. I just knew it did.

Frett had probably been dumped in the mangroves on Friday afternoon. Why murder him if he was integral to the sale? I was sure he was taking bribes. Maybe he wanted more? Or maybe he was threatening exposure? But killing him had probably killed the deal. Why not just go along till things were finalized? Then Saturday morning the plane had gone down.

Right now the only leads I had were that boat the old man had seen and Jack Westbrook. He had met Frett right before Frett had gone to the mangroves and disappeared. I found a phone just down the road at a little grocery store and tried Dunn again. Still no answer.

I didn't want to spend the rest of the day looking for a speedboat with a yellow stripe along the side, but I knew who would. When I called the office, Jimmy picked up the phone. He told me that Stark had still not returned and no one else was around.

"What are you doing, Jimmy?" I asked. I had the feeling he'd been napping. If there wasn't something intense going on, Jimmy tended to get bored. Typical kid.

"Just hanging out," he said, yawning into the phone.

He was happy to spend the rest of the day out looking for the boat. I gave him the description. He'd take the *Wahoo* and cruise through the harbors near Road Town, then head over to the West End, check out Cane Garden Bay and Soper's Hole.

"Why you lookin' for that boat?" he asked.

"Just a lead. It probably won't go anywhere. If you see it, I want you to simply get the name of the boat. I absolutely do not want you approaching anyone until we find out who they are. Got it?" I knew how the kid was—too anxious to get involved and still too young to realize he was mortal.

"Sure, no problem," he said.

"I mean it, Jimmy. I'll call you at the office later."

I needed to find out more about Westbrook. I wanted to know why he was having lunch with Frett the day Frett disappeared. Maybe there was a whole lot more involved here than Westbrook's simply being determined to buy land with or without his wife's approval. I'd disliked Jack Westbrook since that first encounter in the hospital when he'd been poking his finger at Dunn and demanding an explanation for my leaving his wife in the water.

I'd been willing to entertain the idea that he'd been ruthless enough to bring down a whole plane to kill his wife. Now that it was clear the crash had been accidental, that obviously wasn't the case. Still, I wouldn't put it past the guy to kill either Frett or Kiersted. Again, the question was why? With Westbrook, it would have to be about money and power.

Frett's secretary was on her way out for a late lunch when I got back to the government building.

"Why don't you join me? I'm going around the corner to the Mongoose," she said.

"Sure," I said, even though the old woman's lemonade and cookies still slogged in the pit of my stomach.

The Mongoose was packed in spite of the impending storm. Most people weren't taking cover yet. I could hear the chatter and conjecture. Some optimists in the restaurant still believed it was going to veer off. Others were sure it would be the worst hurricane to hit in decades. Most had been through enough of them to know that anything could happen.

Customers proceeded through the line, heaping plates with goat stew, jerk chicken, and conch fritters. I opted for coffee and we found a place in the corner. This was a good place for casual conversation. I hoped that Frett's secretary didn't have some silly notion that licensing approvals were strictly confidential. She didn't. In fact, she was willing to tell me anything I wanted to know. And she clearly didn't like Westbrook.

"He came in right after you left and picked up the final paperwork for the property he's buying. All he cared about was whether Mr. Frett had had a chance to sign the license before he died. Didn't have one word of condolence. That man thinks the world revolves around him and his doings."

"What property was it?" I asked, sure it would be the mangroves at Paraquita Bay.

"It's that big house out near Soper's Hole. The man can't wait to get his hands on it. He was worried that someone else would buy it before he could get the necessary licenses. Paying a big price too."

"I was talking to the old man who owns that property on Paraquita Bay. He said he saw Frett with Westbrook that Friday when he met him to show him the property lines. You sure Westbrook wasn't interested in that property?"

"I'm sure. Why would a big senator want that piece of swamp?"

"Someone was looking at it," I said. "Do you have any idea who?"

"Mr. Frett never mentioned it to me. I'm the one who types up all the final forms. Never saw any paperwork for that property down there."

"Surely you saw or heard something." I knew that she was no dummy. I was betting nothing went on in Frett's office that she didn't know about.

"I did hear him arguing on the phone with someone about that property."

"Do you know who it was?"

"Only that it was a woman. I took the call and transferred it to Mr. Frett."

"What did you hear?"

"I don't want to say nothing bad about the dead. Mr. Frett was a good boss," she said, pushing her food around with her fork.

"Maybe what you tell me will help find his killer," I said.

"Well, I wasn't eavesdropping, mind you. His door was cracked open a bit."

"Sure. I understand that you wouldn't do that."

Satisfied that I was not going to condemn her, she said, "He was telling her how much that property would be worth. He said he'd been getting calls from the chief minister and he was putting his career on the line by helping them. Anyone who looked at things closely would see that he should not have approved the transfers. He said he wanted more money."

"When was this call?" I asked, knowing this was why Frett had died.

"Friday, right before he left."

Chapter 29

Jimmy was sitting in my chair looking smug when I got back to the office. It had taken him all of a half hour to find out about the boat that the old man had seen in the lagoon. He was a little disappointed that it hadn't involved racing in and out of the harbors of Tortola and questioning every dockhand, fisherman, and sailor he encountered. Today he'd have been skipping that boat across six- to seven-foot waves.

Jimmy reveled in the title "Deputy" and loved flashing his badge. It had nothing to do with authority or power. He was a nineteen-year-old with raging hormones who would use any device at hand on the easily impressed and bikini-clad. But the thing was, Jimmy had grown up in these islands and he knew how to get information. All it had taken was a couple of questions to some of the locals on the docks down in Road Town Harbor. He had not even needed to fire up the *Wahoo* to learn that the sleek speedboat was called the *Mystic Runner*.

Evidently half a dozen fishermen who'd been tied at the docks unloading fish traps had witnessed an argument between a woman on the *Mystic Runner* and Enok Kiersted.

"Dey all be laughin' 'bout it. Said dat woman couldn't of been much bigger dan a child and Kiersted be one big man. She done grabbed him, twisted his arm so hard she 'bout broke it. Told Kiersted to be stayin' out of somethin' he couldn't be finishin'."

Only one person fit the description—Zora Gordon. I was on my way out the door when the phone rang. It was a call from Stark's old partner in Miami. He'd checked on Zora's boss and learned the guy was known to be involved in illegal gambling and prostitution, but they'd never been able to convict him on anything. Seems he had a good lawyer: Zora.

I asked Jimmy to keep trying to contact Stark and have him meet me at the marina over at Brandywine Bay. When I got there, the guard recognized me and let me in without so much as a hello. I found myself wishing that Stark was standing by my side. It was stupid to be out on my own, but I didn't have the time to wait. I knew that once the storm moved in, my investigation would come to a screeching halt. I wasn't about to gamble that I'd be able to pick up where I'd left off or that Zora or anyone else involved would still be around.

Zora was in the salon and she was put out with the fact that I was there. She didn't bother to offer refreshments. Today she was wearing a tank top and leotards. In spite of her size, it was clear that the woman was capable of following through on her threat to Kiersted. I wondered what motivated her to train to the point that her body resembled steel. "I don't know what else I can tell you about that crash that I haven't already told you," she said.

"This isn't about the crash. Actually, the investigators have determined it was an oversight in fueling."

"Doesn't that just figure," she said, shaking her head.

"What do you mean?"

"Nothing. If the crash is resolved, why are you here, Detective? Surely you have better things to do than continue to harass the passengers."

"Well, you know, Zora, this whole week has been just one thing after another—airplane crashes, a break-in, and poor old Capy in the hospital. Now why would someone break into that warehouse when it turns out there was nothing to cover up? Then we find a body over in the mangroves yesterday and then the local environmentalist shoots himself. And you know what? It was the very gun that was stolen from the warehouse. A gun that I recovered from that wreck. Now the thing is, I can't figure out how that gun ended up in that dead guy's hands."

"Seems pretty obvious he stole it from the warehouse."

"Guess that's what someone wanted us to believe, anyway. But you know what? I don't buy it. And whose gun was it to begin with? I don't suppose you brought it on board that plane, maybe lost it in the wreck, maybe worried about it being traced to you?"

"Don't be ridiculous. If it was my gun, it would not be traceable."

"Oh yeah?" I challenged.

She realized she'd made a mistake even suggesting she knew how to keep a weapon under the radar.

"What do you want here?" she said.

"I hear you're interested in buying the property down at Paraquita Bay?"

"I don't know where you heard that."

"The owner said he saw the *Mystic Runner* out there when he was showing Conrad Frett around. He saw him board your boat."

"I'm sure he's mistaken. Why would I be interested in a bunch of swampland?"

"So you know the lagoon?"

"What are you getting at, Sampson?"

"You know that we pulled Frett's body out of those mangroves over there yesterday?"

"Are you insinuating that I was involved?"

"I heard you work for some unsavory people in the States," I said.

"Everyone has the right to a lawyer. I'm good and I'm well paid."

"What about Enok Kiersted? Did you know him?"

"Never heard of the guy."

"That's not what I heard. A whole bunch of people saw him arguing with you down at the docks."

"Oh that guy. I didn't know his name. Never saw him before he showed up down there. Now, I'm very sorry, Detective, but I've got better things to do than listen to veiled accusations from you."

She was on her way to the lower deck, no doubt to the gym, when I left. I knew she wasn't about to admit anything, but I wanted to push her. Maybe she'd make a mistake.

I went out to the Rambler and sat inside, hoping Stark would show up and watching the waves crashing into the concrete seawall nearby and trying to figure out what was missing. If Zora had killed Frett and Kiersted, what the hell was she waiting around for? The more time I spent running events through my mind, the more I began to wonder whether I was dreaming up the entire scheme and Zora's involvement.

Chapter 30

Zora lay on the bench, straining to lift the weights and work off her anger. He was standing behind her, spotting.

"Poltolski is going to be pissed when he finds out the whole deal is off. No big casino, no big resort, and no opportunity to launder all his dirty money," he said.

"Don't worry about Poltolski. Besides, there are other islands in the Caribbean. We'll simply find another, darlin'," Zora said.

"None as perfect as this. And we spent a lot of time and money getting Frett on board. If you hadn't been so eager to kill him, we wouldn't be in this situation now. What would it have cost us? Half a million is chicken feed to Poltolski. Instead you let your temper get out of control. We've got to put an end to this now."

"Don't worry about it. We'll take care of it today and get out before that storm hits," she said as she finished another set.

"Right. Don't worry. That's what you said before you followed the kid out to the airport. Couldn't even take care of a nine-year-old. Then you follow him onto a plane and the thing crashes."

"Hardly my fault," Zora said.

"Maybe not, but the warehouse was a debacle."

"We couldn't get what wasn't there, and I got my gun

back, didn't I? It was a stroke of genius to use it on Kiersted. That asshole pissed me off. Nobody threatens me."

"It didn't throw Sampson off for a minute. She's on the verge of putting it all together. This whole thing has just spiraled out of control."

"Our luck is about to change. I can feel it. Come on, sweetheart, relax," she said, setting the weights in the rack and pulling him on top of her onto the weight bench.

"I don't know why I put up with you, Zora."

"I know why, darlin'. Face it, you like your sex mean. And I'm the one to give it to you," she said and bit him hard on the lip.

"Christ!" he yelled, brushing the blood away. "Knock it off. Look at this," he said, getting up and peering into the mirror. "It's swelling."

He went back over to the weight bench, grabbed her, and threw her to the floor as thunder rumbled somewhere out in the ocean.

Chapter 31

I'd been sitting out in the Rambler in Brandywine Bay for fifteen minutes, watching the lightning play across the distant sky and staring at the *Mystic Runner* through a fogged windshield. The runabout was tied up alongside the yacht. Something about the thing silhouetted through the rain was very familiar. That's when it hit me. It looked a lot like the boat that had marred the pictures that Simon had taken of the egret high in the mangroves. It had that sleek silhouette, with the sharp bow jutting out over the water, that had been visible even in the small frame of the digital camera. Had Simon and his father been in the lagoon the same day that the speedboat had picked up Frett?

I headed straight to the photo shop. Gus had printed the photos that I'd asked him to enlarge. There were five—two of Simon and his dad and three of the series that Simon had taken of the egret in the lagoon. It was all there, the proof unfolding in the eight-by-ten color photos.

The first showed the *Mystic Runner* in the mangroves just at the edge of the frame, drifting. In the next I could clearly make out the people on board. There were three—one that I was sure was Conrad Frett, the other unmistakably a short redhead—Zora Gordon—and another man, his face hidden under a baseball cap. In the next photo the boat had drifted farther into the frame. Zora was holding a gun and Frett had his hand to his chest and was going down. In the final photo, Frett was out of sight, no doubt lying on the deck, and Zora looked like she was staring directly at the camera. The other guy's face was still hidden under the shadows of the cap.

"Gus, can you load that CD and pull this photo up on your computer?" I asked.

"Sure, no problem." He slid the CD into the drive. It seemed to take forever for the photos to load. Finally he had them all up and moved quickly to the sequence.

"Go to that last one of the egret. Can you zoom in on the guy in the baseball cap?" I asked. He moved the cursor to that portion of the photo and when he clicked on the zoom, a face emerged from under the cap—Daniel Stewart's face.

Jeezus, I had been a fool. I couldn't get to the school fast enough. Traffic was backed up for a herd of goats. At least a dozen people were standing out in the rain trying to corral them. All they were succeeding in doing was scattering them and scaring them down the middle of the damn road when they would have crossed on their own. Horns were blaring and several people were taking the opportunity to get out of their cars to stand under umbrellas and shoot the breeze.

I glanced at my watch. It was two forty-five. What time did school get out? Three? In an act of desperation, I laid on the horn. I knew it wouldn't do any good. It didn't. No one paid any attention.

A stomach-churning, mind-numbing fear hit me as I sat helpless in the middle of the bleating goats that had finally made their way back to my car. With the tail of the last one swishing against my back fender, I cut the Rambler out of the traffic, bumped over the curb and swerved back onto the clear section of road, leaving others wondering at the American cop in her old Rambler, who was always in a hurry.

When I got to the school, the playground was deserted, the swings hanging empty. I ran inside, sure the kids must still be in class. It was only a few minutes to three. The halls echoed with the unmistakable emptiness of one pair of feet, mine, racing to the main office. I knew already that the kids were gone.

A custodian was on his way out, locking the door behind him.

"Where are the kids?" I demanded, breathless.

"The principal let 'em all go home early, count of da storm comin'," he said. "Buses left 'bout a half hour ago."

Could someone have gotten to Simon? That's what this had been about all along. The kid didn't go anywhere without his camera. That's why Zora had been on that plane. And when they hadn't found the camera in the warehouse, they'd realized he had it. The man in the trees. It had to have been one of them, probably Burke, watching Simon. They'd sent that kid to the market to try to grab the camera and I was betting that Simon had not had a nightmare last night. One of them had been on the *Sea Bird*.

"Did you see the new kid, Simon Redding, get on the bus?"

"Sure, he be leavin' with da others," the custodian said. "You know, another guy be up here lookin' for him too."

"What did he look like?" I asked.

"Big guy, hair all spiked, almos white it be so blond," he said.

It had been Burke. Daniel Stewart would have sent him to the school. I'd actually told Stewart that Simon had taken the camera to class today. Why hadn't I seen it? He and Zora had been trying to grab the camera for the past three days. I'd blown it. My visit to the *Mystic*, my pushing Zora. It would force their hand. That had been my intention. But I had never imagined that it would jeopardize Simon. Now they'd be getting desperate. They'd go after Simon and they'd take the camera and the kid too. They couldn't afford not to.

I tore back down the coast highway to Pickering's Landing. I prayed that I got there before it was too late. I skidded into the parking lot and ran to the marina. I could see Calvin steering a boat out into the bay and the *Sea Bird* still tied to the dock. Tilda was inside getting the girls ready to go to her sister's to ride out the storm.

"Hannah, what on earth is the matter?" she said when I burst through the door.

"Simon. Did he come home with Rebecca?"

"Of course he did," she said. "You be turnin' into one mother hen, Hannah. He be out on da *Sea Bird*, waitin' for you. Tole him you be takin' him up to O'Brien's before dat storm hits."

"Jeez, Tilda, I was really worried." I could feel the panic subside. She was right. I had never felt that kind of fear before, a fear that I could not think past or smother with logic.

"He be fine. That Daniel Stewart fellow came by. He be out dar with him."

"Christ," I said and ran down the dock to the *Sea Bird*.

Chapter 32

They were sitting at the table in the salon. Stewart had one arm over Simon's shoulder. In the other hand he held a revolver. The smashed camera card lay at his feet. Simon was trying hard not to show how scared he was.

"Let the kid go, Daniel. There's no point in hurting him. It won't do you any good. I had copies of those photos printed. I left them with Dunn on my way over here."

"That's not going to work, Hannah. You see, while I was heading over here to find Simon, Zora was following you."

His cell phone rang. He dug it out of his pocket with one hand, the gun pressed against Simon's belly. He never took his eyes off me.

"Yes, she just got here," he said to the person on the other end, no doubt Zora. "What about the guy at the camera shop? he asked, then paused.

"You didn't have to kill him," he said. "I know, baby, but . . . Fine. I'll meet you out in the channel. We need to get out of here before that storm hits."

Gus, I thought. *They killed Gus.*

"Take her out, Hannah," Stewart said, putting the phone down. "Tell Calvin you decided to secure the *Sea Bird* in Paraquita Bay. And don't screw it up. I'll be sitting down here keeping Simon company."

I grabbed a rain poncho, went up top and started the engine, then cast the lines off. I motored slowly out to where Calvin was tying boats together and yelled at him that O'Brien had offered to secure the boat over in the mangroves. Not much I could do but explain later, if I had the chance. A big if. I knew that Zora and Daniel Stewart would kill both Simon and me. They didn't have a choice now. Stewart was obviously in way too deep. And Zora? Hell, she'd enjoy it.

If I'd thought it would have done any good, I'd have alerted Calvin. But I figured it would only serve to get him killed too. I pulled away before he had a chance to argue with me. When I looked back, he was still standing in his boat staring at the *Sea Bird*. Had he seen through the lie? He should have. Calvin knew that I trusted him completely and depended on him to take care of my boat.

I grabbed the horseshoe-shaped float from its rack and raised it above my head. Hoping he'd get the message. The horseshoe had but one purpose—rescue.

Once I was clear of the harbor, Stewart came up top.

"Where is Simon?" I asked, the fear breaking in my voice.

"Don't worry about him. He's all right. He's just got a bit of tape around him. He got a little out of hand down there while you were talking to Calvin."

"If you hurt him, I'll kill you, Daniel."

"You're in no position to make threats, Hannah," he said, handing me the duct tape. "Now, I want you to wrap this around your wrist and secure it to the steering wheel."

He stood back with the gun pointed at my chest and watched as I did what he said. Then he secured my other wrist to the wheel and stood under the bimini.

"You know, Hannah, I'm sorry about all this. I can see that you've gotten attached to that boy. I'm really upset that it came to this. I mean it. All we needed was that camera, but nothing worked out. Now there aren't any options left."

"Come on, Daniel. It's a damn excuse. You're good at

it. It's all rationalization to do what you really want to do anyway."

"Don't psychoanalyze me, Hannah. You don't know me."

"I know you. I deal with your type all the time. It's all about what you need, isn't it, Daniel? But tell me, how did you get involved with Zora Gordon?"

"Zora and I have been together ever since a spring day under the football field bleachers when we were juniors in high school. I never knew sex could be like that. She came from the same crappy town I did and we got out together. As soon as we graduated, we headed for L.A.

"Zora's always been the smart one. She knows what she wants and she goes after it. She hooked up with Poltolski in a bar in L.A., and she's had him wrapped around her little finger ever since. He paid for her law school and I got to be a movie star on his buck. She's been keeping him out of jail forever. He'd do anything for her."

"You ever wonder why?" I asked him.

"Of course, I know why. The sex. And it's fine with me. We both see it as a means to an end. When he asked her to set up the money-laundering operation down here, there was never any doubt I'd come with her. She made it clear to Poltolski that she wanted to run the whole operation and that I'd be part of it—a celebrity with a name, to add credibility, was the way she explained it to him."

"Why would you get involved? You're successful enough."

"I could never say no to Zora," he said, running his tongue over his bruised lip. It didn't take much imagination to figure out how that had happened.

"Besides, all the big stars have their own places—nightclubs in Vegas, bars in Hollywood," he said. "I'm just keeping up my image."

"Sammy know what you're up to?"

"No. Sammy doesn't even know Zora exists. We've managed to keep the relationship a secret, even out of the tabloids. Amazing, huh? We meet at her office, at her condo. It's the one thing that Poltolski insists on, his lawyer staying out of the news, and he makes sure of it.

"Sammy's the last one I wanted to know about her or this deal. As conniving as Sammy can be, he's got this standard he lives by. He'd never get involved in anything illegal. Man, he almost dropped me when that whore I was with accused me of hurting her and threatened to go to the police. I convinced him she was lying and then I paid her off big time."

"What did Zora think of your being caught with a prostitute?"

"Hannah, you are naive. Zora was with me. In fact, she's the one who got too rough. She was having a little fun with handcuffs and a knife."

"Are you the one who left all the papers piled on Kiersted's chart table yesterday?"

"Yes. I wanted to make sure he'd left nothing on his boat that would implicate us. I thought leaving that article out was a nice touch. I had just begun searching the *Sea Bird* for the camera when you showed up. I couldn't believe Simon took that camera to school. It was like we were always about half a step behind him. Jeezus, that camera should have been ruined in the crash. Why the hell didn't that kid take the thing out of the waterproof case? Kids."

We were well out in the channel by now. In the distance, I could see the *Mystic*.

"Head over to her," Stewart said. I managed to turn the boat upwind as Stewart pushed the throttle all the way down. At top speed, the *Sea Bird* wouldn't go above eight knots. In this wind, I was fighting to keep the boat at four knots and on course. The *Mystic* slowed to wait for us. I knew that once we reached her, my opportunity for escape would diminish exponentially. If Simon had not been tied up below, I'd have been over the side long before Stewart had handed me that damn duct tape.

When we got closer, I recognized Zora standing at the rail. It was almost dark. Sheets of wind-driven spray blasted across the *Sea Bird* as we followed the *Mystic* across the channel and headed into Salt Pond Bay at Salt Island. I saw one of the crew, the woman with the ponytail, scurry up to the bow and open the hatch that held the windlass. Seconds later, the anchor chain rattled across the bow and the anchor splashed into the water a hundred feet offshore. Then the engines shut down.

"Head us over there, Hannah, and don't do anything stupid or Simon suffers," Stewart said, shifting the *Sea Bird* into neutral. I swung her toward the *Mystic* and eased her alongside.

I knew the anchorage well. It was a little harbor, deserted now. The tiny settlement on shore looked dark and abandoned. Normally a handful of islanders lived in the cottages on the strip of land between the harbor and the salt pond, where they harvested the salt. But no one would be stupid enough to stay out here with a category four hurricane moving through.

Burke was standing at the rail. He lashed lines around the cleats on the *Sea Bird* and Zora jumped on board.

"This is no place to be with a hurricane bearing down," I warned. I knew that the holding here was bad—a grassy bottom and wind that would funnel down into the anchorage. In the best of conditions the winds were too fickle and the surge too intense to anchor in the harbor for long.

"Nice of you to worry, but we'll be out of here long before that storm hits," Zora said.

"You can't outrun a hurricane," I said. I could feel it coming.

"You think I don't know what I'm doing?" Burke said. "It's just a couple of miles over to Hurricane Hole on Saint John. In this boat we can be there, cozied up in the mangroves, in a half hour. Got a spot all picked out. Not much better protection around. Once that storm passes, we'll be on our way to the Bahamas."

"You know, it's especially gratifying to see you tied to that wheel," Zora said. "Maybe we should have a little fun, Daniel."

I hadn't seen the knife until she moved in close and smiled, a warped, seductive smile. She ran the blade down my neck, paused for a second, sliced down the raincoat, through the buttons on my shirt, tipping it open with the point. Then she moved the knife to her mouth, ran her tongue along the steel, placed the tip between my breasts and ever so slowly glided it down to my navel, leaving a thin strip of blood. The pain was nothing compared to the anger. All I could do was struggle uselessly against the bonds that held me to the wheel.

She held the knife pressed against my stomach for what seemed like an eternity. I waited for the thrust. It's funny what you notice at times like this. I found myself staring at Zora's purple running shoes while I anticipated the cold steel that would nick a rib on its way to my heart.

In one swift move, she ran the knife down my arm and slashed through the tape.

"Get her aboard the *Mystic*," she said, turning to Burke.

Stewart was already pulling Simon aboard. The kid turned and gave me this look like I was going to be able to do something about this. Then he saw the blood that stained the water-soaked shirt I'd pulled back over my chest.

Chapter 33

Simon and I were sitting in the salon of the *Mystic*, each of us tied to a chair. It was pitch-black now. The wind howled and the boat shuddered against each violent gust.

Simon and I had been talking nonstop. I'd been trying to keep him calm. He told me about his mother, how he remembered her reading to him at night and taking him to the park. I told him about my family and about O'Brien. Then I started telling him stories, some of the same ones O'Brien had told me about the sea.

Finally, Simon got around to asking about Stewart.

"How could he be so mean, Hannah? I thought he was the Avenger and the paper said he was a hero rescuing that lady from the plane."

"Some people get lost along the way, Simon. They get confused about what's right."

"How do you keep from getting lost, Hannah?" he asked.

"You have people who care about you and show you the way," I said, then immediately regretted it.

"Don't worry, Simon," I said. "I won't let you get lost."

All the while we'd been talking, I'd heard muffled voices up top. There had been an argument with the female crew member. She'd said she had not signed on for anything like what was happening on the *Mystic*. She wanted out. They'd obliged her. I'd heard a gunshot, then something hit the deck and tumble into the water.

"Just the boats bumping against each other," I said to Simon, but the kid was not stupid. He knew the score.

"Don't worry, Hannah. I know you won't let them hurt me," he said, his voice small in the chaos of waves and wind smashing against the hull and foaming over the windows. I hoped I'd be able to live up to his expectations— live at all, actually.

I could hear someone on the *Sea Bird*, slamming a sledgehammer into her hull.

"You've got to make it look like it went down in the storm." It was Zora yelling at Burke and Stewart.

"Don't worry about it," Stewart said, breathless.

Then I heard another loud bang and the hull cracking under the blow.

"That's got it," Burke hollered. "She's filling with water."

I heard them scrambling back onto the *Mystic* and the sound of water rushing through the *Sea Bird*. Then it was quiet. The *Sea Bird,* along with everything I owned, was sinking to the bottom.

Finally, Zora and Stewart came down, followed by Burke.

"Too bad about your boat," Zora said. "Guess you shouldn't have been out here with that storm bearing down. Sooner or later someone will find what's left of it, and then maybe they'll discover your bodies washed up on the shore."

"No one will ever buy that," I said, knowing damn well it was the perfect ploy. It would look like I'd had problems getting the boat over to Road Town and into the shelter of the lagoon and had been swept into the rocks at Salt.

"We've got just enough time to have a little fun," Zora said, leering at me. "It will be the best sex Daniel and I ever had. We've never gotten to take the violence to the level we will with you. You'll be dying to the sounds of our climax."

"Zora," Burke warned, "we don't have that kind of time."

"It won't take long," Stewart said. He had the knife now and was holding it against my chest. He leaned over and ran his tongue down my cheek and across my lips, then bit down hard. All I could do was struggle uselessly against the bonds that held me to the chair.

"No point in fighting it, Hannah," he said, licking my blood from his lips. "Although that does make it more enjoyable."

I could see the look of shock in Simon's eyes. Jeezus, he didn't need to see this.

"What about the boy?" Burke asked, clearly uncomfortable with what was happening in front of the kid.

"Take him up top and wait for us," Zora commanded. "As long as he's alive, Sampson will cooperate. I know her type. She'll believe until the very end that there's something she can do to save him. Won't you, Hannah?" She was taunting me, hoping I'd give her an excuse to strike.

I didn't give her the satisfaction, but she was right. I was waiting for the first opening. She was cocky enough to think I'd fail. I admit it, things weren't looking too good. But I was not going to let Simon die.

Burke untied the kid and pulled him kicking and screaming all the way out of the salon.

Once they disappeared up top, Stewart moved back in. Zora was right behind him, a look of hunger in her eyes. She grabbed my hair and yanked my head back, exposing my throat. There wasn't a damn thing I could do about it. I tried to hide my fear, but my breath was coming in short rasping gasps.

"Good, Hannah," she said, her face just inches from mine. "I like the fear. I can see it in your eyes. You're like a trapped animal. This will be fun. Get her out of that chair, Daniel."

Stewart cut me loose with one quick swipe while Zora

pointed the gun at my head. He pulled me out of the chair and shoved me into the master suite and onto the bed face-first, my hands still tied behind my back.

"Turn her over, darlin'," Zora said, moving around to the other side of the bed. Stewart was kneeling next to me. When he pulled me onto my back, I caught sight of the leather straps attached to the bedposts. This had to be the epitome of their fantasy—the bondage scene—woman bound, helpless victim ripe for abuse. Once they had the straps tightened around my wrists, it would be all over. But they were going to have to untie my hands. This was my one chance. I would either die now or I would get out. I was not about to be the sacrifice for their perverted needs. It was just not going to happen. My mind was racing, my body tense, waiting for the opening.

Stewart still had the knife and was taking his time, relishing every moment. He'd climbed on top of me and was sitting on my hips, teasing, running the knife around my breast, over my collarbone, and across my throat. As Zora watched, mesmerized, he slid the blade under the shirt again, baring my chest and the thin wound that seeped red. Then he circled the knife around my belly. Finally, he reached behind my back and sliced through the tape that held my hands and clutched my wrists in an iron grip. Zora put the gun on the bedside table and moved in next to me on the bed. She grabbed one of my arms and was working it toward a leather strap as Stewart bent over and took my breast into his mouth, the hand with the knife dropping to my side.

I moaned in the best imitation of ecstasy I could muster and pushed my hips into his groin while twisting out of Zora's grip. Stewart was too aroused to react and Zora wasn't fast enough. I had the knife before either of them knew what was happening. I caught Stewart with a slash across his chest, and followed through, catching Zora across her cheek. The next one sliced across Stewart's neck. He grabbed his throat, stunned, blood gushing from between his fingers. Then he fell, his weight pinning me on the bed. I could hear Zora screaming and I knew she would be going for the gun.

I wrapped my arms around Stewart and rolled with him off the far side of the bed in a tangle of bloody covers.

"You bitch! You killed Daniel!" she shrieked. I kept moving, rolling away from the mass of blankets and Stewart's body.

I was crouched and opening the door when Zora started firing. I felt a stinging blow in my side, then more bullets crashing into the door as I slammed it closed and tipped the bronze statue against it. It wouldn't hold her for long.

I scrambled up the stairs, ignoring the blood that splattered on the steps. The only thing that mattered now was getting to Simon. I knew the bullet had gone all the way through, tearing flesh, but I'd live.

When I stepped up on deck, I was struck by a blast of wind. The storm was moving in fast. A deck chair let loose, narrowly missing me before it flew over the side. A sudden bolt of lightning lit up a sky of contorted ink-stained clouds. On shore, I heard the sharp crack of a tree snapping like a dried bone.

I was about to climb up to the wheelhouse when Burke came out. No doubt he'd heard the blast of gunfire above the roar of the wind. He had hold of Simon's collar and was pushing him ahead of him.

"I'll break his neck if you come any closer," he said, wrapping his arm around Simon's throat. I knew he'd do it.

"Put the knife down," he said, tightening his grip on the kid.

Down below, I could hear Zora trying to shoot her way out of the bedroom. It would be only a matter of minutes before she succeeded.

Then Simon gave a nod toward Burke's feet. Burke was shoeless. I knew what the kid had in mind. I stooped down to lay the knife on the deck and stepped toward the rail as

Simon made his move, slamming his shoe down hard on Burke's arch. The kid was light, but the surprise as much as the pain threw Burke off. Before he could recover, I had Simon in my arms and we were over the side and falling into the raging sea.

We'd barely hit the water when the shooting started and a slurry of bullets peppered the water around us. I dove down, Simon in my arms, kicking hard, ignoring the pain in my side, the cramping in my calves, the water surging against us. I kept swimming, moving farther and farther from the zing of the bullets that still ripped through the water. I swam until I could no longer hold my breath or lift my arm to take another stroke.

Finally, I surfaced, gasping for air, Simon sputtering and coughing up seawater beside me. We were out of range now, and I could see the white sandy strip of shore less than thirty feet away. I turned on my back, held Simon in my arms and kicked, mindless now except for the focus on moving my legs. Finally my ass scraped bottom. Simon helped me struggle to my feet and up onto the beach, where I dropped into the sand and lay, spent, as the storm raged around us.

"Come on, Hannah. We've got to keep going," Simon yelled, pulling me up as another muffled shot sounded through the riot of wind.

We were staggering across the sand when I heard the speedboat engines roar to life. I took Simon's hand and we ran toward the settlement, pushing against the needles of rain and sand that exploded into our faces. I heard the speedboat crash up onto the shore, then spotted Zora struggling onto the beach.

We darted into the nearest cottage. It was one room with a cement floor. I knew I'd lost a lot of blood. I sat on the floor and pulled my shirt away from the wound—very messy. Simon found an old piece of clothing balled up in a corner, knelt down next to me, and tied it around my waist tight enough to stem the bleeding.

"What are we going to do, Hannah?" Simon asked, trembling with the cold and the fear.

"We'll be okay, Simon," I said, getting to my feet. I stumbled around in the dark, feeling my way over countertops, pulling drawers open, looking for anything I might use against her. The most lethal weapon I found was a soup ladle. I ran my hand along the wall and worked my way around the room, tripping over bags of what I presumed was salt. Finally my fingers found the handle of a rake. Christ, at least it was something.

I could hear Zora out in the storm yelling. "You killed Daniel, Hannah," she screamed. "I'm going to kill you and the boy. You can't hide from me, Hannah. You'll watch the boy die first."

I peered through a window, trying to see through the wind and the blowing sand. The rain was coming down in horizontal sheets now.

I caught a glimpse of her as lightning shot through the dark. She was running between the cottages. Her eyes were crazed, her hair a wild mane that looked like tangled snakes.

She had the gun in one hand and the knife I'd left on the deck of the *Mystic* in the other. She disappeared around the corner of a building, then I heard her inside and the sound of glass shattering.

I tightened my grip on the rake and stepped back into the shadows of the cottage.

"Simon, get out of here now. Go straight past the salt pond and keep running to the other side of the island. There's a bluff there. You can climb down into the rocks. It will be protected."

I knew that these cottages offered no refuge, either from Zora or from the hurricane-force winds that would soon be turning them into a pile of rubble. Anyone inside would be pummeled by debris or swept away in the water that would rush over the sandy spit. With the wind blasting in from the southwest, the rocks below the butte would be the only protected spot on this godforsaken island.

"I don't want to leave you, Hannah," he cried. "Come on, Hannah, come with me!" He had hold of my hand and was pulling with all his strength.

"Simon, I can't go," I said.

"Why not?" he asked.

Why not? I asked myself. Because I felt compelled to face this seething woman who had two weapons, no concern for her own life, and was raving out there in a hurricane? And I was going to go out there after her, bleeding, with a damn rake? To protect Simon? *Get real, Sampson.* I knew what this was about. Sure, it was the cop mentality, but I also wanted revenge, and I was willing to risk Simon to get it. Christ, Zora was going to die out there with or without my help.

"You're right, Simon. Let's go," I said.

"Okay, Hannah!" he said.

We edged out the door, around the back, and took off running across the sand.

I stopped once to make sure that Zora was not following. She wasn't. I caught a glimpse of her as she pushed her way inside another cottage, searching for us. Again, I heard her yelling. The wind and rain swept away the words. I grasped Simon's hand again and we kept running.

At the salt pond, the ground turned to sludge that sucked us in. We were drenched, our clothes pasted to our skin. I tripped, fell, sprawling into the ooze, pain shooting through my side.

"I'm okay," I said as Simon pulled me up.

We kept running, fighting our way through a smothering curtain of rain and wind that tried to blow us back. Heads down, we pushed against the storm. I knew the butte had to be just ahead. The island was barely a mile across. Right now it seemed like a hundred. Finally our feet found the stony outcropping.

"Slow down, Simon. We've got to be close to the edge." In seconds we found ourselves looking down into a raging sea. Angry, foaming water thundered against the cliff and exploded into the air.

I held on to Simon and we started down, struggling to find footing on the slippery boulders. I knew that one misstep would send us over the edge and onto the sharp rocks below. We kept going, the wind ripping at our clothes. We were on our hands and knees now, fingering our way down until suddenly we were out of the worst of it, sheltered behind a huge and remarkably solid rock wall.

"Look, Hannah," Simon shouted. "It's a cave." He scurried into it, and I followed just as the storm hit like a steam engine. Tree limbs, boards, shingles hurtled past our sanctuary and swirled into the blackness.

We made our way into the far reaches of the cavern and collapsed against the back wall, too exhausted to speak. I leaned my head against the granite, closed my eyes, and listened to the bedlam outside. At some point I was sure I heard screaming, like the sound of a banshee screeching in the wind.

The next time I opened my eyes, it was dead silent. Simon was asleep, his head on my lap, his breathing deep and regular. I gently moved out from under him and crawled to the opening. A sickly greenish yellow light reflected devastation—trees floating in the water, a rooftop lying below in the rocks, a burlap bag hanging from a bush. I knew it wasn't over. We were in the eye of the hurricane.

I heard rocks tumbling down the butte. An unreasonable fear caught me—the image of Zora climbing down the side of the rocks, her face a mirror of evil.

"Get a grip, Sampson," I whispered to myself and scrambled back to the recesses of the cave. I awoke one more time to the howling of the storm that once again raged outside.

Chapter 34

"Hannah, Hannah, wake up!" Simon was kneeling next to me, gently shaking my shoulder.

"What is it, Simon?" I asked, immediately on the alert.

"Come on. Come outside."

I followed him out and stood. My whole body felt bruised and the makeshift bandage was stiff with dried blood.

"Look, Hannah," Simon whispered. "It's beautiful!"

That it was. Rubble and debris littered the ground, but the ocean was a fine sheet of glass that reflected the first rays of the sun as it crept above the horizon. Soon the sky and water were exploding in color that bounced off the hanging clouds. Gold, orange, and pink saturated every surface.

We sat on an outcropping for a long time, numb and grateful to be alive to see this sunrise. Finally, we climbed back up through the rocks and headed to the settlement. The island had been leveled. We walked through the devastation, stopping to examine broken pottery, a torn pair of overalls, a radio with its parts spilling out. A piece of roofing was swaying precariously from the only tree that remained. A two-by-four had pierced the trunk like a toothpick through Jell-O.

Simon found a stuffed bear, soaked and matted, caught

in some brambles. He pulled it out and carried it with him as we headed down to the shore.

The *Mystic* was still in the harbor, one side completely submerged, the other tipped toward the sky, no movement on board, no sign of life.

The *Sea Bird* was gone. I knew she was lying on the bottom somewhere or in pieces on the rocks, propelled by the fury of the waves. I could see the *Mystic Runner*, the speedboat Zora had slammed into shore, now just a shattered hull resting in the sand with the engine hanging off the back.

"Stay here, Simon, okay? I want to have a look around." I picked up a board with a nail sticking out of the end and headed down the beach.

I found Zora on the point, floating in a tidal pool. She was lying on her back, her eyes open in an empty stare.

I left her where she lay and walked back down the beach to where Simon was poking at the sand with a stick.

"She dead?" Simon asked.

"Yes."

He just nodded and kept poking at the sand.

He sat on the shore clutching the bear while I swam over to the *Mystic* through an ocean filled with dead fish and debris. I climbed on board and crouched, listening for any movement, looking for any sign of Burke. The boat was silent except for the occasional grinding of the hull against the sandy bottom. Then a gull cried overhead and landed on the bowsprit. I crept quickly across a deserted deck, then up to the wheelhouse, where I found Burke's body wedged under a bench with a bullet in his head. That had been the gunfire I'd heard as Simon and I made it to the beach last night. More than likely Burke would have wanted to forget about us and get out of the harbor. Zora had wanted something else.

I made my way below. The boat listed heavily to port and the entire left side was underwater. Everything that could float did, including Stewart, whose body had washed into the doorway between the bedroom and the salon. Fortunately, the galley was on the dry side of the boat. There was water and enough food to feed Simon and me in gourmet style for weeks. We wouldn't be here that long though. I gathered a few items, along with some dry clothes and a tarp, and loaded them into a waterproof bag that I'd found under the chart table.

Finally, I climbed back up to the deck and took the time to survey my surroundings. I was stunned by the devastation. It was frightening to know what the ocean was capable of becoming. All around me things were dead, broken, twisted, shattered. From here the shore looked like a sandbox littered with matchsticks. Simon was sitting in the middle of it all, clutching the bear. I climbed down the side ladder and swam back to shore.

Simon helped me rig the tarp for some shade and then we took a walk down the beach. Like the water, it was littered with dead sea life. At the end of the beach, we came across a young dolphin, flopping in the sand. Then I saw a fin break the surface. An adult dolphin was circling in the harbor.

"Can we get it back in the water?" Simon asked, hopeful that somehow we could save the animal.

We found some old fabric tangled in the wreckage on shore and laid it out in the sand beside the dolphin. Then we very gently rolled the animal onto the cloth. We each took an end and dragged the dolphin out into the water. When it was deep enough, we dropped the fabric away, but the animal just lay in the water, unmoving.

"Come on, fish, go," Simon pleaded. Finally it flicked its tail, splashed once, and was gone. We saw it join the other, and they disappeared.

I thanked God it had not been another death in Simon's short life. In mine either.

*   *   *

We were sitting on the beach eating peanut-butter-and-jelly sandwiches and drinking from a water jug when I heard the boat approaching.

It was Calvin.

He had called the police department yesterday evening when he'd seen me raise the horseshoe, and realized I was in trouble. No one had answered at the office. Then he'd called SeaSail to find out from O'Brien whether I was headed over there. O'Brien had already gone out to rescue the charterers. At that point there was nothing Calvin could to do but get Tilda and the girls to safety and ride out the storm.

He'd started looking at first light, saw the wreckage of the *Mystic*, and motored into Salt. He told us what he knew about the damage in the islands. Information was still sketchy, but he'd heard that only a few deaths had been reported. Electricity was out and many homes had been destroyed.

We weren't prepared for what we found in town when we motored into the harbor. It was a shambles. Buildings and houses had lost their roofs and glass littered the streets. Scores of boats that had tried to weather the storm on anchors or tied to docks lay grounded on the shore, some three deep.

Calvin tied up at the dock at SeaSail. It had fared better than other parts of the island—only a dozen boats with damaged hulls and a couple dismasted. Dockhands were already lifting booms back into place, hauling out sails, and storing tires for the next time.

But O'Brien had not come back.

Simon and I stayed at his villa and every night I sat on the patio gazing out at the sea, expecting O'Brien to come sailing down the channel.

Everyone on the island worked together on the cleanup. Sammy Lorenzo was in the middle of it—pulling plywood off of windows, sweeping the streets, and flirting with Claire. He hadn't been surprised about Stewart.

"Daniel thought he had kept his aberrant sex under wraps, but the rumors were flying all over Hollywood, especially when that prostitute started making accusations. I tried to talk to him, but I was wasting my breath. I had hoped that the stories about his heroics after the crash would muffle the gossip."

We were sitting at a sidewalk café, Simon intent on keeping his ice cream from dripping down his cone. Sammy and Claire were holding hands. I could hardly believe it, but in spite of the fact that Claire was a tall Caribbean beauty and Sammy a short, balding Italian guy, I could see the chemistry between them.

"I'm thinking about staying down here for a while," Sammy said, smiling at Claire. "We've been talking about promotion for Claire's business out in L.A. I've got a lot of contacts there, and after Daniel, I'm tired of representing actors."

The Westbrooks had flown out that morning. Evidently they too had found romance at the peak of the storm.

"I'll take what I can get right now," Debra had said.

I'd been down at SeaSail checking to see if there'd been any news of O'Brien and stopped by the Westbrooks' boat. It had survived the storm without a scratch.

"We'll see how it goes," she said. "Jack's been contrite, attentive. I don't know, maybe it was the storm, maybe he's realized how fragile life can be and how important family is. I never thought I'd see it. He's given up the idea of a house here."

On my way up to the marina office, I'd run into the senator. He gushed about the hurricane, the events out at Salt, the murders, Stewart, and leered at me the entire time. Not much change as far as I could tell.

When I got back to the villa, the phone was ringing. It was Simon's aunt. She'd finally found the time to call. She was still in Europe, somewhere in southern France. She made all kinds of excuses. Her secretary couldn't reach her; she couldn't get through because of the hurricane.

She said she'd be back in the States in a couple days and was arranging for boarding school for Simon.

"I simply cannot manage a nine-year-old boy," she said.

"What about vacations, summers?" I asked.

"The school has a summer program. I suppose he'll have to stay with me at Christmas."

I could tell by the tone of her voice how put out she'd be.

"Maybe he should stay with me for a while," I said before I'd even thought it through. Christ, how could I take care of the kid?

She never even hesitated. "That would be fine. I can send money for him."

"I'm not worried about the money."

"I insist."

"Fine," I said. She'd never even asked about me or where Simon would live or go to school.

She agreed to contact her lawyer immediately to discuss my getting temporary custody and to have him place a preliminary call to let the authorities down here know that arrangements were in the works. I told her she needed to make a trip down here soon to see Simon. After that we'd talk more. Until then, we agreed, Simon could stay with me and we'd see how things went.

But I insisted that she talk to Simon about living with me. I wanted the kid to have a choice. He was out at the pool playing with Sadie. When I told him his aunt was on the phone, his face fell, and he dove under the water. Finally he pulled himself up onto the deck, shuffled into the house, and picked up the receiver.

I could hear his aunt on the other end going over the options, the first being boarding school. He was close to tears. Eventually, she got to option two.

"Yes!" he said. "I want to stay with Hannah!" Then he turned to me. "Is it okay?" he asked.

"It's okay, Simon. I want you to stay with me."

He dropped the phone and jumped into my arms.

"I love you, Hannah!" he said.

"I love you too, Simon," I said. So it was settled.

Every day Simon and I went out looking for O'Brien in one of the SeaSail chase boats. We searched a different area using GPS coordinates, but it was a big ocean. For a while, scores of friends, SeaSail employees, and Search and Rescue volunteers were also out searching. The sailors that O'Brien had gone out to find had somehow made it through the storm. They'd been rescued the next day off St. Thomas. They'd never seen O'Brien and some speculated that the chase boat had been swamped and had gone under in the high seas. Some said the waves had reached twenty-five feet at the peak of the storm. By the end of the week, most people had given up.

Calvin, Carmichael, Snyder, and even Stark and Billy were still going out when they could, but I knew they were doing it for me, not because they had any expectation of finding O'Brien. I refused to give up. I knew that if anyone could survive out there, O'Brien could. If his boat had gone down, he would have been prepared with a survival kit that included water, food, flares. Knowing O'Brien, he would even have had sunscreen.

It was ironic that I had the kid and not O'Brien. God, I wanted him, needed him with me.

The last time I'd seen O'Brien was that day on the docks when he'd told me he intended to go out and rescue those charterers. We'd agreed to talk as soon as we could. We'd both been too caught up in events—storms, plane crashes, murder—to make sure we took care of the important stuff.

Now I was sitting out on the patio, trying not to let the regret and grief overcome me, when I heard the door open.

"Dive in, but with caution. You never know what's lurking beyond the reef."
—*Springs Magazine* (Colorado)

DANGEROUS DEPTHS:

An Underwater Investigation

Trying to save an endangered species doesn't normally make one a target for extinction. But police diver Hannah Sampson has her doubts when she pulls her friend Elyse out of the sea, barely alive. Although the chief believes it was an accident, Hannah knows Elyse is a staunch environmentalist, and never hesitates to harass anyone who threatens her beloved natural habitat. Hannah is sure this is no accident— but attempted murder. Now, she must find the would-be killer before he finishes the job.

"A likable, exuberant heroine."
—Margaret Coel

"A thrilling, fast-paced series."
—*Roundtable Reviews*

0-451-21493-5

Available wherever books are sold or at penguin.com

Murder runs deep in this thrilling series featuring
C.S.I. diver Hannah Sampson

BY KATHY BRANDT

SWIMMING WITH THE DEAD

An Underwater Investigation

Summoned to the sun-drenched beaches of the British Virgin
Islands, Hannah Sampson is fully prepared to face unknowable
dangers beneath the crystal-clear waters of an idyllic paradise.
But the possibility of murder runs deeper and darker than the
sea itself. Her police commissioner's son—an expert diver and
researcher—was found dead, pinned under the submerged
wreckage of a cargo ship. Whatever the victim was looking for,
he found.

0-451-21020-4

**Available wherever books are sold or at
penguin.com**